The Whole Wide Beauty

To Ann,

The Whole Wide Beauty

EMILY WOOF

All Those years ago....!

love,

Emily Woof
x
Aug 2010

ff

faber and faber

First published in 2010
by Faber and Faber Ltd
Bloomsbury House
74–77 Great Russell Street
London WC1B 3DA

Typeset by Faber and Faber Ltd
Printed in England by CPI Mackays, Chatham

There is a partial quotation from 'The Wanderer'
by W. H. Auden on p. 291.

A CIP record for this book
is available from the British Library

ISBN 978–0–571–25399–9

2 4 6 8 10 9 7 5 3 1

1

The wind was blowing hard from the north and would bring rain. The bus took a sharp corner into York Way and Katherine watched the flat, scarred earth of the King's Cross development area open up in front of her. The sky above the site seemed vast and unnaturally empty, except for a solitary crane, turning slowly like a giant weather vane. In the distance she could make out a snatch of rainbow among the rushing clouds. The band of colour broke into her thoughts and she felt a simple gladness. It wouldn't last long and she felt the luck of catching it.

It was a journey she made four times a week. The dull parade of shops passed beneath her; House of Kebab, A&K Electricals, Londis, StarBurger. Litter chased into the road and was thrown up in dusty whirlwinds by passing cars. A scrap of magazine caught in the metal grille of the KleenMachine laundrette where it quivered flame-like in the wind.

A couple was crossing a side street, talking intensely. A man joined them, and as the pavement narrowed he was forced to step into the road to stay abreast. He kept jumping and hopping from pavement to road and back again as they all three talked. Katherine watched them, pleased by the simple choreography. As the bus turned into Caledonian Road, the shifting collage of reflections in the bus window caught her attention, and she saw her own face. She had been so lost in the world outside that she was almost shocked to see herself: her head a neat oval, the wide cheekbones, the lid of short brown hair. Something wig-like about it, a dull helmet, she thought. Her hand moved instinctively to mess it, plump it, somehow improve it. Her green eyes, like jade beads, glared back at her. She opened her mouth. Her front two teeth had been smashed in a bicycle accident when she was small, and one of the caps was greyer than the other. She closed her mouth to hide them. A train was crossing the Camden railway bridge, and she sat up in her seat, her focus shifting back outside.

At Agincourt Road, she got off the bus. The air was cold, the summer warmth sucked out of it. She zipped up her jacket and walked quickly towards the gap in the red-brick wall. There was no sign to announce Ashwood; a remedial school for problem children was nothing to advertise. She tapped in the code at the security gate and crossed the playground to a 1970s complex of two-storey units. The atmosphere was hushed, the boys already in their classrooms. Katherine worked part-time and always arrived in the eerie mid-morning after lessons had begun. She walked through the double doors, the sound of her heels reverberating down the pale green corridor, past the school office where Michelle, the school secretary, sat behind her window like a gate-keeper.

'Summer's over before it's begun!' said Michelle loudly, without looking up, but detecting the form and heat of an approaching adult. 'And I've not worn one of my new tops!'

Katherine stopped to find an appropriate response.

'Yes, autumn's here,' she said.

Michelle pursed her mouth as if to say that responses to her outburst were not required. Katherine hesitated, unsure whether their exchange was over. She had started the job at Ashwood five months previously but still felt like an outsider, especially with Michelle, who seemed equally unfathomable whether she was being stonily silent or loudly opinionated.

'All I know is that my new summer tops have been a total waste of money,' said Michelle.

Katherine stood looking at the crown of Michelle's head as she busied herself with the papers on her desk. She had never been able to understand how clothes could cause such acute levels of anxiety. Her own sartorial style, a friend had once told her, looked like she dressed by throwing all her clothes up in the air and wearing whatever landed on her.

'Perhaps you could wear one underneath,' said Katherine, 'as an extra layer, for autumn.'

Michelle gave her a sideways look and sucked in her stomach, accentuating her tightly-packed breasts beneath a hugging white T-shirt. Katherine saw the bra straps scoring the flesh like string round a joint of meat. The tightness of it seemed like a decision Michelle had made. The bra was keeping Michelle's life on course, controlling elements of her that might otherwise burst forth and run riot. 'See you later, Michelle,' said Katherine brightly.

She walked down the long corridor past the metal-framed windows which looked out over the playground. Her mobile buzzed in her pocket: a text from Adam. *Okay 2 mt Jack tonight? A x.* Katherine had a vague sense there was something else they were supposed to be doing, but couldn't remember what it was. She climbed the concrete steps towards a small music room. She closed the door and sat at the piano. It was an upright Knight in yellow wood, the kind found in every school across the country, sturdy and loud, perfect for banging out songs in school assemblies. There were two small guitars in soft plastic cases in the corner and a lone snare drum, its black and silver paint scuffed and showing the white beneath. Three glockenspiels and several tambourines were heaped on the piano in an unwieldy pile.

She was early. Her first pupil wouldn't arrive for fifteen minutes. She played a slow run of jazz chords, modulating through minor to major and back again, letting the sound build. She loved to improvise. She'd danced professionally throughout her twenties, and during that time it was improvisation that she had loved most, letting the flow of expression just happen, one movement following another, without censure. Dancing had been everything; acutely shy as a child, she'd found an escape in it, a refuge from the world of

4

words her parents occupied. She had danced obsessively in her teens, and though she had never completed a formal training, by the age of nineteen she was choreographing her own work.

She started a melody with her right hand, letting her conscious mind rest, each strain leading to the next, like waves. When she thought of that time in her twenties, living permanently on the edge of her emotions, dancing with manic intensity wherever she could, on the street, in pub theatres, at music festivals, she barely recognised herself.

There was a bell and the roar of boys' voices. The square face of Liam Baldwin popped round the door.

'Hello, miss,' he said loudly, emphasising the 'miss' as if it was an insult.

'Liam. Good to see you.' He was taller than her, thickset and chubby, and her keenest pupil. Like most kids his age, he dreamt of fame. He seemed to think his weekly lessons with Katherine were a guarantee of a place on one of the TV talent shows.

'Right, Liam.'

'Have you got it, miss?'

The previous week he had told Katherine he wanted to learn 'How Deep Is Your Love?'. It was one of his Nan's favourites, he explained reverentially. Katherine had written out the lyrics from the Internet the night before, and she handed them to him.

'Thanks, miss,' said Liam, grinning, his tone still bafflingly ironic.

5

She played the opening chords loudly, in anticipation of the barrage that would follow.

They made their way through the song, Liam bellowing like a barrow boy, while Katherine accompanied him on the piano, urging him to find a gentler tone. 'Keep it soft, soft, Liam,' she said. 'Imagine you are singing to your Nan.'

They made their way through the song a second time. Liam's voice was becoming more and more accusatory: 'How deep is your love?' Katherine glanced up at him and was unnerved to see him staring directly back at her. She wondered if the brightness in his eyes was mockery. It occurred to her that he was shouting on purpose. There was a meanness in his eyes. He had been shouting ever since he had started lessons with her five months ago. It occurred to Katherine that Liam was a little shit.

He stopped abruptly. 'Miss, am I ready for *The X Factor*?'

'Nearly. Nearly, Liam.'

'Are we finished, miss?'

'Yes . . .'

'See you, miss,' said Liam, backing out of the room. She heard him in the corridor shouting as he went, '. . . cos we're living in a world of dreams . . .'

After he had gone, the door opened an inch and Michelle appeared. She held it ajar to the absolute minimum, as though opening it any more might invite further conversation.

'Conrad Obadino has been sent home,' she said, in a

voice which seemed full of resentment about their earlier exchange about her tops. 'His music lesson is cancelled.'

'What has he done?'

'You don't want to know,' replied Michelle darkly.

'Can Jared Hinton come earlier?' Katherine asked.

'It is not school policy to disrupt the schedule,' said Michelle. She pronounced 'schedule' with the hard American *sk* rather than the English *sh* and shut the door. Her clicking heels became faint in the corridor.

Katherine took out her phone and looked down at Adam's message. Today was the first hearing of his case. He was representing the families of victims of a train crash. Eight people had been killed. She wanted to call him but couldn't face hearing his professional voice, patient and distracted. She walked over to the window. The glass was criss-crossed with metal wire and through the mesh the high brick walls at the edge of the playground were crested by rolls of barbed wire.

She did not notice Jared Hinton enter the room. He stood by the door. It was 11.20. He was ten minutes early. She was shocked to see him. Jared had been forced to do music: one of the other teachers had put his name down on the list as a punishment. He usually failed to turn up at all and Katherine would wait out the half-hour imagining him somewhere in the school, smoking in a toilet cubicle, his scrawny body hard like a fist.

'Jared,' she said, saying his name to be less afraid of him. 'I'm glad you have decided to come.'

She heard the edge of sarcasm in her voice. It was a teacher's sarcasm, the kind of teacher she didn't want to be. Jared's small eyes were moving around the room, his lips mouthing words, fast and silent. She knew what he was doing; counting, everything he could see, every groove in the radiator, every crack on the wall. He looked at the floor and counted every factory-made fleck.

'Jared,' she began.

His eyes roamed over the window, counting the squares in the reinforced glass.

'What do you like to listen to?'

Jared did not answer. He seemed oblivious to the fact that she was in the room. She smiled at him and he turned and stared at her. He seemed to be counting her features, two eyes, one nose, two nostrils, one mouth. She'd heard from other teachers that he could become violent. The tension inside him was wound up like a tight band.

'It's okay, Jared.'

He blew out through his teeth in a hissing sound, turned on his heel and left the room, slamming the door behind him.

Katherine sat back in her chair fighting the inevitable feeling of failure. When she'd applied for the job at Ashwood six months ago, she told herself she'd be doing something important, something valuable. She had no experience of teaching or of working with difficult children, but had cited her grade eights on piano and violin, and written an accompanying letter stating how passionately she felt about the power of music to transform lives. To her surprise she was invited for an interview and turned up at Ashwood with all the confidence of someone with nothing to lose. In a white-walled classroom, she told Henry West, the head teacher, that every child had musical gifts which needed to be nurtured. Henry West had looked out of the window with a haunted expression and asked her if she thought she was tough enough to cope with troubled adolescents. Katherine had surprised herself by asking him whether he had ever broken his ankle. She found herself explaining that when she had been a dancer, she had been tough enough to continue performing for an hour and a half after breaking hers during a show. Henry West replied that he had never broken any bone in his body, sounding almost disappointed that he hadn't. A few days later she'd received a call to say she had got the job. Whether Henry West had admired Katherine's courage in the face of broken bones was unclear. It seemed more likely that he had confused her application with someone else's; he had concluded the call by saying how good it would be to increase the ethnic mix of his staff.

It had seemed to be a fresh start. After the relentless introspection of the dance world, Katherine had been excited at the prospect of really helping people. The troubled boys at Ashwood needed special teachers, and she would be one of them. The reality was not so straightforward. Although she didn't like to admit it, when she was teaching, she often felt completely at a loss.

She walked back down the corridor and slipped out of Ashwood. As she reached the gates, she suddenly remembered what she was supposed to be doing that night. It was her father's fund-raising evening for the Broughton Foundation. Her mother was coming to the house to see Kieron and they were supposed to be going on to it together. She felt depressed at the idea of it: her father's ceaseless anxiety, the long hours of conversation with people she didn't know. She wondered if she could get out of it. She looked at her watch. Her parents would already be on the train. She had an hour to herself before she needed to set off home, do a shop and pick up Kieron. A precious hour. She'd go swimming.

The pool near Ashwood was Olympic-sized and Katherine went whenever she could. She'd swum regularly as a dancer, to keep fit without risking injuries, and it was the one activity from those days she tried to maintain. She would pound up and down the lanes, alternating crawl and breaststroke, enjoying the immersion, the glide, the heave through the water, the not thinking. She would go as fast and as far as possible until her body ached with the effort.

She stopped at a hole in the wall for some money. It was out of order, so she headed into Felling Hospital, where there was a cashpoint in the canteen. A young man, one of the patients, stood outside at the entrance with his eyes closed as the wind billowed his hospital gown. Katherine passed him and went through the sliding doors. She was walking fast, her hand already reaching inside her bag for her purse, when she saw a woman lying on the floor in front of her. Two nurses were leaning over her. The woman was unable to speak or move. Her T-shirt had risen up around her breasts, and her sagging arms and belly flopped against the hard vinyl, the skin like curds.

'Are you in pain?' asked a nurse.

The woman groaned, her mouth slack and open.

'Is this new pain? Is this old pain?'

Two orderlies hurried down the corridor with a trolley. They lifted the woman up on it, and she groaned as they wheeled her away.

Katherine went into the canteen and withdrew some money. She bought a coffee and thought about the woman who'd fallen. She sat at one of the tables. Under the hard strip lights, all the people around her looked isolated, abandoned. An elderly woman was crying into her hand. A man sat smoking in a wheelchair, sucking the smoke deep inside him. A nurse came over and told him to put it out. A father sat silently with a child in school uniform, an untouched doughnut on the table in front of them. Katherine sat there for an hour. She didn't go swimming, she just sat there watching the people, and knowing she didn't want to go home.

2

Oh God oh God oh God! His back, neck and arms tense as rope, all thoughts obliterated, the breath high in his lungs, David Freeman threw open the passenger door as the car sped on to the forecourt of Carlisle train station. Before it had even stopped he was grabbing his bags and running through the stone arch, his heart thumping, towards the platform, lungs heaving, bags banging, calling out, 'London? London? Is this for London?' Interpreting a nod from a guard in a high-visibility waistcoat as affirmation, he leapt on to the train and stood against the door, taking in great gulps of air and adjusting to the sudden calm of the interior. His second-hand greatcoat, fraying at the hems and with a tear in the right arm, hung off his shoulders. His hair, still black at seventy, stood up in wild peaks, blown by the north-east wind. He smoothed it down, and with his briefcase in one hand and a clutch of plastic bags in the other, he made his way into the carriage.

After the madness of catching it, the train now stood frustratingly still, as though in stubborn reproach at his panic. He leant against a seat and lifted the briefcase on to the table. It was full of papers and would not close. In his haste to leave, he had swept everything from his desk into it: notes for his speech that night, a copy of the Broughton Foundation's annual accounts, minutes from the last board meeting, a thick bundle of draft letters to potential sponsors which needed editing. There were several books; a *Complete Works of William Blake*, a *Collected Works of Duncan Harris*, and two thin volumes by new poets that he'd promised to read.

He looked out of the window as Ken came lumbering along the platform, hugging his coat round his enormous body, as if to stop himself falling apart. He was smiling anxiously at David, looking for a sign of his approval after the drama of the car journey. It was because of Ken that David had missed the earlier train; Ken had driven too slowly along the winding roads from Braymer, scared of the corners. They had missed the connection to Newcastle at Hexham by two minutes, leaving them no option but to race down the motorway at breakneck speed to Carlisle to catch this, the slower West Coast train to London. Ken was the gardener at the Broughton Foundation. He had only driven David because his assistants, Paul, Guy and Matthew, were already at St Mark's in London getting ready for the big night. David watched Ken through the window as he shifted from foot to foot, his open face full of the same selfless devotion he had shown when David had first offered him work almost thirty years ago. He couldn't stop a wave of irritation as he watched him. What an idiot he was! God knows what this delay would mean, today of all days, when nothing could go wrong.

The train pulled out of the station. David raised his eyebrows in a mock 'here we go' and Ken waved happily, relieved to have David's attention at last. Ken's smile was an unassailable thing, as uncomplicated as a baby's. Despite himself David smiled back and a snatch of Coleridge came to him:

O happy living things! no tongue
Their beauty might declare:
A spring of love gushed from my heart,
And I blessed them unaware.

The train picked up speed, and Ken disappeared. David sat back and watched the slate roofs of Carlisle pass. Poetry was essential to him; as essential as breathing. It reassured him that feelings, no matter how complicated or hidden, could always find expression. Fragments often flew into his head from nowhere, like rags caught in branches. The pertinence of the lines in this instance was not absolutely clear: whether his smile was blessing Ken or Ken's was blessing him, but whatever it was, they brought him a sense of benevolence. His mind calmed, and he was able to admit to himself that it hadn't been Ken's fault they had been late, but his own. In fact, Ken had been early; David had seen him from his office window, polishing the mirrors of his car, proud to be asked to take the Director to the station. David had caused the delay, panicking at the last moment and rushing back into the office, convinced there would not be enough catalogues to hand out at St Mark's that night.

What if Sir Richard Seaton needed one and they'd run out? The thought had been too much for him to bear. He'd gone through the shelves stuffing copies into a plastic bag until it had split. He'd had to put it inside another to make a double bag, by which time he had misplaced his briefcase and lost his jacket. Finally, when he burst from Sellacrag Cottage and climbed into Ken's car, they were already too late to catch the train at Hexham.

The train slowly gathered speed through the superstores and business parks on the outskirts of the town. It passed a scrapyard with an old pantechnicon parked in full view, an advertisement on its side: *Tommy's, Carlisle's Best Car Dealership.* The view changed to fields, and sunshine broke through the clouds. The fields lost their greyness and shone green. Summer was over but the trees still held on to their leaves. Black and white cows patterned the fields so perfectly they might have been arranged. David felt the relief of finally being on his way.

> *And from my neck so free,*
> *The Albatross fell off, and sank*
> *Like lead into the sea.*

In the buffet carriage he ordered a coffee and some shortbread. A sour-faced woman served him quickly and disappeared. He took a sip of coffee and stared at the Scottish piper on the shortbread wrapper, his mind on the evening ahead. He went over and over it. Sir Richard Seaton. Sir Richard Seaton. Everything depended on Sir Richard Seaton awarding them an endowment, the new library, the future of the Broughton Foundation itself, *everything*.

He opened the shortbread. The cellophane wrapper tore in a sheer line through the tartan man. The biscuit inside was broken and spilled on to the counter. He put a piece in his mouth and the sweetness soothed him.

He had visited the site of the library earlier that morning, dashing across from Sellacrag, head down in the bitter wind, clutching his jacket round him, a hopeless protection against the driving rain, wanting to feel his vision in the bricks and mortar and fuel his zeal for the evening ahead.

The new Broughton poetry library was to be a perfect mixture of modern and old. The roof would be Shillismoor slate, to match the surrounding farmhouses. The walls were to be built from granite like the dry stone walls which chase up and down the surrounding hills. The interior would be finished in oak, beech and chestnut. In the basement, display drawers of manuscripts would glide from cabinets like silk on silk into a climate-controlled atmosphere. The reading room would be dominated by three arched windows, capturing the majesty of the hills in triptych; Bastlegyle, Lyne Top, Kield Hope. There would be hand-carved desks for readers, and poetry would reach within them, seeping deep into their souls and beyond into the moors and fells themselves.

Standing in the unfinished building that morning, the wind beating against the plastic sheeting, David fought a sense of despair. The library stood abandoned, the windows shuttered with chipboard, the walls smeared with pink plaster dried into rough eddies and creases. Every unfinished wall and exposed wire mocked his vision. The rough mosaic of boot prints on the boards which covered the floor was all that was left of the builders.

Nine months previously, Nicholas Durant, Director of Endeline Insurance, and the Broughton Foundation's most significant sponsor of the new library, had suffered a massive heart attack and died. His family had immediately pulled the plug on his promise to underwrite the project. Nicholas's daughter had visited David to explain. A pinched, birdlike soul with none of her father's generosity, she clearly felt that the best way to convey bad news was to be blunt. She had told David that the family wanted to use the money to support the Heart Foundation. 'If we can save one life, my father's death will not have been in vain,' she had said, sounding rehearsed. David had argued valiantly for honouring her father's passion for poetry but it had been no use. The family's mind was made up. With Nicholas's money gone, construction of the library had stopped. The workmen had downed tools, and the building had stood like a ruin in reverse ever since. David faced bankruptcy, and his critics had declared, not for the first time, that the expansion he had undertaken was a hubristic pipe dream. The Broughton Foundation, they argued, should be a modest place with a tea shop, not the international leviathan he envisaged. David had almost drowned in

17

the flood of rhetoric: poetry was out of date, they told him, marginal, elitist, redundant, above all in the North-East, they argued, where work, not art, was what people needed. The Board of Trustees paid for an independent financial adviser to submit a feasibility report on the library's future. David had argued that the money would be better spent on plasterboard. The building was already in existence, the horse long since bolted, he said, jocular in the face of his critics. Privately he was desperate. He knew the figures. To finish the library, pay the interest on the acquisitions bill and secure the Broughton Foundation's future, he needed two million. No amount of cost-cutting would raise that kind of money.

When Sir Richard Seaton announced an arts endowment of six million pounds for arts organisations in the North, David had felt the timing was almost personal. David had met Sir Richard Seaton on several occasions and had been inspired to find a man with qualities close to his own; the same infectious passion, the same stubborn pride in the North. Above all, they shared the same drive to pursue a goal at any cost, even when others could not see or understand it. It was this sense of vision that had made Sir Richard's telecommunications company the empire it was. The evening at St Mark's that night was ostensibly to celebrate the Broughton Foundation's achievements that year, but in reality it had only one real purpose – to impress Sir Richard Seaton and secure an endowment.

The train braked hard, stopped, jolted forward, and stopped again. David picked up the coffee to stop it sliding down the counter. From the window he saw an inland dump bordered by dark pine trees, and above it, seagulls circling, like shrieking scraps. The tannoy crackled into life.

'This is your guard speaking. There will be a short delay to your journey today. This is due to signal failure . . .'

David's heart sank. A delay would mean being late for his brother-in-law, Gregory. He was supposed to go straight from the train to meet him at the flat. For years David had stayed at Gregory's London flat when it wasn't being used by Gregory and Charlotte. He'd had his own set of keys but Gregory had changed all the locks after a burglary on a lower floor, and David had arranged to meet him there to get the new ones. He knew Gregory disliked waiting. The last thing David wanted was to anger him. The whole situation about the flat was already so delicate.

He set off down the carriage, holding his bags in front and behind so as not to bump them against the sides, and sat down at an empty four-seat. Across the aisle, three old women were settling in, putting Tupperware boxes on the table, their faces sweet and lined, their hair done for the journey. One of them looked at David. Something about her disturbed him; a nervous doubt in her eyes, as though she was searching for something. He knew he was about the same age as her, but he felt he was from a younger generation. He did not feel old and uncertain, and he did not look it. People often told him he looked fifty-five, and although he affected a self-deprecating modesty, he had quietly come to believe it. When he looked in the mirror he saw that his face was still impish. It had a way of suddenly lighting up, like a slatted blind on a sunny day. The woman stared at him with her eyes that seemed to tremble, and suddenly it occurred to David that perhaps she was ill, terminally, forever ill. Her face had an unearthly pallor to it. He looked away, out of the window, not to see her.

The train started up again. The sunshine disappeared as fast as it had arrived and the fields lost their lustre. A terrible thought came to him. What if Sir Richard Seaton was ill? What if he became ill? Nicholas Durant had been the fittest of men. David put his hands to his face as if to shield himself from his spiralling thoughts. He cursed Nicholas for his sick and fattened heart.

A sense of dread descended on him. There was no one with whom he could share his burden. He alone bore the weight of the Broughton Foundation. He alone knew how much depended on success at St Mark's that night. It had always been that way, and he felt a sudden crushing loneliness. He reached over to his briefcase and took out some papers. He would go through his lists. Lists helped, they always helped. He put his hand in his pocket and felt the thin reassuring hardness of a pencil.

For the hundredth time, he went through the list of guests, writing small reminders alongside their names in the margin. He made a note to take particular care of

Harold Flacker, his old friend, the ex-government minister who had done so much to help with St Mark's. Next to Harold's name he wrote *Katherine*. Harold liked young people and Katherine was still young at thirty-three. May had insisted on inviting her. She'd said Katherine needed cheering up. David had agreed she should come, not out of concern for his daughter but because Katherine had a vitality that, should she care to display it, would open up some of his more difficult guests. She would be perfect for Harold. He wondered what would be the best way to introduce her now. He had liked it when he had been able to say, 'This is my daughter, Katherine, a dancer'. He couldn't understand why she'd given it up. Dance had seemed to consume every moment of her life until out of the blue she'd thrown it all in for motherhood and, more recently, some teaching job. Teaching what . . .? He couldn't even remember. He jotted down *job?* next to her name and felt a prickle of irritation as he did so.

The women across the aisle were slowly eating sandwiches from the Tupperware boxes. On the table in front of him, David saw his own hands clasped, and dull-skinned with age. He ought to call Gregory to let him know he would be late. He reached for his phone and tried to turn it on. His fingers fumbled for the button at the top. It was such an awkward slither of a thing. He pushed, trying different angles. Eventually he realised the battery was dead. He cursed Matthew, his personal assistant for neglecting to charge it. He cursed the train for being delayed. If Gregory couldn't wait for him, where would he and May spend that night? Katherine's house was impossible; it was miles from the centre of London in some never-ending suburb, and with no spare room. He needed the flat, and for that, he needed to keep Gregory happy.

The thought of his relationship with his brother-in-law depressed him. He had found him difficult from the moment they met fifty years ago. A sullen stone had settled in his belly. The reason was his sister Charlotte. As a boy, David had adored her. Charlotte was the only one in the family who had shown him affection. His father was a farmer, and his parents worked all hours. David was often ill. His mother had little time for him; as far as she was concerned he was a useful pair of hands missing. He would sit in the big chair under a blanket reading books and she would look at him with her grey, cold eyes as she wiped down the long sycamore table. If he ever got under her feet she would slap him. He would run upstairs or escape to the cowshed to hide his tears. Charlotte, five years older than him, always came to find him. She would pick him up in her arms and cosset him like a little lamb, 'Davey, Davey,' she would say. 'Never mind, Davey, never mind.'

Gregory had married Charlotte when she was just seventeen. It had seemed to David that he had taken her as far away as possible on purpose to hurt him, down to Fairhampton on the south coast. Charlotte's life changed and so did she; she became a society hostess, got involved in charity work, and was wealthy enough to pursue her interest in high fashion. David saw her occasionally at family weddings and funerals, or when he borrowed the London flat, but never again found the closeness they had shared as children. David had been unable to shake off his crude, childish resentment of Gregory, and over the years it collected like low and stagnant water. In later years, Charlotte began to drink heavily. Privately, David blamed Gregory for her pain. She would ring late at night, a slurred voice on the end of the phone. 'Davey, Davey, never mind, little Davey, never mind . . .' she would say. He would hang up the telephone, finding her unhappiness unbearable, but what was worse was to feel her drunken words still soothe him, as they had when he was a child.

Charlotte slowly became a stranger to herself. One night Gregory had called David out of the blue to tell him that she had suffered a mental breakdown, and that her deterioration had been so rapid that she had been hospitalised. He had added almost as an afterthought that he was now sharing his life with a woman called Margery, a friend of Charlotte's, and that she was coming to live with him.

The news had shocked David, and the sullen stone shifted inside him. He felt a pure, clear rage and it alarmed him. He decided never to visit Charlotte in her care home, never to see her brought so low. He resolved never to visit Gregory and meet his new partner, in case he should betray his true feelings. But he needed the

London flat, and it was necessary to remain on good terms with Gregory. He redoubled his efforts to please his brother-in-law, and tried wherever he could to involve him in the Broughton Foundation's activities. It was not just that his fund-raising trips to the capital were crucial to David. The flat had become a haven for a side of himself that he could not share with anyone.

The train pushed on, at a grudging pace, into Wigan Station. The crowd of passengers on the platform started to funnel towards the train doors, their voices raucous, the broad tones still Lancastrian but leaning towards the slacker, more open-jawed Yorkshire. Men and women bundled past him down the carriage, searching for seats, their voices known to him from his childhood, from the farm, his father and the farmhands coming in from the fields for tea, sitting at the table, talking about the livestock and the weather, as his mother served bread, cheese and cold beef, and made tea in the brown pot.

A young man in his early twenties stopped at David's table. He slung a kit bag effortlessly on to the overhead rack and took the seat diagonally opposite. He sat effortlessly upright. David noticed the bulk of his torso under his blue T-shirt, his dark hair closely cropped, his level stare; a soldier; a man whose mind is blank, whose body moves unthinkingly. David leant forward in his seat.

'Going far?'

'Crewe.' The man spoke without hesitation, but gave no invitation for David to continue.

'Lancashire Fusiliers?'

'That's right.'

'You're stationed in Afghanistan, aren't you?'

'Kabul.' The soldier looked out of the window.

David searched for an opening. 'I was reading somewhere. Some of the soldiers are fed up with the war . . .'

The man turned and looked at David.

'Some,' he said.

He looked away again and passed his hand over his shorn head, and in the gesture David saw what he had left unsaid; he read the man's mind as clearly as though he had spoken out loud. The soldier, far from being indifferent to talking, was afraid that if he started he might never stop. He was frustrated not by the madness of war but by others' lack of commitment to it.

'I don't understand them,' said David.

The soldier looked directly at David. 'They're a fucking disgrace.'

The swearing excited David. He received it like a physical touch.

'We've come too far not to get it done properly,' he said.

'To come home now would be an insult to those who never will,' said the soldier, and in his quiet fierceness, David heard the voices of others, voices from the past; not an opinion but a belief, passed down through generations.

'Your father an army man?'

'Used to be. He got injured in Belfast.'

'So you were always going to be a soldier?'

'Ever since I was eight . . .'

. . . and the young man let go. His defences fell away and he gave in to David's attentiveness, grateful to speak, to articulate the thoughts he had learnt so well to discipline. David sat back and listened, his eyes bright with pleasure as the soldier spoke of his father, a fitter at the Ford factory, struggling to hold on to his job after a life in the army with tours of duty in Germany, Hong Kong and Ulster. He spoke of his father's pride when he had joined up at the age of sixteen. He spoke of his brother and two sisters, all younger than him and of how they had looked at him when he had arrived home from his first tour of duty in Afghanistan, how they'd insisted he wear his uniform for the first five days of his leave, and how proud he was that they'd made him. He had been asked to talk at his brother's school and had stood on the stage at assembly and the children had clapped as though he'd won the war all by himself, and that evening, his brother had announced that he wanted to join the army too. It was then the soldier's face changed.

'Mam went mental.'

David waited for him to continue.

'Harry's the sensitive one. She wants him to go to university, become a doctor or something, you know . . .'

He fell silent. David saw the soldier's mind turning. He felt the difficulty of the man's return from the war to the petty tensions of his family, his confusion at realising that home was no longer a place to which he belonged, or wanted to belong. The train was pulling into Crewe.

'My stop,' said the soldier.

He stood to take his kitbag from the rack above them. As he stretched up, his T-shirt lifted and David saw his taut belly in shadow, the curl of black hair at the navel. He felt the familiar ache inside him. A man with whom he had begun a connection was already leaving. With more time they would have become close, gained each other's trust, exchanged addresses. David saw himself writing to the soldier in Afghanistan, saw the soldier opening his letters in the hard sunlight, lying on his bunk bed penning his reply, a short dusty missive, and as he thought of it, his fantasy grew.

He reached into his pockets and pulled out their contents: tissues, old receipts, keys. Among them was a clip of business cards. He handed one to the soldier.

'If you're ever in Northumberland,' he said.

'Thanks.'

David smiled. The soldier swung his bag on to his shoulder like a dead weight, and disappeared through the sliding doors. David didn't watch him go. He didn't look out of the window down the platform. He knew how painful the sight of the disappearing figure would be. He didn't want to watch him go or see his business card lying discarded on the platform.

He wished his wife May was with him. She would be on a train herself now. She would have finished her teaching in Carlisle and caught the first East Coast train south to meet him at St Mark's. He had never understood why she insisted on keeping her teaching job. She seemed to insist on being busy just when he needed her most.

The train pulled out of Wigan Station. David looked at the leaden sky, the blurring fields, the rain streaking the dirt down the window. He began to feel sleepy. A memory came to him of Katherine as a little girl, alone in a garden. It was rare to see her without her brothers; the children, all close in age, had usually swarmed together squabbling and noisy. She was dancing in bare feet, leaping and twirling on the wet grass. He saw himself in the garden too. He started to join in her dance. He hopped delicately from foot to foot. He danced through the trees like a spirit. He danced along a silver river. He beckoned for Katherine to follow him into the glittering horizon. He would dance her all the way to the sea.

He awoke, his face softened by sleep. His doctor had told him that these sudden, deep sleeps were normal; just refuelling, he said. David looked out of the window. Black crows flocked over a field like shreds blown from a fire, and a kestrel flew high and alone.

3

May stepped off the Flying Scotsman and on to the platform at King's Cross fifteen minutes ahead of schedule,
happy that she had made the best of her journey. She had
read the first three books of Milton's *Paradise Lost*, writing her notes on torn strips of paper and placing them
between the pages so they stuck out of the top of the
book like a ragged fan. She was ready to lead her class the
following week on 'Milton's World'. She found Milton
stimulating; every time she read *Paradise Lost* she rose
afresh to meet his mind and marvel at his greatness.

She particularly enjoyed the ambiguous attractions of
Satan, both the villain and hero of the poem. She
thought of the illustrations by Blake, Doré and Westall
depicting Satan's virile romantic form, his muscled legs,
smooth torso and sculpted, powerful shoulders. She
admired his rebellious stance against the tyrant God.
Satan's righteous desire for independence chimed deeply
with May. She too felt the strong pull of rebellion, the
fierce demands of her own will. Though ten years past
retirement age, she continued to teach classes at the
Carlisle Adult Education Centre, much to her husband
David's dismay. 'You are independent, May, independent,' he would say as though it was a deeply regrettable

character flaw, but for May, having her own job, away from David and the Broughton Foundation, was more than sheer obstinacy; like Satan, her independence was how she defined herself. *Here at least We shall be free . . . Better to reign in Hell than serve in Heav'n.* She walked with other passengers along the platform towards the main concourse, Milton's words swimming through her. They wouldn't stay with her for long. She would remember their essence but she did not have David's perfect recall. How amazing it would be to be able to store what you read in your mind forever as he did! She berated herself privately: I am a sieve, she thought, scolding herself, a hopeless sieve.

The crowd walked quickly down the platform, released into purposeful strides after a long journey. May was carrying several bags and kept a slower pace. She was not as quick as she once had been but still walked erect, her back straight, with a confident stride. She had always prided herself on being able to walk well. As a child on Blackpool's beaches, she would walk along the wet sand and look back at her footprints with pride, seeing how perfectly one foot fell in front of another. Her mother boasted how May didn't need one of those fancy finishing schools. 'My daughter,' she would say, 'can walk as straight as a Roman road.'

She stopped on the platform and adjusted her bags. She always travelled with a number of them and today had a rucksack, a handbag, a silk satchel, a canvas bag on a long strap and a zip-up briefcase. She liked to spread the weight; a bag for books, a bag for shoes, a bag for papers, a bag for her coat should she wish to take it off, and her handbag for cards, money, handkerchiefs and pens. She also carried a bag for the shirt she was bringing for David and another for the post that had arrived at their house in Carlisle, and pulled a small case on wheels containing her clothes.

A homeless man was coming towards her wheeling a shopping trolley festooned with bags on every possible rail. Inside it, two dogs sat on a bed of hundreds of scrunched-up plastic bags, like toddlers in a pushchair. He stopped in front of May. She stopped too. It seemed to her like a tryst, a secret meeting between two elders of the same bag-carrying clan. She looked at the man's bunched face, his skin the colour of bruises, his lips flaky and white. She reached into her handbag and handed him a pound.

'You're a lady,' he said quietly, 'a real lady. Lady Luck.'

She looked downwards and aslant, abashed like an adolescent girl. A surge of people came down the platform and she sailed on with them, lifted by the tramp's words. There was something lady-like about her. The way she walked, the way she spoke, the way she wore her blouses with a high collar, pinned with a brooch. She had worn blouses like this ever since she was eighteen, when she had a terrible encounter with a bat. It was just before she left her parents' house to take up her scholarship at London University. She had been upstairs in her bedroom. Her mother was haranguing her father in the kitchen below, 'You're no good, no good. You should live in the shed!' Her father started shouting too, and their house, a small two-up two-down, filled up with their quarrel like a Punch and Judy show. May opened her bedroom window to let in the silence of the night. The house gave out on to the fields at the edge of town and the darkness was limitless. Suddenly she was under attack. Bat wings flapped madly in her face. She tried to scream but no sound came. The bat was stuck in her hair. She couldn't bear to reach to her head in case she touched its squealing, frantic form. She felt the bat would get inside her clothes, inside her body. She ran down the stairs, threw open the front door and ran out into the street. The bat went still. She could feel its mouse-like weight, its breathing against her head. She stood in wordless agony. It began flapping again, more desperately than ever, becoming more and more entangled in her hair. She ran into some bushes towards a tree and groped on the ground for a stick. She found one and beat her head with it till the bat was dead. She prised it from her hair and heard the quiet thud as it fell to the ground. When she went back inside, her parents were still arguing.

In the station concourse, a crowd stood looking up at the huge computerised train timetable, people so still and intent that they seemed to May like animals. She weaved her way through them. It was five o'clock. David had asked her to go straight to St Mark's but she didn't need to be there until 6.30; she had plenty of time to go to Katherine's as planned and give Kieron his birthday present.

She reached the taxi rank and stood in a long queue. An American in front of her was speaking into his mobile phone. His accent made her think of the days she and David had lived in San Francisco in the sixties, the salt breeze from the ocean, the fragrance from the eucalyptus trees, the tremendous hope they shared when first married. As always, she felt a distant regret that she had insisted on coming back to England.

A number 73 bus stopped opposite. May left the queue and crossed the road. She could hear David's voice, *For God's sake, May, don't be so bloody-minded!* He had told her there was not enough time to go to Katherine's before going on to St Mark's. He had warned her not to be late – and now here she was, taking the risk of a bus.

She stepped on board, her case bumping up behind her. This bus journey was her little glittering gem of defiance. The driver waved her past. This delighted her. She was really saving money. It would have cost over £15 to get a taxi to Katherine's, and now she was going for free. She sat next to a young black woman and looked out at the grubby shops of the Essex Road. It was raining. Two mums with prams were pulling down rain covers over their babies. May could only vaguely make out the sleeping infants underneath the plastic; like dolls in cellophane packets, she thought. She wouldn't be so late for St Mark's, not really late. She never rebelled too much. Just a little late, she thought, relishing this small margin, and the delicious sense of herself it gave her.

The young woman next to her took off her coat. She wore a T-shirt, and her bare arm touched May's. She was not used to being in close proximity to black people. In Carlisle and in Braymer, people tended to be pinkish-white or greyish brown. Her evening classes at Carlisle Adult Education Centre hadn't attracted one single black person in over thirty years, despite her once putting on a course called *Africa: A Literary Journey*. She felt the black arm resting next to her own. Beautiful, thought May, just beautiful. The woman would be about the same age as Katherine, and she wondered wistfully if Katherine might know her. She knew so little of her daughter's life. It had always been impossible to guess what Katherine was really feeling, or what she might do next, like her taking that job at the school, or her giving up dance and settling down with someone like Adam.

She had always been troubled, too wilful. As a child she had been awkward in company, with a particular intensity. Dance wasn't something May had encouraged, but Katherine had begged for lessons. May took her along to the local ballet school and enrolled her in the grade one class. Katherine was already nine years old, and May remembered her towering above all the four-year-olds in pink tutus, her face set with determination as she tried to master the steps. After ten lessons the teacher told May that Katherine was talented and should audition for a dance school in London, but May was so busy with the other children, her own job and David's demands, that she did nothing about it. It had been typical of Katherine that she had found her way into dance quite independently. She found the only contemporary dance class in Carlisle and signed up. It was run by an unconventional Dutch woman called Gelda van Schut. May worried Gelda was a bad influence on Katherine. She remembered Katherine as a teenager, coming home from class exhausted and bruised from head to toe. Katherine had explained she'd been doing contact improvisation and told her all about it. It didn't sound like dance to May, more like people throwing themselves carelessly around a room. She had been dismayed when Katherine at seventeen, encouraged by this strange teacher, announced she was leaving school to go to Berlin to study dance with a radical choreographer. Nothing could persuade her to finish her studies. She knew no German and had almost no money, but had gone nevertheless. At first May had received long descriptive letters about where Katherine was living and the interesting people she was meeting, but after six months they petered out. May had been sick with worry. When Katherine finally came home, eighteen months later, she seemed lit up by a different fire. She moved to London and started creating her own dance pieces. She sent May a review from a dance journal, with a passage underlined in red pen describing Katherine as having 'a shocking visceral intensity'. When May watched Katherine perform, she barely recognised the shy, silent girl she had brought up. There was something of David in her, the same vitality, the same restlessness. She had no idea whether the pieces were brilliant or dreadful. She only knew that they disturbed her. May had secretly been relieved when Katherine began to be employed by well-known dance companies and stopped making her own work altogether.

She looked at her watch. 5.30. She'd be able to spend half an hour with Kieron. It would be enough time to read him one of the books she had brought him; *Peter Rabbit*, *Tom Kitten* and *Jemima Puddle-Duck*. She wondered if Katherine was happy. Her daughter had always been far more of a worry to her than her brothers William and Michael. William was a teacher living in Scotland with his wife and four children, and seemed satisfied with his life. Michael was a struggling musician living in Canada. He was single and penniless but, like his brother, had an ease in himself that Katherine had never found. May had seen her daughter in a series of intense relationships with difficult men, none of whom had seemed right, until out of the blue she had met Adam, a mature student studying law. No one dreamt Katherine would give him a second glance, but within a year she had stopped dancing and begun a new life with him. They had a child and in motherhood Katherine seemed to have found a new harmony. Ostensibly, Adam brought Katherine nothing but goodness. He seemed to shelter her from herself, but May sensed a restlessness in her daughter, a flickering, like a flame struggling to stay alight.

4

'Did you do a shop?' said Adam as she walked into the house.

Katherine paused in the door.

'I forgot,' she said. He didn't reply but carried on cooking, pouring frozen vegetables into a steaming pan, the atmosphere solid with disapproval.

'I'm sorry.'

She felt a sigh, like a tiny structure collapsing inside her. She walked over to the window.

'Oh my God!' she exclaimed.

Everything had changed. The walls were down and the back garden was open to all the neighbouring gardens.

'Had you forgotten?' he said, not looking up.

The builders had come. Tree roots had been causing dangerous cracks in the garden walls and all the neighbours had clubbed together to pull them down and rebuild them. Kieron was standing on the rubble staring out at this new world without boundaries. A group of kids, ten or twelve years old, were passing a football between them. Kieron, half their age, watched them, fascinated and fearful.

'How was the madhouse?' asked Adam.

'Fine. It was sort of . . .'

She didn't want to tell him how it unnerved her.

'Has this sentence got an end to it?' said Adam, the jokiness covering his frustration.

'Sorry. Yes. It was fine,' she laughed.

'I don't know how you do it,' he said and kissed her.

'I'll go to Sainsbury's tomorrow,' she said.

Kieron picked up a stone from the debris and held it tightly in his hand. She ran outside and grabbed him from behind.

'How's my beautiful boy? How was school?'

His cheek touched hers and she would have held him for longer but he squirmed away from her before the other kids could see. She went back inside. Adam glanced out at him.

'He wants to join in with those boys,' she said.

'He's fine. He likes to watch.'

'He feels left out.'

'He's fine. I used to observe a lot when I was a boy.'

He flipped the fish fingers and did not look at her. It depressed her that he didn't make eye contact. He wasn't angry, it was just habit: a tendency to ignore her, to allow himself to be distracted, lost in his own thoughts. She wondered if it mattered. She wondered if the problem was not with him but with her.

'How was your day, dear?' she said, trying to joke.

'A fucking nightmare.'

'What happened?'

'Same old stuff.'

He took some chips out of the oven.

'What?' she insisted.

'It's not interesting. Still, it pays the rent!' he laughed without humour. The chips were scattered sparsely on the baking tray; just enough for their only child.

Fucking nightmare – pays the rent – not interesting; his words were so many dead ends. She took off her coat and walked into the hall.

'Have you got the holiday insurance?' he said.

'I'm doing it tomorrow.'

'You were doing it last week.'

'Don't get tense,' she said.

'I'm not.'

She took off a shoe, pressing hard with one foot against the heel.

'Adam,' she said, 'I'd forgotten, it's my dad's fundraising thing tonight.'

'You said you didn't want to go.'

'I think we should. My mum's coming. She wants us to go.'

'I can't. I'm seeing Jack.'

'Are you in a bad mood?' she asked, abruptly.

'Not yet,' said Adam.

'It's a big deal for him. It's at St Mark's Club.'

'Don't go, I tell you. You always come back from those things feeling miserable and *someone* has to pick up the pieces,' he said.

'Someone? You mean *you*. If you mean you, why not say you?'

'For God's sake Katherine, what does it matter?'

Their voices had risen. They both looked round instinctively to see if Kieron had noticed.

'You are working too hard,' she said quietly.

'You're tired,' he said.

'You're the one who's tired.'

Katherine went upstairs for a shower, wishing away the tension. She took off her clothes in front of the long mahogany mirror and looked at her body. The dancer's physique was still discernible despite the stretched flesh from her pregnancy. She brushed her hand over the slackened skin, the thin scars like shiny slug trails, and stretched into an arabesque, lengthening her arm above her head. It calmed her to do it. She loved the line the body could make. An arm and leg simply positioned in space. She turned a few inches, making an angle in the mirror, tilting her head, and the line transformed. It became something that had nothing to do with her. It depicted a thousand possibilities – a branch, a building, a refusal, a bid for emptiness. She held the posture for a moment, moved by how expressive it seemed, more than words could ever be.

She dried her hair with a towel, and got dressed. She and Adam would work things out. Minor tensions often rose up between them. They would pass as they always did, until the next time. She hadn't been sure about going to St Mark's, but the fact that Adam was so against it hardened her resolve.

She put on a paisley blouse and leant over the stair rail.

'I'm going,' she called down.

'You hate poetry.'

She didn't hate it, but poetry was the language of her father. It was his profession, almost his religion. Her parents' lives had always been full of it. They spoke about dead poets as vividly as though they were relations or close neighbours, and new poets as though they were precious offspring. Her father, in particular, never ceased to reference poetry, or to quote it. Katherine had grown up finding his words impenetrable. They seemed like riddles, and however hard she tried to decipher them, the meaning always eluded her. As a child, she believed it was her own fault. After all, when her father talked with other people they understood everything, they received his words like precious counsel. She thought she was simply too stupid to understand. She had always believed this, and no one ever tried to persuade her otherwise.

Despite Adam's advice, Katherine knew she would go to St Mark's; she was programmed to respond to her father's needs. The whole family was. All through her childhood, she had been instilled with a sense of how precarious her father's world was. She had grown up longing to make things easier for him, to share his burden. As a child, she reasoned that if she could help him there would be less for him to do, and he might stay at home in Carlisle more often. He worked so late at the Broughton Foundation in Braymer that he often stayed overnight in the little cottage, Sellacrag, and the rest of the time he was always rushing to catch trains to London. She dreamt of him becoming the man she glimpsed once a year at Christmas, when he would spend the whole wonderful day at home with them, listening to their stories, and watching them play. He would carve the turkey and hand out the presents from under the tree like he was Father Christmas himself. By Boxing Day he was back at work.

On rare occasions, he had let her comb his hair. He would come home exhausted from one of his trips, and she would stay up late to see him. He would hold out the small black comb from his jacket pocket and she would stand behind his chair and draw it nervously through the black strands, watching the flecks of dandruff and the dreadful whiteness of the scalp beneath. Her father would close his eyes and become calm and still. It seemed like a little miracle to her, and she imagined his silence filled with gratitude.

Katherine finished dressing quickly and came downstairs.

'Come with me. It might be interesting. There might be some interesting people,' she called to Adam.

'That's exactly the kind of thing your parents would say. Kieron's tea is ready. Can you get it out for him? I've got to write a thousand e-mails . . .'

Rain was dotting the flagstones in the back garden. With the wall gone, Katherine could see into the kitchen of the house opposite. It was bathed in the yellow light of an orb lampshade that stood on a shelf of large hardback books. A short-haired woman was chopping vegetables at a table next to a fridge covered in colourful magnets.

In the garden, the older boys were still playing football. Kieron stood underneath the willow, tugging at a rope he had thrown over a low branch to make a pulley. He had tied a basket to one end. The boys took no notice of him. Adam is wrong, she thought, Kieron is not happy watching. He wants to join in. He is hoping the big boys will notice his rope and basket. He wants to be part of their world.

The rain started to fall more heavily and the group of boys went into one of the houses. Kieron was left alone. He stood staring up at the house. Katherine imagined him thinking about the older boys, playing computer games, watching TV together on a sofa, eating crisps and sweets. He frowned. She didn't want him to be upset.

'Kieron! Come here! You'll get soaked!'

He turned and ran to her. She picked him up and snuggled him, making a coin-sized patch of heat on his neck with her mouth.

'Mummy, throw me.'

She swung him round and tossed him on to the sofa. He landed with his head thrown back, winded for a moment, and laughed.

'Again! Throw me again!'

The bell rang. He scrambled up and ran to open the door.

'Grandma! Have you brought me a present?'

May hugged her grandchild.

'Have I? A little something. Let me see.'

'Kieron, let Grandma come in first.'

Her mother was wearing navy as usual: a navy blouse, cardigan and wool skirt, navy stockings and navy shoes. Her clothes were almost a uniform. She always bought navy. It was part of her sense of thrift; she could match any of her clothes to make a passable outfit. 'Making do' was deeply ingrained in May. She had been brought up with the pain and bitterness of money.

'Do you need a drink? Some tea?' said Katherine.

'I don't *need* anything,' said May, looking in one of her bags, 'but I might have a little warm water.'

Katherine went into the kitchen and flicked on the kettle. Her mother drank ten cups of water a day. She seemed to have an unquenchable thirst. As the kettle began to rumble, she could hear her talking with Kieron in the sitting room.

'Do you know this story, Kieron?'

'About a duck!'

'Yes, a silly old duck. Do you know what she does?'

'No.'

'She gets seduced by a clever fox.'

'Why?'

'She thinks she's better than the rest of the animals, so she goes away from the farm. It's dangerous to go away from what you know, isn't it?'

Katherine listened to her mother's voice, soft and loving. She remembered it so differently as a child; she had always sounded fractious and impatient. Her mother had always been busy. There was no home help, and with her father constantly working May had been stretched to the limit with three small children, but she still insisted on maintaining her teaching post. She remembered her always busy, her attention constantly split, at the cooker stirring a pan with one hand while reading a book in the other. Katherine poured the water into a china cup knowing her mother liked to drink from a thin edge. In the sitting room, May was in an armchair with Kieron on her knee. Katherine gave her the cup and watched her mother drink. It made her throat feel dry to see her drink so thirstily.

'We should go,' she said. 'We mustn't be late. You know how Dad gets anxious.'

5

It seemed the clouds were being wrung dry. David stood at the top of the marble staircase in the lobby of St Mark's Club watching the rain. The marble tiles in the courtyard shone in the lamplight, the water like spitting fat. Beyond the ornate iron gates, people were running in the street, clutching umbrellas, holding newspapers and bags over their heads; they crammed into bus shelters and jumped back as passing cars sent up black sheets of water.

Paul Whitley and Guy Wallingford, two of David's assistants, stood on either side of him, their young, ruddy faces shining on top of stiff new shirts and ties. Towering behind them stood a stone Venus, naked, her hands carefully placed. Everyone was motionless, watching the door.

'We need umbrella stands,' said David tensely.

Yes, yes, they nodded, umbrella stands. The two young men couldn't have looked more different. Paul, who had worked for David for ten years, was built like a rugby player, and stood guard-like at his side. Guy, who had joined the staff more recently, was short and eager, his face as round as a soup spoon, polished and ready to be put to use. Both looked at David with avid attention.

'Time?' said David.

'Five forty-five,' said Guy.

'Where is she?' muttered David. 'Where the hell is she?'

'Traffic,' said Paul.

David pushed his hair back from his forehead in frustration, making it stand upright in a quiff. The rain drummed on the windows.

'Stephen,' said Paul suddenly.

'Where is he?' said Guy anxiously.

'Don't worry. He'll be here,' said David.

David's trust in Stephen Jericho, the poet, was unshakeable. They'd met eight years ago through a mutual friend. David had read Stephen's work and found it promising enough, but when he'd met him in person, he saw a far more fascinating character than was revealed in his work. There was something beyond the charm – a searching quality, a fragility. In Stephen's need and passion for poetry, David saw something of a younger version of himself. He felt Stephen had the potential to write something truly great if he could only find the confidence and the focus. Five years later, there was an opening at the Broughton Foundation and David invited him to Braymer as poet-in-residence.

'This damn rain,' said David. He walked down the marble stairs, which splayed out before him like a stone skirt.

'It won't put people off,' said Paul.

The very mention of people being put off was more than David could bear. He stroked his head again in three rapid strokes, making his hair wilder than ever.

'Did you speak with Sir Richard Seaton's PA?' he asked.

'This afternoon. Sir Richard is coming straight from a board meeting. We are to expect him any time after seven,' said Guy.

'Right, right. Good,' said David.

Their anxious voices rose through the lobby, the Lancastrian tones bouncing softly off the stone and marble.

'Tonight is very big, very big,' whispered David. Paul and Guy nodded. For a while no one spoke.

'Harold Flacker called,' said Paul. 'Third time today. He's anxious about the seating plan . . .'

'We must look after him,' said David firmly. 'It's because of Harold that we are all here.'

Getting St Mark's Club had been a coup, and David had Harold Flacker to thank for it. David had known Harold as a boy at Lancaster Grammar School. Harold's father had been a signalman on the Carnforth line, and the two boys used to sit in his signal box for hours talking about socialism and whether it was best achieved by slow reform or bloody revolution. At eighteen both had gone to Oxford University, where to David's astonishment, Harold had joined the Tory party. After graduating, he rose rapidly through the party ranks, eventually becoming Minister of Education in the Thatcher government. Their paths did not cross again until they were in their fifties, when Harold had been forced to resign from the cabinet after the *News of the World* disclosed a homosexual affair with his parliamentary secretary. Harold's political career was over, and he was ostracised by even his closest friends. When everyone else was deserting him, David got in touch. He listened to Harold, never judging him, as he talked through his fears and confusion. Once again the two men spent hours together, talking as earnestly and passionately as they had in the Carnforth signal box. Harold had never forgotten David's kindness, and when David had told him he was looking for a prestigious London venue to promote the Broughton Foundation, Harold had been delighted to use his contacts to secure St Mark's. An imposing building built in the late nineteenth century as a guest house for royal visitors and now leased to the Foreign Office for official functions, it was the perfect venue to impress Sir Richard Seaton, conferring as it did on the Broughton Foundation the status of an enterprise of national importance.

'Catalogues?' said David.

'On the table inside the main room,' said Paul.

'Get them,' said David, suddenly urgent. 'You must always have one on you, in case you can catch a rising wave of enthusiasm. You never know when that wave will strike, and when it does, you must be ready.'

Paul hurried off into the main reception room, his shoes clicking on the hard marble floor.

'Where the hell *is* May?' said David.

Guy looked around as if she might appear from one of the upper corridors.

'Have you got the plug for the mobile phone?'

'Plug?' said Guy.

'The thing, you know . . .'

'A charger?'

'Yes.'

'Yes, yes I have. Yes . . .'

'My mobile? Where is it?'

'You left it in your coat.'

'And my coat? Where is my coat?'

Panic, like a cloud, rose between them.

'I'll find it. I'll find it,' said Guy, scurrying off to search, to do something, anything that might alleviate the tension.

The sounds and vibrations of his assistants' frenetic activity kept David's darker feelings at bay, the fear that compacted inside him like a tight bud, that he would fail and be seen to fail. He believed pressure and stress could never hurt him. He was protected by his miracle pills. He had suffered a mild brain aneurism ten years before and his doctor had prescribed Inderal to keep his blood pressure down. These pills are your safety net, the doctor had told him. If you take them regularly, you will never have a heart attack. David loved this guarantee and whenever the opportunity arose, boasted playfully that he had the blood pressure of an eighteen-year-old.

He walked across the mosaic floor of the lobby into the cloakroom. An attendant was placing coat hangers on hooks.

'Do you have any umbrella stands?' he asked.

'Of course, sir,' said the young man in an East European accent.

He stepped to one side to reveal a wooden stand holding several umbrellas. There was a puddle of water on the floor below it.

'Good. We're going to need it,' said David.

He went to the door and looked out at the rain. A queue of headlamps blurred towards a distant traffic light. He closed the door and turned back to the attendant.

'Have you worked at St Mark's for long?'

'Six months,' said the man.

'Where are you from?'

'Poland.'

His straw-coloured hair fell over one eye. His skin was so pale it was almost luminous.

'What do you want to do?' asked David.

The young man looked up in surprise.

'I sorry?'

'In your life, I mean. Did you work in a cloakroom in Poland?'

'I make camera for film,' said the man.

'Film? How wonderful,' said David, his face lighting up. 'Film is my secret love. If I could have my time again I would be a film maker. Polish film makers are the best in the world. Andrzej Wajda's *Ashes and Diamonds* is one of my favourites.'

A smile spread across the attendant's face. David was grateful for it. The smile gave him focus and allowed his curiosity to flourish. Where did this young man live?

With other Poles, in a shared house? Did he stay up all night editing his films? He looked at him more carefully: his soft skin without bristle, his eyes blue like lavender. Could he become involved in the Broughton Foundation somehow? Make a film for it perhaps? He was reaching in his pocket for a card when the front door opened and a man and woman ran in.

'David! Good to see you!'

'Tom! Sarah! Welcome!'

Mr and Mrs Dillon, eminent book dealers and supporters of the Broughton Foundation, emerged from dripping coats and umbrellas.

The Polish attendant snapped back into his formal role and helped them off with their coats. Guy and Paul rushed down the stairs to take their positions. Paul was clutching half a dozen heavy catalogues. Guy held David's mobile phone and charger. They all shook hands vigorously.

'So good of you to brave the storm, Tom,' said David.

'We wouldn't have missed it. It is always lovely, David,' said Mrs Dillon.

The Dillons were not vastly rich but they were childless and David hoped that one day they might bequeath their rare book collection to the Broughton Foundation.

'It's good to see you, David,' said Tom Dillon warmly.

All David's panic evaporated in the heat of their affection; the way they said his name, acknowledged and supported him. It was an electricity he could tap into and he switched himself on like a light.

'Who is reading tonight?' said Tom Dillon.

'Duncan Harris,' said David proudly.

'What a coup!' said Mrs Dillon.

'And Stephen Jericho, our former poet-in-residence. You may remember him? His first collection won the Lexicon Prize. He is now writing an epic poem.'

'I remember him,' said Mrs Dillon. 'Very good on childhood.'

'We only get the best,' said David turning to the attendant. 'We even have our very own Polish cinematographer taking your coats!'

'Really?' said Mrs Dillon, caught up in David's irresistible way of presenting the world as a place rich with infinite possibility, where poems were epics and cloakroom attendants international film makers.

'Paul, take these brave people upstairs and give them a drink. Wine or whisky? Do we have whisky? Whisky Macs on a night like this. Tom, we must talk about your Chaucer. I've found its companion, Wordsworth's copy of Gray's annotated Chaucer . . .'

The door opened again, and a tall imperious woman in a rain hood and long fawn-coloured coat strode into the lobby.

'Ghastly!' she announced to no one in particular.

'Louise!'

David rushed to greet her. Lady Highsmith was David's most loyal supporter. She was nearly a foot taller than David and bowed her cheek gently towards him to be kissed.

'Not too early, I hope,' she said, sniffing the air as if she could smell how many people had arrived. 'What ghastly weather!'

She saw David's anxiety.

'It's perfect,' she said. 'Rain always brings people together.'

She undid her clear plastic rain hood, covered in diamond drops of water. Lady Highsmith was in her eighties, with a long face creased like unironed silk. She kept herself softly powdered, her hair expertly dyed, her eyebrows perfectly drawn into two squirrel-red arches above intelligent eyes. People still referred to Lady Highsmith as beautiful, and they meant her kindness as much as her elegance. David was always reassured by her. Her upper-class demeanour seemed to reassure the working-class man in him.

'I've brought someone!' she said, her eyes twinkling. 'He's in his car finishing a phone call.'

'Who is it?' said David excitedly.

'Paolo Giordano,' she whispered, as though it was a secret joke between them.

'Shoes?' said David.

'I know him from Tuscany,' said Lady Highsmith nodding. 'We had lunch with him today. I persuaded him to come along.'

David grinned at Lady Highsmith. She had spoken to David previously about Paolo Giordano, the Italian shoe manufacturer, telling him he was a rich and cultured man, often in England on business, the kind of man who might donate to the arts. The purpose of the evening at St Mark's was primarily to woo Sir Richard Seaton, but any potential funder was welcome. As though on cue, the door opened. A handsome man in his fifties walked into the hallway.

'This English weather!' he said.

'Weather? What weather?' said David walking forward to meet him. 'This is vital rain. How else are we to be a green and pleasant land?' He smiled and shook Paolo Giordano's hand. 'David Freeman,' he said. 'An honour to meet you.'

'Paolo Giordano. A pleasure to meet you,' said the Italian formally.

'Louise has told me all about you,' said David. 'It is wonderful that you have come.'

And it was. It was wonderful that Paolo Giordano should arrive at an obscure, esoteric event like this on such a cold, wet night. Paolo Giordano, world leader in fashion and commerce, like all business people, was obviously a creative man. People like him needed to be reminded of other worlds, abstract beautiful worlds in which their minds could roam free. He felt sure that he and Paolo could both gain much from each other. How apt of Lady Highsmith to bring him, he thought, how perfectly judged.

He led them upstairs, full of optimism, joking with Paolo: was Italian rain as robust as this? Had he had ever visited Northumberland – 'a rain-filled paradise', 'a miniature Tuscany'? As they reached the top of the stairs the front door opened again and May and Katherine came in out of the rain. David signalled to Guy to take Paolo Giordano and Lady Highsmith upstairs and ran back down. The Polish attendant was already helping May with her bags.

'Everything all right?' she said, a little too brightly.

'For God's sake, May! Where have you been?'

'To see Kieron. I left you a message on your phone. We got stuck in traffic.'

'I told you to get a taxi straight here . . .'

'We're here now, Dad,' said Katherine, kissing her father on the cheek. 'Hello.'

'Yes, yes, hi, Katherine. Great you are here,' he said, noticing how bedraggled his daughter looked in her big coat and jeans. Like a student, he thought. Why couldn't she have worn a skirt? She must know how important the night was to him.

'Did you get the keys from Gregory?' asked May.

'My train was late.'

'Have you not spoken with him?'

David shook his head to silence May. It was not the time.

'I've got your shirt,' said May, understanding perfectly.

'The Dillons are already here and Louise has brought Paolo Giordano.'

'Who?'

'Paolo Giordano of Giordano Shoes, May! They're upstairs,' he said, his voice full of accusation.

'They're all very early,' said May, ignoring his tone.

David sighed. What did it matter if they were early? They were upstairs right now and needed looking after.

'Haven't Paul and Guy been helping?' said May.

'Of course, but . . .'

'And Matthew?'

'Matthew is coming later.'

'He should be here.'

'He had to see a friend.'

'He's supposed to be your personal assistant,' said May testily. 'Doesn't the Broughton Foundation pay him to be here?'

David looked at May darkly, warning her.

'Come,' she said, taking his arm. 'Let's find somewhere to change your shirt.'

'May, no!' said David. It was too late for a new shirt. Why didn't she ever understand?

May did understand. She knew that this was not the moment to nag about Matthew, another in David's long line of young and selfish personal assistants. She knew that Sir Richard Seaton could arrive any moment. She knew her husband was a brilliant man on the verge of securing a major endowment, but she also believed in the importance of a clean shirt.

'Come.' She took his arm more gently.

'There's no time . . .' he said weakening.

'Please, David, just nip into the loo.'

'Oh God.'

He glanced around. The Polish attendant was hanging May's bags inside the cloakroom.

'I'll come with you,' insisted May.

'No, no.'

'Yes.'

'Please, May! All right, I'll put it on. Just go and be with the guests. Introduce yourself to Paolo. He's Italian. Paolo Giordano. He could be important to us. Don't put on an Italian accent when you speak to him.'

'Really, David . . .'

'And talk to the Dillons about the Chaucer exhibition next year. They own Gray's annotated Chaucer, remember? Maybe they would lend it, and if you see Harold. And Sir Richard Seaton, he's expected from seven . . .'

'David, I can't talk to them all!' she said, teasing him.

He sighed in exasperation. Despite his protestations, May knew he was reassured by her mischievousness, as she was by his indignation.

Katherine was left alone in the lobby. She undid her coat. The attendant took it from her shoulders with a hint of gallantry; he had caught some of her father's enthusiasm. She walked slowly up the stone stairs past the alabaster Venus. The damp, unheated air made her shudder involuntarily.

'Katherine! Katherine!'

David ran up the stairs behind her, stuffing the tails of his fresh white shirt into his trousers.

'Has your mother gone in?' he said, looking past her.

When he spoke to Katherine about May, David always

referred to her as 'your mother' rather than the familiar 'Mum' which presumed an intimacy he resisted. It was part of his stubborn Northern heritage. 'Your mother' was used by men to distance themselves from the family; 'your mother' seemed to Katherine to mean, 'she's your mother and neither of you have anything to do with me'. It jarred again as she heard it and the old feelings of resentment contracted inside her.

'Yes, she's gone in,' she said quietly.

'Right,' said David, not listening. 'About dinner . . .'

'I'll sit wherever you want me to,' she said.

'Actually we're short of places . . .'

'I don't need dinner,' she cut in quickly.

'You don't mind, do you?' he said.

'Of course not.'

She knew she mustn't mind. This was her father's work, and his work was known by the whole world to be important. Why should she mind? Why did she? She didn't even want to stay.

'Harold Flacker needs looking after,' said David. 'I wonder if you could, Katherine? He likes young people.'

'I'm not young,' she said.

'He's just written his memoirs. You'll have to speak up. He's going deaf. Talk about your dancing.'

'I don't dance any more.'

'Can't you pretend?'

She looked at him in silence and as their eyes met there was challenge in them both. When David spoke there was anger in his voice.

'For God's sake, Katherine! What's the matter with you?'

She wanted to shout back at him but her antagonism was inexpressible and she stood there like a dumb child.

'What is the point of your being here if you are not concerned with the guests?' His voice was cooler now, softer, as though he knew she could not speak.

She folded her arms, the whole mess of her response packaged into one stubborn gesture. She held his gaze, trying to match his will, but she already knew this was a battle she mustn't win. She couldn't make trouble, not on a fundraising night. Her eye was drawn to her father's hand, clutching the stone banister. Did he hold it so tightly because he was upset, or because he was fearful he might fall? The fight in her subsided. She uncrossed her arms and tucked in his stray shirt collar.

'I'm sorry, Dad,' she said.

He let her fuss him, craning his neck so she could fold the collar into position.

'You look nice,' she said, not knowing what else to say.

'Always important,' he said smiling, the impatience gone. He put his head on one side to show he was grateful for her capitulation. Katherine could see the cloakroom attendant below them, his black trousers and white shirt blurring against the floor tiles. The front door banged open. New guests were arriving, and David headed back down the stairs.

'Don't forget Harold, Katherine,' he called over his shoulder. 'Talk to Harold about your dancing.'

*

Katherine reached the top of the stairs. A waiter stood by the double doors to the reception room, holding a tray of drinks. The room had a light blue carpet, giving it an institutional look, like a function suite in a hotel. Chandeliers hung from the ceiling. Katherine could hear people talking within, and a tightness entered her chest as she imagined the next few hours: the failing conversations, the nodding, the smiling, the shrinking inside.

Adam was right, she thought. She shouldn't have come. She remembered another of her father's events. She had been younger, around nineteen, just returned from Berlin. The guests' voices had seemed so loud she couldn't hear her own thoughts, let alone join in a conversation. She tried to escape. She wanted to walk up Bastlegyle, to run, to move, but her father stopped her by the door. 'Don't be shy,' he said. 'If you're feeling shy it's because you are thinking of yourself. Forget yourself. The secret to being comfortable in life is never to think about yourself. Always think of others.'

It was the only advice he had ever given her. Katherine took a glass of wine from the waiter and walked in. The wine tasted strong and good. Think of others, she told herself, think of others.

New guests were still arriving, running in from the rain, climbing the marble staircase, taking wine from the trays, laughing loudly as they entered the party. Some had the crumpled look of academics, others were

61

glamorous. David welcomed them all, and moved amongst them making introductions and connections. The waiters passed through the rooms with trays of fresh asparagus tips wrapped in Parma ham, scallops on tiny toasts and oat wafers with caviar. The canapés alone were costing a fortune, but it was worth it. David imagined the moment Sir Richard Seaton would walk through the double doors. The two men would look across the room at each other and the recognition would be a taut line held between them: we understand each other, their look would say, my world is your world.

David spotted Duncan Harris, the Scottish poet on the far side of the room. He was standing with George Gull, who was staring sulkily at the floor as though he was all alone in the room. George was a forty-five-year-old conceptual artist whose strange paintings did not sell, and who had a knack of alienating everyone he met. No one had wanted to bring him to the Broughton Foundation but David had seen something fascinating in his fierceness and had offered him a year-long residency.

David was making his way over to rescue Duncan Harris from George's misanthropy when a tall, thin young man in a velvet jacket too short in the sleeves, sauntered up to him.

'Matthew!' said David. 'There you are at last!'

'I have been here for hours, in spirit,' said Matthew, smiling archly, his thick Manchester accent levelling all the words.

'Come and be useful,' said David, ignoring the sarcasm and steering him towards Duncan Harris.

'Duncan! This is Matthew. He's my . . .'

'Slave,' butted in Matthew.

Duncan Harris laughed.

'Matthew is my assistant. He has the precocity of youth.'

Duncan Harris turned to Matthew, relieved to have a new focus. George Gull slunk away and stood at the edge of the room beneath an oil painting of a lady with a dog on her lap.

'I admired your last collection,' said Matthew to Duncan, his voice deadpan, 'almost as much as I admire Ezra Pound's *Cantos*.'

Duncan Harris roared with laughter, delighted at the young man's arrogance. David left them talking. He took a bottle of white wine from a waiter's tray and moved amongst everyone filling their glasses. May was talking earnestly to the Dillons by the marble fireplace. The two young sculptors, Rita and Pomona, seemed amused by the whole occasion. They couldn't wait for the poetry readings, they said, laughing, they'd waited all year. Wonderful, thought David, as he weaved his way through the crowd. People being witty, people being scurrilous, people talking deeply; it was a celebration of everything he treasured – conversation, conviviality, art.

Guy was standing by the door.

'Has Sir Richard arrived?' said David looking towards the stairs.

'Not yet.'

'Check the mobile,' he said.

Where was he? It was past seven. He took another bottle of wine from a waiter and walked over to a small group that included Paolo Giordano and Harold Flacker. Harold was clearly straining to keep up with the conversation, his face gaunt and uncertain. David was irritated that Katherine wasn't looking after him as he'd asked. He looked around the room for her but there was no sign of her.

'Let us eat and drink, for tomorrow we die!' said David, holding the wine bottle high.

An attractive woman with flawless skin stood next to Paolo Giordano. Her thick black hair was cut into an expensive bob and her figure was neat, her pink dress hugging her bosom and flaring at the waist. She wore a string of pearls around her neck.

'My wife arrived late. Ilana,' said Paolo Giordano, stroking her arm, 'David Freeman.'

'I love poetry. I love it, really I love it,' said Ilana in a thick accent, looking meaningfully at David.

'This is certainly the place for you!' bellowed Harold Flacker, relieved that David had joined them.

'Yes,' said David, ignoring him and turning to Ilana, 'we have two excellent poets reading tonight. Duncan Harris, who you might know, and Stephen Jericho who you will enjoy getting to know.'

'*Bene, bene*,' said Ilana Giordano. 'Darling, it is wonderful to be here.'

She kissed her husband and he smiled like a boy who had pleased his teacher. David was anxious to talk to Paolo Giordano alone but the presence of his wife made it more difficult. He asked her whether she liked Dante.

'Of course,' said Ilana Giordano.

'Then you must meet my wife. She is an expert on Dante,' said David looking round for May.

'Are you staying for the dinner?' said Harold Flacker loudly.

'Dinner? There is dinner?' asked Ilana.

'You must stay,' said David. 'I won't allow you to leave until you have tasted our pâté. The best in London, I'm told.'

'The pâté! The pâté! The dinner! We must stay for the dinner!' cried Ilana, as if pâté and dinner were divine revelations.

May was by the fireplace, still talking enthusiastically with Mr Dillon. Katherine stood near her, vaguely hoping for reassurance. The evening had been worse than she had imagined. Since she'd arrived she had talked briefly to Guy about Sir Richard Seaton and the endowment. She had spoken to Bob Clayton, an old friend of her parents from their days in San Francisco. She had spoken to one of the waiters about their shifts. She had said a guarded hello to Matthew, her father's new assistant, whose bristling irony she found exhausting. She had been unable to sustain a conversation with any of them. Her mother on the other hand was in full flow with Mr Dillon, her fingers conducting the air with ardent precision.

Katherine stepped forward and touched her arm.

'Mum . . .'

May looked around, emerging from the depths of her conversation, lifting her head like a swimmer unsure of her coordinates.

'What is it?' she said, unable to disguise her irritation. She hated being interrupted, especially by her children. For a lifetime they had demanded her attention, tugging at her skirt, indistinctly wanting something, needing their squabbles stopped, their endless questions answered.

'Tom, this is my daughter Katherine. I don't know if she has read *The Canterbury Tales*. The school she went to hardly made them read at all. Tom Dillon,' she said to Katherine, the introduction almost a reproach.

'Hello,' said Katherine.

May dived back into the discussion.

'The Wife of Bath might appear to be a comic figure,' she said with teacherly persistence, 'but surely Chaucer is presenting us with a serious discussion about the power struggle between the sexes . . .'

Katherine took another glass of wine from a waiter, and moved away. She didn't know how to talk like her mother. She didn't know anything about Chaucer. Chaucer was a wall. Chaucer, Dante, Milton, Shakespeare, Wordsworth, the great writers who had peopled her childhood, existing for her parents as living, breathing individuals, had always been walls to her. She stood apart, hating the feeling of being on the outside. She remembered her father's precious advice, but she felt too uncomfortable to do anything with it. In this room full of erudite guests, she felt her ignorance like shame.

Katherine's formal education had been a failure. She'd attended Moreton, a rough comprehensive where clever children were bullied, and the whole ethos was to do as little as possible. Her mother and father had always been so busy with their own lives that they'd been blind to what a dreadful school it was. Katherine had found her challenge and her sanctuary in dance. She adored her dance teacher Gelda van Schut, who had danced with Hans Müller in Berlin when she'd been younger, and spoke of it with such reverence and excitement that Katherine felt inspired to do the same. Katherine had barely ever left the North of England before, but aged seventeen she set off to Germany. She waited tables and with an introduction from Gelda, did class with Müller's company. The technique was rigorous but Müller had a freedom in his thinking that opened Katherine's mind. He believed there was nothing more essential to dance than emotional truth, and encouraged all his dancers to mine their own experience. Under his influence, Katherine's shyness transformed into a fearless urge to express herself, a desire to create in movement a world that made sense to her.

'Katherine!'

It was her father, his arm round Harold Flacker.

'Harold, you remember my daughter Katherine.'

'Of course,' said Harold. 'How are you, young lady?'

'Fine, Harold. How are you?' said Katherine.

Her father was already gone, introducing Ilana Giordano to May.

'Your father is a great man,' shouted Harold. 'You are lucky to have such interesting and clever parents.'

'Yes,' she said. 'Yes, I am.'

'You're a dancer!' Harold said loudly, nodding his head, trying to get something going.

Katherine looked at his hearing aid. The pinkish plastic looked somehow naked, like a newborn mouse curled in his ear.

'Must be an interesting life,' he said, still nodding.

'I don't dance any more,' she said. 'Now I am a part-time music teacher.'

'Pardon me?' said Harold.

The chandeliers hung above the guests, their glass pendants heavy. They seemed to sway; Katherine had the feeling they were going to crash to the floor and smash into the guests. She saw them all screaming, their faces bloodied.

'I don't dance any more, Harold. I kept getting injured.'

'Right, right,' said Harold.

He couldn't hear what she was saying above the noise of the other guests, but clearly felt too defeated to ask her again.

'Excuse me, Harold,' she said and walked into the cool

lobby. She stood in a shadowed corner and reached for her phone. Adam answered.

'You okay, Kath?'

She was grateful for his voice.

'I'm just getting Kieron to bed . . .'

'Right . . .'

'What's up?'

'I don't know.' She could hear Kieron shouting in the background.

'I'm talking to Mummy,' called Adam. 'Are you okay, Katherine? Be quiet, Kieron . . .'

'I'm fine.'

'You're not, I can tell. You shouldn't have gone. I told you,' said Adam.

Kieron was shouting, 'Daddy! Daddy Daddy!'

'Come home. Your dad won't miss you,' said Adam.

'Go to Kieron. I'll see you later.'

Katherine put the phone back in her pocket and walked down the stairs to the cloakroom. Adam was right; she wouldn't stay. Her father hadn't invited her to the dinner; he didn't really want her there at all, and she felt the injury of it. She waited for the Polish attendant to fetch her coat, feeling odd, weightless, insubstantial as paper as her thoughts floated above her. She took her coat but didn't put it on. She was afraid its thick cloth and dark, inky colour would be too heavy. She wanted to drop it and slip away through the door, through the crack by the hinges and disappear into the night like dust.

The door opened and a man wearing a woolly hat ran inside. He was laughing as he shook off the rain.

'Hopeless,' he was saying, 'hopeless.'

A woman wearing a dark green pleated skirt followed him in. Katherine stepped back.

'Are we very late?' said the woman.

The man turned to the cloakroom attendant.

'The Broughton Foundation. Is it upstairs? I'm reading . . .'

It was Stephen Jericho. Katherine knew him vaguely. He was one of her father's poets. She saw a nervousness in his smile.

'Upstairs,' she said, stepping forward. 'They are just about to start.'

'Katherine!' he said. 'Good to see you again. You've met Alison, my wife?'

'Yes,' said Alison, 'we met in Braymer.'

'Good to see you again.'

'I'll meet you upstairs,' said Alison to Stephen, and headed towards the ladies' room.

Stephen unzipped his jacket.

'Are you leaving?' he said, glancing at her coat.

'I've just arrived,' said Katherine. Her lie surprised her. She didn't know why she had done it.

One of the straps of her bag fell off her shoulder; she lifted it back on. She noticed herself correcting the strap. Stephen noticed it too, and she saw that he did. He smiled at her and it filled her out like sails.

'Excuse me,' he said and ran up the stairs.

Katherine handed her coat back to the attendant and followed Stephen up the stairs.

Duncan Harris stood mountain-still at the back of the podium, his eyes unflinching as he looked out at the guests. David stood next to him, waiting to begin. Stephen Jericho pushed through the crowd. He nodded to them both and began to flick through a paperback of his poems, hurriedly turning down the corners of the pages.

Katherine stood at the back of the room next to Matthew and Paul. Guy ran up the stairs.

'He's not coming!' His face was white. 'Sir Richard Seaton is not coming. I just got the message.'

Her father's three assistants looked at each other, speechless. Matthew stepped past Katherine into the crowded room. 'Oh God . . .' he muttered under his breath. David looked over towards him, detecting his anxiety. Matthew looked back at him but his face went blank, betraying nothing; he could not bear to break the news.

David approached the microphone. The loud applause that greeted him drowned out his fears. Katherine put her wine glass on a mantelpiece. She joined in the applause, clapping her hands together vigorously as though to beat away the bad news. Despite the antagonism she could feel towards her father, she couldn't bear to see him fail.

'Good evening,' said David, 'I would like to introduce

two wonderful poets. Duncan Harris needs no introduction as a Nobel Prize winner. His work always astonishes, always reaches beyond our limitations and takes us to places we have never previously conceived of. It is our great pleasure that you are here tonight, Duncan.'

Duncan Harris received the warm applause with a short nod.

'Stephen Jericho was our writer-in-residence last year. His work takes us to places we think we know, only to discover they are strangely new to us. He has already won two major prizes and is currently working on an epic poem – *The Crossing* – which he began while he was with us in Braymer. It is an exciting project that I am sure will prove to be a huge achievement. Perhaps we will be lucky enough to hear some of it tonight. We live in hope . . .'

David winked at Stephen, who shook his head and looked over at his wife. She was perfectly framed in the tall windows at the side of the room. She looked and smiled, slowly moving her weight from one hip to another.

'Duncan will read first as he has another engagement tonight. He is, I think I'm right in saying, dining with the South African Ambassador. Far more important than us!'

'Just better wine!' said Duncan Harris stepping up to the podium. The audience laughed as his voice reverberated around the room, deep and sonorous compared to David's quicker, more anxious tones.

'With the Broughton Foundation, David Freeman is

creating a treasure house, and he is doing so against the odds. His conviction that poetry should be cherished and enjoyed by all people, without elitism, without barriers, is one I share. He is not only a great friend, but a man who possesses the rarest of qualities – the ability to inspire, to make people believe.'

The guests clapped warmly, eyes turned to David. He smiled graciously and Katherine saw how much the praise meant to him.

Duncan Harris began to recite from heart in a slow tempo, meting out the words to the ends of the lines. He kept his eye on the audience at all times like a preacher. The poems were thick with references to classical myth: Tiresias, Telemachus, Prometheus. He enunciated the names with biting precision, conjuring forth their ancient worlds. His themes were dishonesty in politics and treachery in love. His acerbic tone struck like flint. The imagery was exact and brutal: collision, rupture, blood, bedlam. Katherine recognised the power in the poems but their meaning was opaque and the words did not touch her.

When he finished, there was a long and sustained applause. Stephen stepped up on to the podium. He swallowed, and inexplicably Katherine felt a tightness in her own throat. He leant into the microphone.

'Good evening,' he said. 'Like Duncan, I am grateful to the Broughton Foundation. David has been an inspiration in my life, and if I ever get *The Crossing* finished, it will be because of his faith in me.'

Katherine's attention was taken by David's three assistants approaching him through the audience. She saw her father frown as they made their way towards him. Matthew whispered in his ear and she saw him receive the news about Sir Richard Seaton like a blow; his back slumped and he closed his eyes.

Stephen began to read. His voice moved through the room capturing everyone with its sweetness. Katherine was unable to shift her attention from her father. He remained completely still, watching Stephen with an almost desperate concentration, as though adjusting his focus for even a second might bring the whole world crashing down.

She caught only phrases of what Stephen was saying ... 'the trees were giants ... the snow, linen ... the field, a bridal bed.' The words were sensual, the poems finding beauty in everything. They contained a wonder, as though he was discovering the world for the first time. He wrote about the thrill of looking over the side of a steamboat, the laughter in the revolving splashing paddles; the happiness he had felt swimming in a river with friends like fish in a shoal. The poems drew on his childhood, but he wrote too of his own children and the love he experienced as a father.

The audience were seduced by his words, spun slowly round and round like honey on to a pouring stick. His poems insisted that the world was a tender, wonderful place. He lowered his eyes and hushed his voice to deliver a poem about his wife breast-feeding their firstborn.

The women in the audience were seduced by his vulnerability, the men reassured by his self-doubt. Here was a man not afraid to be a boy. Katherine recognised the sweetness of the words but hardened against the sentiment behind them. She wanted to believe in the world he was presenting, but nothing was so straightforwardly beautiful. The sweetness pressed itself on her and she folded her arms and leant back against the wall to resist it. She would not float away like the others. Stephen's looks and manner seemed to her too studied; his faded green shirt without tie, his soft voice. Her scepticism made a dam against his words, this poet, this favourite of her father's, this man she barely knew.

Stephen looked out over the audience. He had felt nervous about reading after Duncan Harris. Duncan was the most revered poet of his day; Stephen had won a few prizes but he had still to prove himself. To his great relief, he saw people were listening, alert to his words, their faces open, shining up at him like moons, he thought, beautiful moons.

His last poem of the evening was 'Killing Time'. It had been inspired after an argument with Alison. He had walked out of their house to be alone. It had been a wintry day, and the biting wind had seemed to reflect his own sense of bitterness and confusion. He had walked into the centre of Stroud along the dreary pedestrianised streets: W. H. Smith, Greggs the baker,

Curry's, past terraced houses and shops, walking in a sullen daze, wishing he was elsewhere, somewhere more inspired, more free. Suddenly six bullocks were standing in front of him, nostrils flaring, feet stamping, eyes bulging. He had walked through town to the farmland beyond and was standing at the edge of a field. The bullocks faced him, shoulder to shoulder, breathing as one. He thought they might charge but he couldn't run, he felt heavy-legged, rooted to the spot. He met the bullocks' stare; they were empty of thought, pure being. They were so close he could see the wetness of their noses and the muscles of their legs shuddering. He clapped his hands and they scattered, running powerfully across the field. As they did, his worries and fears scattered with them, and he felt empty and free. He read the poem, the imagery tumbled forward in urgent patterns, capturing the exhilaration he had felt. When he finished he looked up; the audience sat silent, like children held by a story.

He stepped off the podium. The audience broke into loud applause and something calmed in him, like ruffled sheets being smoothed out. David put a hand on his shoulder as he passed him to the microphone.

'Thank you, Stephen. Stephen's next work, *The Crossing*, will be published in the spring. I am proud to say it will be the first work to be printed by our new publishing venture, the Broughton Press.'

The audience clapped louder. Stephen felt the adrenalin running through him. He took a glass of wine from a tray. A woman in her fifties was walking towards him, wearing a necklace of pearls. She looked like she was going to embrace him.

'*Bellissimo! Bellissimo!*'

Her voice was husky, sensual.

'Sensational! Sensational!' she said, the words like splashing water.

'Thank you,' he said, happy to taste the wine. The pearls hung round her neck like rows of brightly polished teeth.

'You are a friend of David's?' said Stephen.

'I am a new friend, Ilana Giordano – but it does not matter! It is you, you! You are sensational. I know because I know poets. My mother was from Santiago. She knew Neruda – I too as a little girl. I meet Heaney last year and I faint, almost faint!'

'He is a wonderful poet.'

'Yes, but not so beautiful as you!'

Stephen enjoyed the outrageous praise. She came close to him and he could smell something like toffee on her breath. He stared at the pearls above her cleavage. She had olive skin and her breasts were full. He was in a delicious daze from the success of his reading, and every detail seemed magnified and full of sensual possibility. He imagined nibbling the woman's pearls, his tongue against the hard little balls.

'Do you write?' he asked her.

'I am more rare,' she said laughing. 'I am a reader.'

Stephen laughed. Alison was walking towards them.

'Alison, this is Ilana Giordano. She knew Pablo Neruda. My wife Alison.'

'Good to meet you,' said Alison.

'You have a beautiful husband,' Ilana Giordano said. 'Are you staying for the dinner?'

'I'm afraid our son is unwell,' said Alison. 'We have to get home.'

'I hope we shall meet again.'

'I'm so sorry.'

Ilana gave Stephen a sympathetic look and drifted away into the party.

'Alison, I need to speak with David.' His tone was decisive.

For the past six months, he hadn't been able to write. It was as though there was a lock on his mind. While he had been writer-in-residence at the Broughton Foundation he had been inspired by David. They had fired each other's minds, talking late into the night about poetry, about their beliefs and backgrounds. David was like a father to Stephen, encouraging him to demand more of himself, to delve deeper into the feelings that lived inarticulate and fearful within him. Stephen's imagination flourished and he had begun to conceive of a longer poem, at once intimate and epic. It would be about his family. He would tell the story of his grandparents' escape from Poland during the war; how his grandmother had given birth to his mother during the voyage; how they had struggled to settle in England; how a sense of alienation had pursued them across the

continent, and how it had infected not just his grandparents but subsequent generations, his mother and
himself.

It was a release to acknowledge the pain of his family's
past. The poetry began to pour out of him. He wrote
every day for ten, twelve hours. David encouraged him to
believe in his right to take on such a big subject, and his
responsibility to do so. Stephen's ambition for the poem
grew; it would resonate beyond his family's story to be
the emotional history of a diaspora, an entire people
yearning to belong. It would be called *The Crossing*.

When his residency was over, Stephen had returned
home to Stroud. His writing began to flounder and he
didn't know why. He desperately wanted to talk to David
again to try to find a vital connection to the inspiration
of the poem.

Katherine searched for her father amongst the guests.
Outside the windows, the trees blew dark shapes in the
wind. He was standing ashen-faced in a group of people,
looking dead ahead. She went over and touched his arm.

'Dad . . .'

He barely turned.

'David!'

A dark-haired handsome man strode through the
guests and shook her father by the hand. It was Paolo
Giordano.

'My wife is captured by your young poet! It is wonderful!'

Katherine watched her father. He tried to smile at the man but she could feel he was frantic inside. She threw caution to the wind and stepped in to protect him.

'We haven't met,' she said to the man. 'I am Katherine, David's daughter.'

'Pleased to meet you, Katherine. Paolo Giordano. What a wonderful night!'

'Yes it is,' she said. 'What do you do?'

'I am in shoes,' said Paolo.

'So am I!' she joked, looking down at her plimsolls, thin as slippers. The Italian laughed. Katherine looked at David, but he didn't seem to notice her.

'I love shoes,' she said, wildly trying to say the right thing, 'I just love them.'

The Italian seemed amused.

'What do you do?' he asked.

'I am a dancer,' she said looking again to David for his approval.

'Ballet?' said Paolo.

'Contemporary,' she said. 'You know Pina Bausch?'

'No . . .'

'She's been at the vanguard of modern dance theatre since the early seventies.'

'You are working with her?'

'Yes,' said Katherine, brazenly entering into the madness. 'We are making a new piece. It's about love. Love and shoes.'

Paolo threw back his head and laughed. Katherine looked to her father, hoping he would recognise her efforts, but he pushed past her and disappeared down the stone stairwell.

He had to be alone. He stood by the tiled urinal in the men's toilets and stared through a round window into the dark gardens. Sir Richard Seaton was not coming. His wife was ill. He wasn't coming for the speech, for the poetry, for the dinner. He wasn't coming at all. Around the edges of the window, leaves flattened black against the glass. David waited for the despair to drag him down. He wished it would come fast, like a plummeting bird to pull him into oblivion, but his thoughts tormented him. The effort, the sheer pointless effort of it all! Winning people over, securing commitments, arranging schedules! Duncan Harris's speech; such an endorsement of his work, of his vision! Richard Seaton had missed it all. He thought of the money he had spent, money he could not afford to spend, a thousand pounds on the canapés alone, he thought of his critics and how they would triumph at his failure. He heard the rain against the window, and cursed it. He cursed Richard Seaton's wife with her cold. A chance like this would not come again; people like Richard Seaton lost interest without warning. The failure, the dreadful failure of it all.

The Polish attendant was mopping puddles of rainwater left by umbrellas on the lobby floor. David stood in the shadows, trying to control his despair; with a massive force of will, he walked out into the light and smiled at the young man.

'Does it rain in Poland?'

'Yes, yes . . .'

The young man laughed and looked down. His eyelashes were long. 'My home is in the Bieszczady Mountains, more green as England.'

'Oh?'

'In summer I have . . .'

He made a triangle shape with his hands.

'Tent?'

The young man laughed, nodding.

'Camping?'

'With my horse.'

David conjured the image of the horse; the boy riding through the Bieszczady mountains. He forced himself to see its freedom and its beauty. The image gave him a handhold and he began to drag himself out of his despair. His imagination took hold; he saw the wooded path and dappling foliage, a view of the hills beyond. A man and woman came down the stairs talking urgently. It was Stephen and his wife. David couldn't remember her name. She took her coat quickly and walked towards the door, her heels tapping on the tiles. Stephen started down after her, then stopped as he saw him.

'David! I've been looking for you!'

Alison turned in the doorway and looked back at Stephen.

'Richard Seaton hasn't come,' said David.

Stephen paused. He slowly shook his head and put his hand on David's arm. David was grateful for it. Stephen understood the gravity of it and his touch gave him spark.

'Still,' he said, rallying, 'Paolo Giordano could be useful! You're not leaving? I can do with all the help I can get . . .'

'Al, would that be all right?' asked Stephen.

'I want to take the car,' said Alison.

'I'll get the last train.'

'Good luck,' she said and walked out into the rain without looking back. They watched her go, then turned together to walk back up the stairs.

'Your reading, Stephen. The climbing poem was good. You've captured more of the aspiration.'

'You've read the Shelley I suggested?'

'I did . . .'

With Stephen at his side, David felt his zeal returning. 'We were hoping to hear something from *The Crossing*.'

'David, I can't write it . . . it's beyond me.' Stephen slowed on the stairs. 'I feel blind . . .'

'Write it. Write it all. Write your blindness.'

'I was hoping we could talk . . .'

'We will, but not now,' said David, leading Stephen into the reception room towards Ilana Giordano. 'We've work to do.'

'There is a seating plan!' cried David as the guests made their way into the dining room. A large table was laid with silver and starched napkins. It took up most of the space and the guests had to funnel down the narrow gaps on either side as they searched for their places.

'Where is this seating plan?' cried Lady Highsmith, laughing, as she wedged herself along.

'Louise, you sit next to Harold. Lionel, next to May . . .'

The two young sculptors, Rita and Pomona, sat next to each other.

'No!' David said, 'not together! The world is vast and wide! Come along, over here, Rita! Have you met Harold Flacker? Harold, this is Rita. She's a sculptor. She works entirely in wool.'

'Wood?' said Harold, struggling to hear above the hubbub of voices.

'Wool.'

'I knit nudes,' said Rita.

'How strange. My mother used to knit,' said Harold sadly.

The Giordanos appeared in the doorway.

'Paolo, Ilana! Come to the head of the table.' He pushed his way towards them.

'Thank you, David. We are delighted . . .'

David placed them in the seats reserved for Sir Richard Seaton and his wife. He wanted to keep the seat next to Ilana free for Stephen, but his guests were ignoring the seating plan and sitting wherever they wanted. He looked over at May for help but she was already deep in a conversation with Lionel Treader.

'David!'

A tall, red-faced man stood in the doorway. It was his brother-in-law, Gregory, looking impatient as usual.

'David!' shouted Gregory more loudly.

'One moment!'

Gregory would have to wait. He had to get Stephen seated next to Ilana Giordano. Where the hell was he? David spotted him on the far side of the room talking to George Gull. George looked more relaxed in Stephen's company. The two of them had met when their residencies at the Broughton Foundation overlapped. They would take hikes together in the hills and spend long evenings in the village pub getting drunk and discussing their ideas. Stephen seemed to have done the impossible; he'd made a friend of George Gull.

'Stephen, come round! Come round!'

'Of course,' said Stephen affably.

'For God's sake, David!'

Gregory's voice cut through the room. People turned to look at him. Gregory started to walk away. David had no choice but to go after him. As he left the room, he glanced back to see someone else moving into the seat he had been guarding for Stephen. Stephen hadn't been fast enough. He had stopped to talk to Katherine. Katherine? What was she doing here? She wasn't invited to the dinner . . .

'Gregory, wait!'

David caught up with him at the top of the stairs.

'Come and join us!' he said breathlessly. 'There are some very interesting people. I'd like to introduce you to an artist whose work you might like, George Gull. They would complement your paintings at the flat.'

'For God's sake, David! Isn't there something you need from me? Hmmm?'

Gregory pulled a set of house keys from his trouser pocket and dangled them in the air.

'I'm so grateful, Gregory.'

'It's been a complete waste of my time. I had to come miles out of my way.'

David put the keys in his pocket. There was a roar of laughter from the dining room followed by the percussive clinking of cutlery and crockery over the soft hum of conversation.

'Please stay,' said David. 'You recommended the wine. Everyone is talking about it.'

'Really?'

'Stay for a starter.'

'I can't,' said Gregory, crossing his arms, in no hurry to go anywhere.

David knew the game. Gregory wanted to be cajoled. The more he said he had to go, the more he wanted to stay. He saw his brother-in-law's loneliness, his raw need, and for a moment he hated him for it, for the sheer exhaustion it created.

'I really can't allow you to go without a glass,' he said brightly. 'It's as good as you said it would be.'

'Of course it is. It's a Pétrus '98,' said Gregory.

'An excellent choice . . .'

'Richard appreciates a Pétrus '98.'

'Richard Seaton? He couldn't make it. His wife is ill.'

'She's always ill,' said Gregory, chuckling.

'You know him?'

'Did a bit of work for him once,' said Gregory, dismissively, heading towards the dining room. 'Pétrus '98. Yes, I think I will try a glass . . .'

Katherine had tried again to leave but her mother had insisted that she stay for the dinner. She found herself standing at the table with Stephen Jericho, unsure where to sit, when she spotted her Uncle Gregory in the doorway. He gave her one of those toothy smiles that had nothing to do with pleasure. Her heart sank. She didn't want to end up sitting next to him all night. They would have to talk about her aunt Charlotte. Whenever she visited her at the care home, Katherine made a point of checking ahead that her uncle wasn't going to be there. She pretended not to see him. She turned and smiled at Stephen.

'Let's sit here,' she said, sitting down in one of two vacant seats.

Stephen caught her smile. He liked it. It was complicated. The diamond-cut of her eyes; there was something of her father in them.

He sat next to her and she reached for a bread roll.

'How is your boy?' said Stephen.

'Kieron. He's fine.'

Their two families had spent an afternoon together in Braymer. Their children had played together, making a den in the rhododendron bushes in the garden at Sellacrag.

'Yours?'

'Molly's fine, but Frank's not well. Alison had to go home to look after him.'

Katherine tore the roll in half and put it to her mouth, then lowered it. He smiled at her hesitation without knowing why.

'Kieron still talks about that bonfire.'

'I was sorry we had to leave so soon.'

Katherine put the bread down and took her glass of wine. Stephen noticed one of her fingernails was broken. He reached for his glass and she waited for him to drink. 'You live in Stroud?'

'Just outside,' he said.

'Right.'

He was smiling directly at her. She smiled back.

'Have you ever caught a carp?' said a low voice to her right.

A red-faced man with white hair reached across her for a bread roll. It was Charles Chedwin, a friend of her father's, who ran a restaurant in Otterburn.

'I'm sorry?' she said.

'Have you ever caught a carp?' he repeated thickly, his mouth making breathy plosives near her ear.

'No, I haven't.'

'They swim deep.' He raised his eyebrows and cleared his throat. 'I should take you fishing, Katherine.'

She heard the mucus gathering and being swallowed.

'I don't fish,' said Katherine bluntly. She turned back to Stephen. He was already talking to a woman with short grey hair on his left.

'We enjoyed your work very much tonight,' she was saying in ringing tone. 'Your outlook is such a positive one.'

Stephen could feel Katherine beside him and turned to include her.

'I don't know about that,' he said.

'There is so much bad news in the world,' she continued. 'I keep a book of all the good things that happen during the day. I call it my good news bible. It's so important to remember the positive things, don't you agree? I shall be writing your name in it,' she added with a little sparkle.

'I'm honoured,' said Stephen, glancing at Katherine.

'I don't know if you know my husband, Lionel Treader? He's a great fan of the theatre, but for me, poetry! A poem like one of yours is better than a thousand plays,' she said.

'It's certainly shorter,' said Stephen laughing.

'I loved the one about horses, didn't you?' said the woman, leaning forward to address Katherine.

Stephen looked at Katherine, but she said nothing.

A man leant over the table and tapped the grey-haired woman's arm.

'Bettina, it's true, isn't it? Foot and mouth killed us!' he said stridently.

'Absolutely!' cried the grey-haired woman, all thoughts of Katherine instantly forgotten.

Stephen turned to Katherine. 'You didn't like my poems,' he said simply.

Katherine didn't know what to say. She looked away; through the doorway, she could see a crescent edge of one chandelier and the blazing orb of another.

'I don't know,' she said. 'They feel . . .'

There was an awkward pause, a tension between them.

'Don't you feel the violence?' she said suddenly.

'What violence?'

She didn't know exactly how to articulate it.

'Everything has a kind of violence.'

Stephen hesitated.

'I try to put my experience into words,' he said, 'to respond to what is in front of me.'

'But you don't. Your poems skate on the surface.'

'Do they?' His voice was gentle but defensive.

'Two people meeting is a kind of violence. Us. Right now. Don't you feel it?'

He didn't respond. She looked down at her hands. She wished she had never said anything. Her words gave rise to some feeling deep within her. Stephen saw her blush. Her skin was flawed, imperfect. The redness of the blush crept down her neck.

'I don't know,' she said.

Something in Stephen, startling in its clarity, rose up to meet her. It surprised him; it was clear and strong, like a great wave of compassion, as though she was crying.

'Tell me,' he said.

'We live such muffled lives,' she said. It was as though she knew the truth of her words for the first time and was devastated by them. He watched her. She drank some wine and moved her hands through her hair.

'I don't know,' she repeated.

'I'm sorry if my work makes you tense.'

'It doesn't. I wish it did.'

She laughed suddenly, and everything changed. She stretched in her chair and smiled at him and it was like sunshine. He loved the brightness in her eyes. They ate and drank wine and talked, and beneath their words, another communication flowed between them. Two hours passed. They didn't notice the other guests at the table.

After the dinner, the guests made their way downstairs. Paolo and Ilana Giordano came over and started talking to Stephen. Katherine walked ahead with her mother. When he reached the lobby, he looked around for her. People were saying their goodbyes. Lady Highsmith was placing her rain hood over her hair as carefully as a wedding veil. Mrs Dillon was helping Mr Dillon do up his buttons. There was no sign of her. Stephen suddenly knew he had to find her. He pushed his way through the guests and out into the dark.

David handed his card to the Polish attendant.

'Come to Northumberland. Wonderful scenery, for your films!'

The young man laughed. He looked like he was about to reply when May took David by the arm.

'Come on, dovey. You look tired.'

She nodded curtly to the young man as he opened the door for them, and she and David walked out into the cold air.

'We should call for a taxi,' he said.

'The walk will do you good. You know what the doctor said. A daily walk.'

David had been complaining of chest pains, and had recently suffered a spate of infections. Dr Hegarty had said that fresh air and exercise would help. The idea of fresh air as a cure made sense to May.

'Dr Hegarty is out of his mind.'

She smiled. When they were alone together like this, David would respond as though everything she said was intended to pester him. She would not mention Sir Richard Seaton. She would wait until he was ready.

'Better than those pills you take,' she said. 'Taxis are an indulgence. We're not made of money.'

She used the phrase deliberately, the old-fashioned cliché harking back to their working-class roots. A taxi was not an indulgence after the night they'd had but May knew her affectionate nagging would give David a sense of normality and bring him comfort.

'We will cross the park.'

'It'll kill us.'

'If we get tired we can get one of the night buses.'

'No buses.'

'As OAPs we don't pay a penny.'

'May . . .'

'It's my peasant stock.'

'Your mother was bourgeois.'

'She wished she had been, poor thing.'

David fell silent. His tone had no lustre.

They walked into the dark shapes of the park. David was craving something. Sweetness. He longed for pudding. His mother had made him puddings on the farm, and he wished for a milk pudding now, sweet and formless.

May felt David gripping her arm more tightly. She was already faintly regretting making him walk, even though Dr Hegarty *had* said it was good for him, and it wasn't far.

'Do you think the Italians might come to anything?' said May, trying to bring him back.

'Possibly . . .'

'I spoke to Gregory at dinner,' said May. 'He knows Sir Richard. He told me he was the one who'd made him rich.'

'Typical Gregory.'

'It's true. He managed the hedge fund Richard Seaton invested in.'

A taxi approached, its small brick of golden light floating towards them in the darkness.

'Did he now?' said David, brightening. 'How interesting.'

He smiled as he stepped out from the kerb and raised his arm in salute.

Stephen walked towards the tube station. In the dirty light Katherine stood talking with Rita and Pomona, the two young sculptors from the party. She turned soundlessly, as if she knew he would come.

'Stephen, do you know Rita and Pomona?'

'Nice to meet you,' he said.

'We enjoyed your poems,' said Rita.

'I never read poetry,' said Pomona. 'Never ever.'

'Never! Never!' said Rita.

The two women laughed raucously. Stephen felt unsure of their tone and stood awkwardly, like a boy in the playground.

'Are you taking the tube?' said Katherine, smiling at him.

'I have to get to Euston. I might walk actually. The night is young.' He felt the dire clumsiness of the cliché.

'Yes, it is young! And we are young!' laughed Rita and Pomona.

'Come to our house!'

'We have wine!'

'And music!'

'Dancing!'

Katherine hesitated. She was thinking of Adam. He would be waiting for her, watching TV, or in bed, reading. She thought of his warmth, of lying next to him. She thought of Kieron; of getting him up in the morning. The thoughts came at her like fear.

'It's been great to meet you all,' she said. 'I have to get back.'

'How?'

'I'll catch a bus.'

'I'll walk you,' said Stephen.

*

They walked into St James's Park. A bright half-moon shone in a hood of clouds. They crossed the iron bridge over the ornamental lake, and walked into the wet grass. Katherine felt the water coming through her thin shoes.

'Slow down,' said Stephen.

She had not realised she was going so quickly.

He stopped by a tree. Katherine looked up at the branches veining the sky.

'Good of the moon to come out,' he said.

'Like a segment of apple.'

'Satsuma,' he said.

He put his hand on the trunk of the tree and leant towards her. She pulled back abruptly.

'Do you often walk women across the park?'

He put his arms around her. She experienced his touch like shock. He pulled her into him. His skin was warm. Her feet were numb with cold. I am in someone's arms. I am against someone's chest. Someone who is not Adam.

The clouds moved away from the moon, and she saw that Stephen was right. The moon was a satsuma, covered in a thin membrane of skin. Skin, she thought, Stephen's skin. My skin. His smelt musky, delicate like fresh mushrooms. He turned her towards him but she pulled away again.

'Do you like travelling?' she said.

He smiled. She set off again across the grass towards the silhouette of a bandstand. The words felt suspended, unreal.

'Why are we talking about travelling?'

'My dad told me you wrote travel stuff. I thought it would be a good subject for a conversation. In lots of ways,' she said, 'travelling is pointless.'

She reached the edge of the park and stepped over a low fence. Stephen followed. A car passed them on the opposite side of the road.

'Why is it pointless?'

'I went away when I was seventeen. I didn't ever want to come back, but I did, and when I did nothing made sense. Travelling is pointless because you always have to come home.'

There was an anger in her voice. Stephen saw her shiver. He wiped raindrops off a railing with a finger.

'Where is home?' he said quietly.

She turned to look at him. She realised he was speaking of himself. She saw the uncertainty in him, and it was immeasurable. She stepped forward and kissed him.

'I should go,' she said.

He put his fingers to her mouth and pulled her into him. She lifted her lips to his, and they kissed.

A gaggle of people ran across the Mall, their laughter broke the silence. They stopped a taxi and climbed inside. It drove off, leaving the road quiet and empty again.

Katherine and Stephen stood kissing. Each was amazed how effortlessly they understood the other's touch, how inevitable it seemed. Their kissing was like talking, a kind of searching. What is this? thought Katherine. This flesh? This tongue? This feeling, like colour reaching deep inside me.

6

Gregory drove through the high streets of Stockwell, Brixton, Streatham, Norbury, Waddon, Purley, each indistinguishable from the last, towards the sprawling suburbs of South London. He was happy and secure in his Jensen; the heated air, the quiet purr of the engine. After a bad start his evening had panned out nicely. When he had realised that David was going to be late to meet him at the flat, a screw had tightened inside him. He hated being made to wait, made to feel the world turning, the tedious seconds of nothingness pass. He had paced up and down the flat, stopping in front of one of his favourite paintings. It calmed him. It depicted a large purple egg standing on what looked to Gregory like a tiny saucer. The egg had a golden crack running across it. The gold colour inside the egg was shiny and reminded him of foil bottle tops on full cream milk.

When David still hadn't arrived after twenty-five minutes, he'd left the flat and gone to his club. He had sat by a roaring fire drinking a cocktail and doing a Sudoku in a puzzle book. Gregory had always been good with numbers. Numbers had made him successful in the city, and they deeply reassured him now. The solutions formed in his mind like percussive beats, effortless, satisfying, delightful. Three cocktails and four Sudoku later, he looked up at the clock, and felt the usual self-reproach. David would have been trying to get hold of him. Gregory knew he ought to have waited for him at the flat. For reasons he didn't fully understand, he hated making things easy for his brother-in-law. Perhaps it was the way David seemed so fulfilled and excited by life, the way he was so tirelessly optimistic, the way he seemed beyond material comforts. He seemed to thrive on enthusiasm alone, and had an infectious way of transmitting it to everyone he met. He was hugely gregarious, generous and witty: in fact everything about him made Gregory feel diminished, narrow-minded and boorish. Gregory always felt acutely shy in company, and often appeared gruff when he tried to disguise it. He felt nothing but envy for David's charm and was angry with himself for still somehow liking the man. He felt sorry enough for him to drive on to St Marks to give him the keys, arriving just in time for dinner.

He was pleased to have missed the poetry readings. Gregory tried to be sympathetic to David's enterprise but he couldn't hide his loathing for contemporary poetry. It amazed him that David had managed to secure as prestigious a venue as St Mark's for his fundraising evening. He was baffled that he had such influence. Poetry was dead after all, wasn't it, and rightly so. If something couldn't survive commercially, it should be left to die. It was the natural law, the law of the market. There might be value in the Broughton

Foundation's original collection of rare books and manuscripts, but poetry's heyday was gone; today it was nothing but an excuse for self-indulgent wallowing.

Gregory had almost hoped, after his wife Charlotte had become ill, that he might cut all ties with his brother-in-law. Instead he had found himself maintaining the relationship by continuing to lend David his London flat. He suspected that David and May interpreted this kindness as his attempt to alleviate some guilt he was supposed to feel about Charlotte. He felt they blamed him for her breakdown. The thought enraged him; Charlotte had nearly driven him mad with the years of sullen silence, of drinking herself into a frenzy, of crying in her locked bedroom. What did they know? What would David ever know about what Gregory really felt? It was not guilt over Charlotte, it was a knot inside him, the tight knot of unspeakable, killing remorse that he and Charlotte had lived a lifetime together like strangers. David could never understand, with his perfect marriage to the perfect May. They had a marriage of equals. Charlotte had never been his equal.

It had stopped raining, but he liked the muffled swish of the windscreen wipers so he left them running. He turned on the radio and flicked through the stations till he found some disco music. It was not really his kind of thing, but the regular drumbeat and the electronic sounds cheered him. He wished he had managed to sit next to his niece Katherine at the dinner. He'd always felt an affinity with her, and wished he could have spoken with her. He had spotted her in the dining room and tried to get her attention but she was already talking with someone else. Gregory knew that Katherine visited Charlotte regularly, unlike her father, he thought bitterly, who had never once visited the Beaumont care home and barely even enquired after his supposedly beloved sister. The nurses told him that Katherine would sit holding Charlotte's hand, and Charlotte would smile, sometimes even laugh. Gregory ascribed to Katherine a kind of goodness. Charlotte never smiled with him. His own visits to his wife were short and painful.

He remembered Katherine as a self-conscious child, unlike her brothers. One particular memory of her nagged at him. It was a family wedding at a country hotel. There was a big lawn swarming with guests, and he had wandered off towards some trees to be alone. A flock of starlings had landed near him and begun pecking at his feet. He had sat surrounded by the birds, smoking a menthol cigarette and blowing soft rings of smoke upwards into the green canopy. Suddenly there was violent crashing in the bushes. The birds flew off and Gregory was jostled from his reverie. It was Katherine, aged eight, in a long party dress.

'Don't scare the bloody birds!' he shouted.

She looked terrified. Gregory immediately felt guilty.

'Come here,' he said, trying to soften his tone. Katherine's eyes were full of tears but she looked at him defiantly.

'I was only skipping,' she said, her small voice hard with indignation.

She ran away. He went to look for her and spotted her standing in a circle of grown-ups. Her father was holding forth and everyone except Katherine was laughing. She was twisting a napkin around her thumb as she struggled to understand the conversation. Gregory felt a welling of empathy towards her. He wanted to rescue her, to march over to David and tell him for once in his life to shut up and give his daughter some attention. Instead, he did nothing. His shyness stopped him. He hadn't had the courage to act, and had walked away thoroughly demoralised by his impotence. Later, he'd seen Katherine with his wife, who was brushing her hair. Katherine was giggling happily. Gregory had always wished it had been him and not Charlotte who had comforted the child.

He knew these roads; for nearly thirty years he had driven this way from London to Sussex, never once stopping. Most of the shops were closed but the windows of pubs glowed amber, and the empty offices spilled blue and white light into the street. The monolithic council estates rose above the terraced houses like mountains, and Gregory shivered at the thought of the unknowable lives teeming within them.

He stopped at the traffic lights by Sunset Parlour. It hadn't changed much over the years; in the top corner of the blacked-out window front *MASSAGE* flashed in red, *SAUNA* in blue. He hoped for a glimpse of something. Occasionally he would see men going in. Some pushed the door open as though they were walking into a corner shop, others hesitated before ringing the bell. Their seedy desperation touched him in a way he didn't understand. He could never see who opened the door: a pimp, he imagined, perhaps a black man, who would call for a girl for his customer, slap her if she complained, push her up against a wall.

He put his foot down on the accelerator and headed on to the motorway. The lanes were clear, and he moved into the fast lane, slipping smoothly into fifth gear and driving at a steady seventy miles an hour. After two hours he took the sliproad for Fairhampton. He pressed the remote and the garage door of Willow House rolled back.

He walked into the utility room. He could smell washing powder and damp. The home help must have been in. The smell made him nostalgic for something he could not identify. He went into the kitchen and poured himself a large glass of Sauvignon Blanc from the fridge. It slipped down easily and he poured himself another. Always good, always there.

He stood by the glass doors and looked out at the garden. The outside lights were on, making the swimming pool glow, illuminating the branches of the trees and the flecks of rain. He looked out at the wooden screen and the jasmine Charlotte had planted against it, the beds of flowers and herbs she had nurtured.

Beyond the pool stood three piles of leaves. The man who looked after the garden had been in. Charlotte had asked Gregory to hire him before she had gone into the home. He never spoke to the man and rarely saw him. Gregory felt angry about the leaves. He didn't care about the garden. He didn't care if the shrubs were overgrown or the grass was long. He didn't care if the leaves from the eucalyptus covered the lawn and filled the pool like a blocked drain. He didn't want the man to come at all, but he came, every week, a valiant soldier against the leaves. He corralled them into mounds with his blower, and carried them down to the bottom of the garden, and burnt them in great bonfires behind the pine tree. Gregory hated him for it; he felt the urge to scream at him from the window, Get away! Get away from here! Leave the leaves! Let them bury the place! Let it disappear under them!

He stood at the window drinking his wine. He thought he saw Charlotte by the pool, swaying, drunk again. It was four years since she'd gone into the care home but when he was on his own in the house, Charlotte was often with him. He turned abruptly and looked at the clock. Where was Margery? She should have been home by now. He turned on the television and perched on the edge of the sofa, reassured by the voices. It was eleven o'clock when she came in.

'It's me-ee!' called Margery. Gregory loved the singsong of her voice. It reminded him of Mrs Quinn who had looked after him for a summer when he was a boy. Mrs Quinn had called him 'dearie' and bought him boiled sweets.

'Sorreeee! Sorry I'm late!'

Gregory was grateful that Margery acknowledged her lateness. Charlotte would never have done so. Charlotte would have drifted in. Charlotte had always let things drift.

Margery kissed him on the cheek.

'Sorry,' she said, breathing out theatrically to show that she had exasperating things to tell him.

'Where have you been?'

'Arts and Crafts evening.'

'It's after eleven,' he said tetchily, crossing his long legs and settling back into the sofa, happy now she was back.

'We didn't get started till after eight. I had to pop into the home. The doctor wanted to change Charlotte's regime. Her new drug is making her unstable. I wish you'd been there, Gregory, I had to sign something.'

She giggled for no apparent reason.

'How was your night? Did you see your brother-in-law?' she said.

'Yes,' he said and shook his head.

'Poor you,' said Margery, not understanding.

Gregory went to pour her a drink. Margery sat back in her chair, and watched him. She loved everything about Willow House: the furnishings, the curtains, the white velveteen sofa, the kitchen with its slate surfaces, so sharp and clean. She loved the garden, the pool, the patio, the changing hut in the Shaker style. Above all, she loved the quiet. Margery had experienced chaos in her life; a troubled marriage had given her four children, an acrimonious divorce, and had eaten up her savings. She was delighted to have put the hard times behind her.

It had been Charlotte who had first brought her here, ten years ago. They had met in the village. Charlotte invited her back for coffee. As soon as they turned into the drive, Margery had fallen in love with the house, and with Charlotte. When she met Gregory she fell in love with him too. She loved them both; she loved the way they drank when they pleased, the way they swam in the pool in the afternoons. She couldn't help but love them.

Charlotte had been grateful for Margery's friendship. She was lonely; her GP had diagnosed depression and prescribed medication. Margery encouraged Charlotte to give up the pills. She encouraged her to take herbal remedies and tissue salts. Together, they fought Charlotte's loneliness. They went on outings, tried on new outfits at the local dress shop. They swam in the pool and lounged in the summerhouse, wearing thick dressing gowns and eating orange-flavoured chocolates. Margery soothed the sadness which had lived in Charlotte for years. 'Bless you, Margery,' Charlotte would say, barely keeping back the tears, and Margery would squeeze her hand firmly in reply.

Within a year, Margery had started an affair with Gregory. She couldn't help it; she was in love with him. As she told him, nothing could stand in the way of true love. She had felt sorry for Charlotte, especially after Charlotte saw them in each other's arms in the garden one night. Margery believed that had been the beginning of Charlotte's illness. It was as if a cold wind had blown through her that night and she never got warm again.

Margery looked out into the garden at the piles of leaves as Gregory handed her a drink.

'The man has been.'

'I pay him, don't I?'

She heard it in his voice.

'You're worried about Charlotte . . .'

'I'm not,' he snapped.

She went and stood next to him and put her hand on his shoulder, stroking up and down, saying *mmmm mmmm mmm*.

'Get off me,' he said. 'Get off.'

He pushed her away. She staggered backwards into the coffee table. She lost her balance and fell, landing heavily against the corner. Her wine glass shattered in her hand, and as she got to her feet, she saw blood on her blouse. Her hand was red with blood and wine. She covered it quickly before Gregory could see it. She felt angry with herself. How ridiculous to be so clumsy, she thought. How ridiculous to feel upset. Her hand was stinging and she pressed it hard to stop the bleeding.

'I think I'll go upstairs,' she said.

'Of course,' said Gregory. 'I'll be up soon,' and he turned to the window, and looked back out at the leaves.

7

The sound of the latch was deafening; the metal tongue cracked into its slot and seemed to reverberate down the street. Katherine pushed open the door. Coats bulged on their hooks, shoes lay scattered on the floor. She climbed the stairs, undressing as she went, her footsteps muted by the carpet, her clothes falling silently. By the time she stood by the bed, she was naked.

Adam was motionless under the duvet. She got in beside him; like a thief, she thought, breaking into her own home. His back was to her and she lay in the warm lean-to of his body, breathing as lightly as possible. She looked at the thin red lines on the clock: 5.05.

She couldn't sleep. She listened to sounds from the street outside, the wind blowing, footsteps, voices. She could hear a girl, her voice high and delighted, and a man's low, intermittent murmur.

Light was coming through a crack in the curtains. She heard the whirring of the milk van. She could still feel Stephen's eyes looking into hers like a physical pressure. Adam was breathing evenly, slowly. Everything she could hear and feel, the milk van, the breathing, the touch of the sheets, seemed to be Stephen. She lay in a strange rapture. The milk van pulled away. New sounds replaced the old: scraping on concrete, metal bins against the ground. Sunshine crept into the room. The flowers on the curtains made yellow splashes, the light diamonds in her eyes. She felt the cotton duvet brush against her skin. She could feel Stephen's kisses. Her lips felt bruised. A bird started singing; there seemed to be no end to its song. She was tired but her tiredness was a kind of arousal and it coloured everything around her.

At 8 a.m. Adam moved his head sharply.

'What time did you get in last night?' he said.

'I can't remember.'

'It must have been late.'

'Dad's thing went on and on. He introduced me to two women he's interested in working with. They are sculptors and we got talking. They took me to a club.'

'A club?'

'Yeah, I know. A real club.' Katherine laughed loudly, too loudly, deep in her throat. 'Oh God, Adam! I haven't been to a nightclub for so long.'

Everything was moving so fast. Adam got up. He put on a T-shirt and underpants.

'God,' he said.

'What's wrong?'

Perhaps he could see she had been kissing someone; her lips were red, the edges smudged. She turned her face into the pillow.

'I've got a meeting at Barthes.'

'Wasn't the case supposed to close?'

Adam didn't reply. Not replying was normal. She

realised everything about the morning was normal. She wrapped the duvet round her. Adam was in the bathroom. She could hear the sound of the shower.

Perhaps it wasn't so bad. A kiss. It was not so bad.

Kieron ran in and jumped into bed next to her.

'Good morning, my sweet little boy.'

She could hear her own voice. He squirmed in her arms.

'Mummy! You smell.'

'*You* do!'

'*You* do, Mummy!'

'Come here . . .'

He struggled, delighted.

'I've got you! I'm never going to let you go!'

She spoke with a warmth she barely recognised. She heard the shower stop. Kieron ran into the bathroom.

'Daddy, I want pancakes!'

She closed her eyes to catch the full memory of Stephen. His hand on her face. He had stroked her cheek, brushed up and down over her mouth with the heel of his hand, almost roughly. He had pressed his hand upwards between her legs. Her face, her mouth, her genitals, willing.

Adam was putting on a shirt.

'You okay?' he said.

'I was drinking dodgy wine all night. Getting too old, I can't take the booze any more!' She heard her voice sounding deliberately humorous.

Adam drew the curtains. A flock of gulls swooped into

the lime tree as if they were caught in a net. She could hear Adam's footsteps as he went downstairs.

Stephen had lifted her against him as he undid her jeans. She hadn't stopped him, her head tilting back as his fingers had eased the elastic, stroked her flesh, pushed into her. They had been like teenagers, astonished by the sheer emotion of it.

She dressed quickly and came downstairs. Adam and Kieron were making pancakes in the kitchen. Adam turned as she came in and put his hand on her lower back. Instinctively, she stepped away.

'We have to pack for France,' she said.

'I'll do it when I get back from work,' he said, feeling the rejection. 'I've only got two hours today.'

She walked into the sitting room and stood in front of the mantelpiece. The tensions between her and Adam were as mute and complex as the patterns in the Persian carpet. They were part of her life. The kiss with Stephen was not; it was from elsewhere. She had stepped outside her life. Katherine watched Adam with Kieron through the doorway, happy, chatting, serving out pancakes. Kieron was cutting open a lemon with a dinner knife. Without warning, she felt a sudden coldness for them, and it terrified her.

8

'Your spending outstrips your annual turnover and has done for the last ten years. It's only a matter of time before the banks refuse to lend you any more money and then you'll face closure. If we are prudent we can avoid it. The figures for the shop, for example . . .'

David sat with his assistants, Paul, Guy and Matthew, in the Broughton restaurant. A plate of fruit cake sat untouched on the table in front of them, as Geraldine Henderson, the independent financial adviser appointed by the Board of Trustees, flicked through her report, barely pausing for breath. Paul smiled nervously, Guy frowned, deep in concentration. Matthew demonstratively stifled a yawn, as if to tell everyone that everything was ultimately unimportant. David watched Geraldine Henderson as the figures poured out of her. She flashed little smiles at him to maintain regulation eye contact, her tight curls bobbing with enthusiasm; a middle-aged Shirley Temple, he thought. Craig the waiter brought over a fresh pot of coffee and started wiping down the empty tables. David often took meetings in the Broughton restaurant in the hope that refreshments might defuse tensions. Geraldine Henderson registered the coffee with a curt nod of the head.

'In terms of subsidised grants, your income has risen by four per cent in the last five years, but your spending has risen by nearly ten. If we look at the shortfall . . .'

David looked out of the window. The sky was blue silk behind the smooth green flanks of Kield Hope, Dungeon Burn and Lyne Top. Their lower slopes of dead bracken and scree plunged steeply into Lake Braymer, which glittered through the trees.

When he'd first met Geraldine Henderson he had tried to win her over. He wanted to awaken a personal enthusiasm in her, to encourage her to see beyond the intractable financial troubles. He gave her the tour, explaining the Broughton Foundation's history, how it had been an eccentric and all-but-forgotten place when he had come across it in the 1960s. Thomas Broughton, an industrialist from the North-East, had established a trust in 1883 to look after his collection of poetry manuscripts and books. A proud northerner, he stubbornly declined requests from London libraries to purchase them and bought a stretch of land by Lake Braymer in Northumberland, where he created a museum in an old barn. Broughton believed passionately in making poetry accessible to working people. He displayed his manuscripts and books amongst artefacts from Northumbrian life, to give the poetry a context; spinning wheels, bobbins, candle moulds, clothes dyed with vegetables, sheep's skulls, flint axe-heads from the Bronze Age. Under each item he wrote their origin and history on little square labels. David tried to communicate to

113

Geraldine Henderson the excitement he had felt when he first walked in. The books and manuscripts amounted to a map through English literary history, from Caedmon to Coleridge. There were paintings by Turner, Poole and Towne. Broughton's passion communicated across the years, chiming with his own, he told Geraldine. Once people were introduced to poetry, they would change forever. Poetry was a quiet permission for people to embrace their own mystery. He proudly showed Geraldine the new museum, the gallery space, the shop, the reading room. He showed her the staff houses. He introduced her to the artist-in-residence. He explained the immense effort of fundraising that had gone into making the Broughton Foundation the artistic beacon it had become. Geraldine had been unmoved by David's passion and his charm. She had told him she would look at the figures and get back to him in a week.

' . . . staff wages, for example. The wage structure is eccentric to say the least. In my opinion, it is unsustainable. One of my recommendations will be staff cuts. There are too many people earning too little . . .'

David could see Ken from the window pruning the hedges, his shears making the sound of a slow clock. How could he get rid of someone like Ken? Ken had been with him since the beginning. David had met him on the London train in the late sixties, when Ken was eighteen and David had recently become involved at the Broughton Foundation. He had reminded David of the slow men he had known as a boy, working on his father's farm. He said he was on his way to London, to see Big Ben. David hadn't been able to bear the thought of Ken trying to survive in London on his own and had instantly invented a job in Braymer and offered it to him on the spot.

'People are what we do here,' said David, making eye contact with Geraldine Henderson for the first time. She tilted her head and gave him a tight little smile.

'Private donations form the majority of the Broughton Foundation's income,' she said, 'but the budget for attracting donations is far too high for an organisation of this size. The recent junket in London ...'

'It was not a junket,' said David quickly, an edge in his voice. 'It was aimed at securing a specific endowment.'

He immediately regretted the show of emotion.

'Let's not get into semantics,' said Geraldine Henderson evenly. 'The rental of St Mark's alone cost four thousand pounds, and with the hospitality bill, the cost of the evening was five thousand, three hundred and eighty ...'

David looked away. His anger was based in pain. Since returning to Northumberland, Sir Richard Seaton had not returned his calls. David had rung every day for a week. He was at a loss to understand what he had done wrong. The silence was such a contrast to Sir Richard's initial enthusiasm; his understanding of David's goals had seemed so acute. David had believed the warmth between them to be genuine and the sense of personal rejection made the silence all the more unbearable.

David coughed suddenly, an expulsion erupting from him before he had time to cover his mouth. He wiped his lips and took a sip of coffee.

'I don't know how you did it, but you managed to borrow from the bank with the endowment as collateral before you've actually secured it. Your powers of persuasion are impressive, David, but it won't help you in the long run. The library will cost three and a half million to finish. I recommend that you pay back the loans and suspend all building works until you find more realistic investment. This situation is serious, David.'

David was enraged by her patronising tone. He took another sip of coffee to stop himself from retaliating.

'You mentioned on the telephone that you had a plan,' said Geraldine, giving David another swift smile. 'Another source of funding?'

Paul and Guy sat forward on their chairs in anticipation of good news. David cursed himself for mentioning it to her. He'd thought he'd found a possible link to Sir Richard Seaton. Gregory's claim to have a close relationship with him had turned out to be true. In the eighties, he had brokered Seaton's investments in telecommunications; with the boom in mobile telephones, both men had made a fortune and had remained firm friends. David had thought he could reach Sir Richard through Gregory and in his enthusiasm had rung Geraldine Henderson. It was not until he had discussed it with May that he realised how difficult it would be to secure Gregory's help. Gregory derided the Broughton Foundation. His involvement in David's life was strictly limited to practical matters such as the flat in London or choosing wines for his fund-raising dinners. David knew she was right. It was all because of his sister Charlotte. Her illness had left a persistent tension between himself and Gregory. Their civility barely covered the tangled mesh of emotions between them.

'There is no plan, I'm afraid,' said David. 'I was mistaken.'

Guy, Paul and Matthew looked crestfallen. Geraldine Henderson sat back in her chair as she received this statement of surrender.

'A realistic financial structure will be invaluable in planning the future, however modest,' she said gently. 'A reassessment of your pricing system might generate more income. The museum and shop prices haven't changed for over five years . . .'

David looked out at the lake, the rocks, the high slopes. He heard the wind roaring in the trees. He did not wait for her to finish.

'Thank you, Geraldine,' he said, standing, 'but we will not be accepting any of your proposals. We will raise the money. We will finish the library. There will be no redundancies. No arts institution can be run purely commercially. We embrace our debt. Debt is transitory; libraries, rare books and manuscripts, the works of our artists and writers-in-residence and our staff, the vital link between the past and the present – are permanent things which bring permanent goodness. They are our heritage. We will carry on as we are and if we must do so without your help, so be it.'

He walked out into the darkening light. Paul, Guy and Matthew followed, leaving Geraldine Henderson to gather up her papers alone. They caught up with him, weaving in and out of each other, buzzing with praise, like young boys.

'That showed her!'

'Did you see her face?'

'Fantastic!'

Their jackets flapped in the wind but they did not button them or hold them in. Their pride was unfastened, their jubilant northern burrs and inflections echoing across the valley. Matthew's voice rang out.

'I believe that what we need is a cup of poison! As De Quincey said,' he declaimed theatrically. 'There hasn't been an exit speech like that since Disraeli! David, will you join us at the Back Rooms?'

'You go ahead,' said David, smiling, and he watched as the three young men strode off into the village.

He walked back to Sellacrag alone, and sat at the kitchen table like a dead weight. How could he raise the money? What could he do? What could he do that he had not already done?

He poured himself a whisky to steady his nerves. He took milk from the fridge and warmed it on the stove. There was a corner of Kendal mint cake lying on the table. He put it into his mouth and sucked it for a moment, then dropped it into a cup and poured in the hot milk. He stirred the mixture for a while, then tipped in the whisky, and sat at the table drinking it for a long time. Over an hour passed. Eventually he picked up the phone.

'May, I have to go to Sussex.'

'Are you sure?'

'I need Gregory's help.'

'Charlotte?'

'I must visit her. It's the only way.'

He was silent, his hand tight on the phone.

9

They were struck by the heat the moment they walked off the plane at Carcassonne. The hot air was filled with mingled smells, acrid and sweet. Adam, Katherine and Kieron made their way through passport control and picked up the keys for their hire car at the air-conditioned Europcar office. They walked out into the sweltering midday heat of the south of France into a car park filled with rows of shining cars and stopped at a silver hatchback.

'Is this ours?' said Kieron.

'Let's see.'

She pressed the remote on the key and the yellow indicator lights flashed.

'I'll drive,' said Adam.

'It's okay.'

'Let me, please . . .'

Kieron, sensing conflict, strapped himself into his child's seat and like a miniature judge said, 'Mummy, you drive.'

Adam sat in the passenger seat. It was an old issue. Katherine had always been the driver. When she first met Adam, he was thirty and hadn't had a single driving lesson. She would race from dance rehearsals to his flat in her clapped-out black Vauxhall, a ghetto blaster blaring on the seat next to her, and beep her horn for him to come down. She'd felt as though she was in a film. Driving was something she felt she was good at.

She put the car into gear and slowly edged out into the narrow lanes of the car park.

'I'll sit in the back with you, Kieron,' said Adam, and climbed over the seats.

She knew he was angry. It didn't matter where they travelled, the parameters of their relationship came with them and were always the same.

'Don't drive too fast,' he said.

'I won't,' she said trying to keep the edge out of her voice.

They turned out of the airport on to the Route Nationale and headed south.

'Look how straight the road is, Kieron,' said Adam.

'Why is it so straight?'

'These roads were built for soldiers.'

'What soldiers?'

'Napoleon's soldiers. He planted the trees too.'

'Why?'

'So that his soldiers wouldn't get burnt by the sun on their long marches.'

'Who is Napoleon?'

Katherine listened to her husband's patient explanations, her son's obedient curiosity. Their chatter became a background hum. The windscreen of the hire car was yellow-tinted and gave the unfolding countryside a Polaroid intensity; fields of alternating yellow, green, and brown stretched away to a horizon spiked with dark cypresses. Her thoughts drifted. She imagined a convoy of Napoleon's army: red-uniformed soldiers walking in weary formations through the dappled shade, stragglers and big-skirted women and boys playing the pipes, ragging the line.

'Was Napoleon a goodie or a baddie?' said Kieron. He was playing with the button for the electric window. Katherine heard the whirr of it lowering, and the loud hiss of rushing air filled the car.

'At first he seemed good, but then he turned out bad,' said Adam raising his voice over the din.

'Like Hitler?'

'How do you know about Hitler?'

'Mummy told me.'

Kieron closed the window and the hush returned.

'Hitler was a baddie all the time,' said Adam. 'Napoleon started out good but went bad.'

'Will Napoleon try and kill us?'

'Don't worry. He's dead.'

'Are all the bad people all dead?'

'Yes.'

'What about burglars?'

She couldn't focus on the conversation between her husband and son. Was she wrong to have walked across the park with Stephen? It was he who had kissed her. Or had it been her? He had led her into the park and kissed her. It had lasted until four in the morning. When they had left each other there had been no sense of future, no

122

exchange of numbers, no plans or promises; but everything had changed.

'Slow down!' said Adam.

Her foot was hard on the accelerator. She eased off.

'You're too close to this side of the road.'

Katherine drove on. They reached Limoux. The stone houses were shuttered, the streets deserted as though long abandoned. The pollarded plane trees seemed to push up out of the concrete like fists, their flaking bark revealing the cream jigsaw pieces beneath. The road opened up again and the houses became sparse. Katherine turned on the radio. It was Bach, a fugue for violin. Her foot pressed down on the accelerator. On either side were fields of hay and bright yellow rape. She let her thoughts fill with Stephen. She felt her hands on the hard rim of the steering wheel as though she were holding his body; her tongue in her own mouth seemed to be touching his. She felt his presence as though he were inside her.

There was the sound of a terrifying explosion, like a blast of gunfire. Katherine saw a flash of metallic blue, another car rushing towards her. She heard screaming horns, sheer hurtling speed. A heavy weight fell into her, then nothing.

In the silence she saw grass and concrete, houses at an angle. All was still and silent.

'For fuck's sake! What the fuck?' Adam's voice was furious, rasping, close to her.

'Oh God.'

He was crushed into her, thrown through the gap in

the seats. He lifted himself off. She looked into the back desperately. Where was Kieron? Kieron was not there.

'What happened, Mummy?'

His voice was bright and calm. He was on the floor of the car.

'It's okay,' said Katherine quietly. 'We hit the kerb.'

The radio was still playing.

'What the hell were you doing? I told you to slow down! Kieron, you okay?' said Adam, picking the boy up.

'I'm sorry,' said Katherine.

The Pyrenees rose up ahead of them, huge mountains of rock and snow frozen in space like an angry wave. Katherine felt their presence like an admonishment.

'You fucking nearly killed us!'

Kieron heard his father's anger and started to cry.

Katherine opened the door and walked round the car. One of the back tyres was blown out. It looked as if it had exploded from within.

'You've shredded the wheel,' said Adam. 'We are fucking miles from anywhere.'

Kieron ran to Katherine and put his arms around her. She hugged him tight, his body so small.

'I'll go for help,' she said.

She walked across the grass. A window in one house was open and she walked towards it. There was a small forecourt. An elderly woman with a lavender perm peered out from a side door.

'Bonjour, bonjour, madame . . . excusez-moi! Un accident. Nous avons un accident.'

An old man with a grey moustache appeared next to her and they replied in unison.

'Oui, oui, oui . . .'

'La voiture. Mon mari et mon fils, ils sont là . . .'

They craned their heads at identical angles towards the hire car.

'Ah, oui, oui . . . ah, oui.'

They saw Adam with Kieron in his arms.

'Attendez! Attendez, s'il vous plait.'

The moustached man disappeared into his garage and reappeared with a jack. Katherine and the woman smiled and nodded, and they all walked over towards the car. The couple did not speak English but Katherine spoke enough French to communicate with them.

'My husband, Adam. My son, Kieron,' she said in French.

Everyone shook hands. The elderly couple did not volunteer their names. The man looked at the tyre and shook his head.

'Are you far from your destination, monsieur?' he asked.

'No parle français, but in any language I would say we are fucked!' said Adam, and made an explosion noise with his mouth, then shrugged. The old man laughed and put his hand on Adam's arm.

'Don't worry, monsieur!'

Together, they got the spare tyre from the boot and knelt down to position the jack under the car, communicating in sign language and broken English. The woman invited Kieron and Katherine back to the house. The downstairs room was tiled, cool and gloomy, the shutters closed against the heat of the day. Katherine and Kieron waited politely on the sofa listening to glasses clinking in the kitchen, liquid pouring, a spoon stirring. The woman reappeared with two lurid green mint cordials.

'There have been many accidents at this spot, many, many!' she said.

'Really?'

'The road is too narrow,' she said.

Katherine looked about her. There were stuffed deer heads on the wall, mounted antlers, skins stretched and hung like pictures and a framed display of boars' tusks.

'My husband adores hunting. Boom boom,' said the woman, laughing and miming a gun at Kieron.

Katherine's eyes filled with tears. The woman took her hands and squeezed them.

'You are shocked. You are shocked, madame.'

Katherine smiled and looked out the window. Adam and the man were still at the car pumping up the jack. Suddenly it snapped. Adam and the man burst out laughing.

'Complètement fucked!' cried Adam.

'It is not easy!' said the man.

Neither understood the other but their humour translated effortlessly between them. They walked back toward the house shaking their heads, like old comrades. The French man said he would call the car hire company. Adam sat with Katherine and Kieron on the sofa and drank a beer while the man spoke at length to Europcar at Carcassonne airport. He persuaded them to send a new car out to the holiday house the next day, and to pay for a taxi for la petite famille to continue their journey that evening.

Katherine was worried about the cost.

'Don't worry. Insurance! Insurance!' said the man, gesticulating in the air.

He made another call to a friend, Laurent, asking if he would take an English family up into the mountains to their holiday cottage. Laurent was the village taxi. He was mending a fence at his brother's farm but would pick them up in an hour.

The man winked and left the room. He came back in swinging a big dead rabbit by its feet. He showed Adam the entry wound at the top of one of its back legs.

'It didn't kill him. I had to . . .'

He snapped the rabbit's neck with sharp twist.

'It is more humane,' said the woman.

'Ah, yes. Yes,' said the man.

He held out the rabbit. Adam took it. Blood seeped on to his hands. Kieron moved on to Katherine's knee. The old man unsheathed a knife.

The woman went on and on about how she was going to make a casserole, how the rabbit was an old one and she would have to cook it a long time to make the meat tender. She told Katherine how they had lived in Lyon all their lives but had moved to the mountains after her husband retired because of his love of hunting, how in fact he had been born near here, and how good it was for him to be out of the city, back in the world of his childhood . . .

While she spoke, the man made a deep incision into the rabbit's belly, sucking in his teeth as he dragged the blade downwards. The intestines burst from its body and hung down, gleaming darkly, soft browns and purples, greys like wet pebbles, colours nurtured away from the light. Katherine felt they should never have been seen. Kieron started to cry and she took him in her arms.

'He is tired. I'll take him for a little walk . . .'

She took him outside. Kieron ran towards a small wood, the rabbit forgotten, and disappeared down a bank. Katherine caught up with him by a mossy stream. They plunged their hands into the cool water. There were shoals of sticklebacks and they moved their hands to and fro, watching them scatter.

After two hours Laurent arrived and drove Katherine, Adam and Kieron up the winding mountain road to Senesse-de-Senabugue. Night fell and the road was pitch black. Katherine sat in the back with Kieron, his head lying on her lap as Laurent chatted to Adam in halting English. The car twisted and turned into the darkness but she felt fearless and held, like a sleepy child being carried in the night with no will of its own.

There were no lights when they arrived at the house, and the sky was moonless. With the help of the car's headlights, they found the key under a stone. Laurent wished them good night and disappeared. Adam carried

Kieron to a bed and wrapped him in a blanket. Katherine found a bottle of wine in a small larder, and she and Adam sat on the kitchen bench and drank it together before climbing the creaking stairs. They slept under damp-smelling eiderdowns.

Over the next few days the tension between Adam and Katherine began to fall away. They went for walks up rocky paths, past mountain shrines, along grassy terraces and through dense and magical woods. When Kieron wouldn't walk they made a seat for him with their arms and carried him like a little emperor. Adam would make up long fantastical stories to keep him entertained. They stopped planning their days and let the time drift. There was a path from the garden to a copse lined with blackberry bushes. They filled bowls with the ripe fruit. From the village, they bought flour and sugar, and Katherine helped Kieron bake his first blackberry pie. Sometimes they ventured out in the hire car along the winding roads. They visited churches, taking it in turns to keep Kieron occupied with games and tasks. They had picnics of baguette, cheese, tomatoes and olives. They sat on flat rocks by the river and paddled in the cool water.

On market day, they went to Mirepoix. They found baby courgettes, bulbous tomatoes, huge ragged lettuces and mushrooms as big as dinner plates. There were oranges and apples and pomegranates, fresh goat's cheeses and home-baked tarts and breads. They bought too much of everything and carried it in boxes to the car.

Kieron was bored and Adam offered to buy him an ice cream. Katherine wanted him to wait until he'd eaten lunch, and for a moment, tension flickered between them. Adam offered to take Kieron to the playground while Katherine explored the town. She agreed to meet them at the car in an hour.

She wandered into the church. She walked round the nave and stopped in front of a painted statue of the Virgin Mary. There were candles of different heights on metal spikes. She dropped a euro in a tin box and lit a new candle. As she set it down, the flame flickered as though it might go out. She sat on a pew nearby and watched it gutter, strengthen and become constant. The air inside the church was cool and still. The outside world receded and the silence enveloped her. She sat motionless for what seemed like hours. A pale light shone through high windows. Her feelings came and went. She felt she could have no control over them. She could only watch and wait to see what happened. She could not dictate or influence the future any more than she could the flame of the candle.

She left the church. Across the road there was a sign in the window of a café: 'Internet'. Katherine took her mobile phone from her bag for the first time in ten days and was surprised to see that she had a signal. She dialled the code for England followed by her father's number.

'Good morning, the Broughton Foundation.'

'Hi, it's Katherine. Is that Paul?'

'Matthew. Not that anyone can tell. We're all alike.

Clones really. Your dad makes us all in a Petri dish,' he said. 'Do you want him?'

'Not exactly. I enjoyed the poetry at St Mark's and . . .' She felt flustered. 'I want to write to the poets. Have you an e-mail address?'

'For Duncan Harris?'

'For both of them.'

He went away from the phone. She could hear clicking sounds and distant voices. She didn't want her father to know she was calling and hoped he was not nearby.

'Here they are,' said Matthew and gave her the addresses. Katherine thought he sounded sarcastic and knowing.

'Thanks,' she said quickly and hung up.

In the café, she was shown into a small room behind the bar. An old Dell computer sat on a cluttered desk. She logged into her account, opened a new e-mail document and tapped in Stephen's address.

When she returned to the car she found Adam and Kieron waiting for her. They were sitting on the ground, and taking it in turns to hit an Orangina can with pebbles. She felt a welling of love for them both. She'd bought an ice cream for Kieron and gave it to him.

'Sorry I'm late. I got stuck into some window-shopping.'

'That's what holidays are for,' said Adam. 'You okay?'

'I'm fine,' she said. 'I love you both so much.'

10

Stephen stared at the crack of light coming through the door and slipped out of bed. It was 4 a.m. Alison stretched out across the bed and reached her hand towards him. He leant over and kissed her. He put on a shirt and jeans and crept past the children's room and downstairs. He opened the back door and walked across the garden to his workspace. They had converted it from a garage when he and Alison had first moved to Gloucestershire eighteen months ago. They had installed a bed, toilet and shower cubicle so that it could serve as a guest room as well as Stephen's study. It had its own separate entrance to the street; sometimes if Stephen was late coming home from a reading, he would sleep there so as not to disturb Alison. He had done so after St Mark's.

He unlocked the door. The air was cold. He turned on the electric bar heater and sat at his desk. He started to write, his pen moving lightly across the page. He did so without censure, putting down whatever came into his head – *in his chair like a saddle, the desk – an old pony, he reports in, makes speech, swimming in words, falling through word clouds into waves and swimming . . .*

He wrote like this for an hour every morning, in a

stream of consciousness. It was an exercise he had started a few months ago to try to break his writing block. A friend of his had told him it was like taking your mind for a run. Stephen had never experienced a creative freeze like this before, and it frightened him. He hid it from Alison; he told her *The Crossing* was going well.

His pen skated across the page. He watched it, hoping to break through to a deeper level, one more free, of pure intuition. If he could only reach that place, his writing would flow easily again. Like a fisherman making a good catch, he would simply have to haul the poetry in, complete and pure.

He had always written. His first poem was when he was eight years old. His parents had been divorced for two years. It was the middle of a hot summer. His father was dropping Stephen and his sister back to his mother's house after a rare weekend with him in London. Meetings between his mother and father were always tense, and Stephen had run upstairs to avoid the awkward handover, her strained voice, the diffident goodbyes. He stood by his bedroom window and watched his father walk away down the gravel path towards his car. Stephen willed him to turn and notice him at the upstairs window. He felt that if he could only make his father stop then everything would be all right, but his father had walked straight to his car and driven away without looking back. Stephen had watched the empty road for a long time, and eventually, as if to fill the void his father had left, words began to come to him. They described the gravel path where his father had walked, how his footsteps had displaced the pebbles that had spilled on to the grass. They described his mother's voice drifting up the stairs like smoke and the grey sky pulled tight like a sheet at the corners.

He had shown the poem to his mother. She had cried and held him tightly to her, saying he was a special boy to write such a poem. Her delight satisfied Stephen in a way he had never experienced before; he felt he had made his mother feel happy for the first time.

Ink running in veins, flat and captured he wished he could bring them alive and fly them like banners pulled by aeroplanes . . .

The pen moved across the page, making words like knots, tiny tangles of thread. All he was generating were thoughts about the pen, his hand, the paper. He threw down the pen in frustration. He longed to be back in Braymer, with its perfect mixture of community and isolation. He could stride off alone into the hills or swim in the lake, or spend time with George Gull, or any one of David's staff. Crucially, he had been able to talk with David, the spark that had ignited *The Crossing*.

A stack of twenty copies of his last collection of poems, *Tree House*, sat on the table. He picked one up. *Tree House* had won the New York Review Poetry Prize and the Lexicon Prize. His readings were popular and the volume had sold well. He still earned money through travel journalism and short teaching contracts but he had finally found the confidence to think of himself, first and foremost, as a poet.

He looked at the lime-green cover with his name beneath the title. His name seemed to have nothing to do with him. He walked over to the bed where pages of *The Crossing* were scattered like so much litter. He gathered them up and sat back at his desk, determined to read through everything and plan the next section. He instantly felt sick to his stomach. It was a physical sensation, as though he were being forced to eat something disgusting. The whole enterprise of capturing his identity and his family's past made him sick.

When he was five, Stephen's father had met another woman. Stephen had experienced the slow process of his parents splitting up as though he was being flayed alive. For two long years he'd listened to the fights, to his mother's weeping, his father's cold rationality. His world slowly collapsed around him, his home dismantled brick by brick. After his father had left them, his mother was diagnosed with depression. She decided to take Stephen and his sister to live near a friend in Dumfries, as far away from their father as possible. As she drove out of London, she cried bitterly. She told Stephen that it didn't matter where they went, their lives were cursed and the curse was on her whole family. It was this curse that Stephen was confronting in *The Crossing*.

He had only shadowy recollections of his maternal grandparents. They had lived in Ipswich and only rarely visited. They had strange accents and smelt of vinegar. After his parents' divorce, Stephen had become deeply suspicious of them. He felt they were the root of the curse his mother spoke of. He remembered his grandfather pulling him on to his knee and saying, 'Be happy you were not born in Warsaw,' and his grandmother snapping, 'You're drunk, Victor! Drunk in front of children!'

For *The Crossing* Stephen had researched their lives. Victor Lewim and Anna Krakowska arrived in England in 1938 from Poland. They had sailed into Harwich on the East Coast with a newborn baby in their arms. They were nineteen and twenty years old and passionately in love. Their parents in Warsaw had opposed their union. Anna's family were wealthy business people who owned a chain of haberdashery shops. Victor's were poor, his father was a labourer, his mother died in childbirth. Neither family approved of the match. Anna and Victor had met in secret and eloped. They left behind everything, their families, their language, their culture. As the ship pulled into the harbour they looked up at the muted English sky and felt the North Sea wind. They felt a new future unfolding for them, a future like the coastline, calm, green and safe.

They settled in Ipswich, living in a small two-up two-down. They loved their new baby and each other. Stephen's grandfather prospered; he was an intelligent and enterprising man, and found a good job in the co-operative bank. He escaped the draft and was promoted to become a manager. After the war was over, the terrible truth of the death camps emerged and Victor and Anna discovered that their grandparents, their parents, their brothers and sisters, had all died. They never recovered from the shock. They couldn't reconcile their family's obliteration with their own escape, and a virus crept into their lives. Victor developed a terror of the English Fascists. He no longer trusted his colleagues at the bank. He began to drink rum in the cellar, to try to loosen his fear.

Anna's way of shutting out her history was bolder. She tried to assimilate herself into the culture. She hated being different. She took elocution lessons to eradicate her Polish accent. Her teacher was Mrs Grant, a local magistrate's wife, who spoke like the Queen. She longed to be part of Mrs Grant's world with her hair perfectly shaped by curlers and setting lotions. One day, Mrs Grant had invited her to a Christian church. She went and almost instantly decided to convert to Christianity. She wished away her Jewishness, her husband in the cellar, the horrors of her past. She spent hours every day at church with Mrs Grant and her friends, preferring the cold interior of God's house to the sad tensions of her own. She bought a set of curlers and changed her hair.

Stephen's mother was their only child. When Victor was drunk he would terrify his daughter with stories of the pogroms and the relatives she would never meet. 'Everyone lost someone,' he would say, 'but we lost everyone'. Anna would chide him. 'We are fortunate, thank Jesus,' she would say in stilted English. 'Leave the girl alone.' The stories seeped into Stephen's mother. She couldn't help but inherit her parents' fear. After her divorce, his mother would creep into Stephen's bed at night and cry inconsolably. Stephen grew up believing the curse on his family was true; a baton of unhappiness, passed from generation to generation.

He turned on his computer. There was an e-mail from the Rockerman Centre. Stephen had applied for a fellowship six months previously to allow him to live and write in America. It would provide a monthly wage and accommodation for himself and his family for up to two years. For Stephen, America was a land of possibility. In his twenties, he had spent time in Arizona and New Mexico. He had picked up work wherever he could: farm labouring, copywriting, reinventing himself as an easygoing traveller, shedding what he saw as his loathsome Englishness. He had an American girlfriend out there called Julia. They bought a campervan and travelled from place to place for a year. His mind had felt clear. He loved the dry heat and the wide vistas.

He opened the Rockerman e-mail. He was on a shortlist of three. He felt a wave of excitement. He was convinced that going back to America could free his creativity and save *The Crossing*.

Alison hadn't been so sure. When Stephen told her he had applied, she'd been confused. They had just bought their house, she said. The children were settled in school. Stephen told her it would be the greatest adventure of their lives. He described the mountains and the roaming emptiness of the desert. He appealed to the artist in her, the part of her undulled by motherhood. He bought her a new lens for her camera. In the desert, she would start taking pictures again, he said. America would be a chance for them to really be together, without distractions. It would help their marriage. He would no longer travel to do readings or write journalism. They would live and work in a simple and honest way.

'Daddy, you were sleeping! You were sleeping!'

His daughter Molly was jumping up and down shouting.

He looked at his watch. It was 11.30. He had slept for four hours. His son Frank was standing beside the bed, looking down at him.

'Mummy says stop work,' he said.

'I'm going to tell Mum you were sleeping!' said Molly.

'Daddy! Get up! You have to come and help! We have to get the fire ready. They'll be here soon, Dad,' said Frank.

He had forgotten it was Saturday. His friend Yuri was coming over with his kids to make a fire and cook potatoes and sausages in the garden. He felt happy at the thought of seeing him. Yuri was a good friend, someone he trusted. He put his arms round Molly and Frank and squeezed them. Frank wriggled out of his clasp, but Molly flopped her weight on his chest.

'Can you write me a book?' she said, picking up one of the pages of *The Crossing* which lay on the bed beside them.

'Mummy says children's books make more money,' said Frank.

139

'Mummy's right.'

'Come on, Dad!' cried Frank, pulling on his arm. 'Get up!'

'Okay, okay,' he said, 'I'm coming.'

'For late September this is amazing!' said Yuri.

The sun was dazzling in a blue sky. They were sitting on the grass; Yuri cross-legged, Alison leaning back on one arm. Stephen walked towards them carrying three bottles of cold Kingfisher beer. They looked like a photograph, he thought. Yuri had shaved all his hair off since Stephen had last seen him, and it suited him. Alison brushed her hand over Yuri's head.

'I like it,' she said.

'Either that or the dreaded comb-over,' said Yuri.

Alison laughed. In one corner of the garden, Molly and Frank were screaming with delight as Yuri's two sons sprayed them with water pistols.

'Any news from the Rockerman?' asked Yuri.

'We're on the shortlist,' said Alison.

Behind her, the three boys had formed a huddle, and were whispering to each other. Molly stood apart, watching them vacantly.

'Al's not sure about America,' said Stephen.

'It will be good for Stephen's writing,' said Alison evenly. She did not make eye contact with him and he knew he had hurt her. Alison was a private person who disliked discussing personal matters even with close friends. He regretted his indiscretion, but her self-control stifled him, made him want to puncture the façade of politeness, to expose the whole tangled underbelly of their relationship to anyone who would listen. Alison was altruistic and generous and he loved her for it, but her capacity to bury her feelings confounded him.

In the early days of their relationship, her strength of mind had impressed him. They had met at university through a mutual friend. Stephen had been stunned by her beauty and intelligence. He did everything he could to woo her, wrote her love poems, sent her flowers, took her to concerts and parties. She seemed to like his earnestness and humour. After things didn't work out with his girlfriend Julia in America, he returned to England and looked her up. She was single too, having just split up with a student doctor. She was working as a photographer's assistant and creating her own portfolio in her spare time.

They started a relationship, and she invited him to meet her parents at their home in Winchester. Her father was a headmaster at a minor public school, her mother was the school nurse. Alison's impregnable stoicism was deeply rooted in her English heritage. She had a sense of belonging that to Stephen, with his fractured, immigrant past, was deeply alien. He found himself coveting her sense of security. After only four weeks of courtship he asked her to marry him.

'How is all your scribbling?' said Yuri.

'Okay. How is your training?' said Stephen, to change the subject.

'I've been on placements for the last three months. It's good to be out of the classroom and working with kids.'

He was in the final stages of training to be a teacher. Yuri had been a travel writer but hadn't been able to make a living from it. After splitting up with his wife, Jules, two years earlier, he had decided to re-train. He'd told Stephen he wanted to live in the real world.

'Are you happy?' said Stephen.

'I don't know. We are so persuaded in this country by the virtues of being miserable. It's like a collective depression. I think the pursuit of happiness is a noble aim: when Jules and I were brave enough to realise we weren't happy, it was like a revelation.'

Stephen remembered it. His own experience of his parents' divorce had left him so wounded that he had watched Yuri's split with his wife with a morbid fascination, as though it were a chance to re-open his own wounds and feel them again. He had watched and waited, expecting disaster, a blood bath, a catastrophe, like the head of a match poised to strike and explode. It never happened. Jules and Yuri had remained amicable throughout their separation. Yuri told Stephen that both he and Jules had felt renewed and transformed by it.

'We have a far better relationship now. We should have done it years ago,' said Yuri.

Alison looked away, as though the conversation no longer interested her. The children were shooting each other with sticks, making noises of explosions and gun-fire.

142

'I'm Ice Man! I cover you with ice!'

'*I'm* Ice Man!'

'Your ice can't touch me. I have a force-field,' shouted Thomas.

'Get her! Get her!' shouted Frank and Gabriel. The boys ran after Molly who put her arms around the trunk of the apple tree.

'Tree is homey!' she shouted.

'You can't just make up homeys as you go,' said Frank.

'I can!' she screamed.

'No more homeys!' shouted Thomas.

'No more homeys!' shouted the other boys.

Molly ran terrified to her mother and buried her face in her lap.

'Do you want to do some drawing, Moll?' said Stephen.

The girl nodded through her tears.

'Don't cry,' said Alison, stroking Molly's hair.

Stephen walked back to the house to fetch crayons and paper. The kids' voices faded as the door closed behind him. The kitchen was dark. The fridge was buzzing loudly. The clutter of plates and glasses from lunch was piled on the table. The computer was on, its screensaver a photograph of Molly and Frank holding up a lobster. There was a window on the screen. *You have mail.* He opened his inbox, half-wondering if it might be the Rockerman Foundation again. He didn't recognise the address. He clicked on it idly and read,

Dear Stephen,
It was nice to meet you and Alison at St Mark's.
I have an idea I would like to discuss with you.
I thought you might be able to help me.
See attached
Best wishes, Katherine

Katherine. Stephen's heart pounded in his chest. The fact of her writing to him. How had she got his address? That kiss. Her mouth. He could feel her mouth pressing against his. He looked at her name again and felt a slight erection. He walked over to the sink. For no reason he could think of, he turned on the tap. He looked through the blind into the garden. Yuri and Alison were sitting on the grass as the children buzzed around them. The day after meeting Katherine, Stephen had written three short poems about her. Since then he had not given her any thought at all. He had told himself he had been drunk. He opened the attachment. All he could take in at first was the shape of it: a block of text, a perfect paragraph.

a woman is walking home one night through the park and she finds a shell on the path. it's miles from the sea. she picks it up. on one side it's rough and on the other it is shining with twists and turns and a depth inside it she can't fathom. she is fascinated by the shell, but she doesn't want to take it with her. it wouldn't be right. it does not belong to her. so she leaves it there on the path but afterwards she can't stop thinking about it. what do you think? how should it end? should she go back and look at it again?

She had written this. Katherine. She had sent this to him. She had not existed before but now she did, as real as though she had walked into the room and stood right in front of him. He understood why she had written like this, partly hidden, using an attachment, not knowing if Alison might have access to his inbox. His heart was pounding as he remembered her willingness to be kissed, the way their tongues had questioned and answered. He desperately wanted to kiss her again.

11

Katherine was walking along Victoria Embankment. It was nearly five o'clock and people were making their way home. In the evening sunlight the black and red arches of Blackfriars Bridge gleamed like a bracelet across the arm of the river.

How about next Wednesday? I'll be in town anyway. Why don't we meet for a drink?

Her linen skirt swayed against her bare legs. She walked along the Strand towards Charing Cross. She was moving in the opposite direction to everyone else. People flowed past her, the colours of their clothes and coats blurring like a rag carpet as she made her way through them. She reached the steps into Trafalgar Square and looked across to the black lions at the foot of Nelson's Column. Stephen was sitting on one of the low walls around the ornamental fountains wearing a thick brown coat. He was leaning forward, his elbows on his knees, his chin resting on his hands, watching something on the ground. His absorption calmed her. He moved, straightened his back, and looked around as she came towards him.

'Am I late?'

'I don't think so.'

She had forgotten his face. It seemed older than she

remembered but it struck her how handsome he was.

'Shall we get a drink?' he said.

They walked to the nearest pub and sat on stools at one end of a curving bar. There were mirrors on all sides of them. The only other people were a couple holding hands on a sofa. They ordered beer and Stephen asked her about her job at Ashwood.

'I don't fit in there,' she said. 'I stumbled into the wrong thing and now it's becoming who I am, and I can't stop it.'

He liked the self-conscious way she spoke, the way she chose her words.

'Do you ever feel like you are doing the wrong thing?' she asked. 'I can't imagine you do. You are so successful.'

'Am I?'

'You are doing what you want, aren't you?'

He heard the challenge in her voice. He remembered her words from St Mark's. A kind of violence. What had she meant? She seemed to demand an honesty from him. He felt he had no option but to tell her the truth. He told her everything, things he had never told anyone else. He told her about the months he had spent failing to write, the wasted days in his study, walking the streets, idling in bookshops and coffee shops and libraries; how he read literary magazines and was envious of other writers and how prolific they were. He told her how desperate he had become about *The Crossing*.

They wandered into Soho. Crowds spilled on to the pavements from the pubs. They stopped by Berwick

147

Street Market. The last traders were packing up their stalls. An Asian man was loading rugs into a three-wheeled van. Two white men, a father and son, sat on crates smoking together without talking. Katherine was telling Stephen about dancing. Stephen listened, and as she talked, her confidence grew. With him she felt the freedom to talk, an ease she had never felt before. She told him about Müller and Berlin, about how when she had returned, she'd felt lost. She told him how the only thing that had made sense to her was to begin choreographing her own pieces, and how she'd done so obsessively, how it had seemed to rescue her. Katherine rarely let herself think about that part of her life. As time had passed, she had become less and less sure of it as though it hadn't really been her at all.

'I wish I could have seen you,' he said and for the first time she felt a pang of regret at the loss of it. Stephen saw it in her, but perceived it as modesty.

'Why did you stop?' he asked.

'I don't really know. I told myself it was because I kept getting injured and I wanted to settle down and have a family . . .'

She trailed off, but Stephen was still listening, waiting for more.

'My last job was with this big company. I'd always wanted to work with them but when I did I felt stifled. We toured a lot and I got into crazy relationships with some of the other dancers. It was an endless treadmill of travel and performance. It wasn't what I'd gone into it for.'

'What do you mean?'

'When I first started it, I wasn't like that. I'd done my own thing. I felt free.'

Stephen watched her and it seemed to him that her body danced as she spoke. Her hands gesticulated, her arms described circles in the air. All her movements were perfectly balanced, connected to her centre. He felt the energy in her body, and longed for her.

'What did your father think of your dancing?'

Katherine gave a short laugh but didn't answer. She caught the faint sweet smell of cigarette smoke in the air and longed to draw it deep into her lungs. She couldn't share her ambivalence about her father with him.

'I want to smoke,' she said.

They wandered through Chinatown, directionless, without speaking.

'I didn't know what it would be like to see you again,' he said.

'We are only talking. There is no harm,' she said.

They wandered into a cornershop. Katherine bought some cigarettes and a box of matches from a man who talked constantly into his mobile phone. She took the little cellophane packet like an illicit gift.

Stephen walked down one of the aisles. The shelves were packed with every possible item: DVDs, nappies, olives, fresh melons, cornflakes, wine. There were fridges full of Chinese and Japanese food and a thousand brands of soft drink.

'They've got *sake*!' he said, as if it was what they'd been searching for. He held up a white pot. It looked like an old-fashioned vinegar bottle.

'Let's get some,' she said.

They took two bottles to a young black woman serving at the counter at the back of the shop. Her long nails were painted red with glitter and curled at the ends of her fingers. They clicked against the ceramic as she searched for the price sticker.

'On me,' said Katherine.

'It's okay,' said Stephen handing over a note. The woman smiled at them. There was a small gap between her front teeth.

Stephen carried the bottles of sake in a plastic bag. Katherine could feel him walking next to her, the small distance between them, the thickness of his coat, the shape of his arms, his bare neck, his face. She lit a cigarette and offered him one.

'Thanks,' he said, taking one. 'I haven't had one for years.'

'Me neither.'

Everything was new now. He led her down an alley at the back of the Duchess Theatre in Haymarket. It smelt of beer and urine. They stopped under a streetlight next to three wheelie bins. Behind them rose the high windowless wall of the theatre. Stephen opened a bottle of sake and passed it to her.

Katherine's phone rang.

'You should answer it,' said Stephen, moving away.

He walked up to Shaftesbury Avenue and leant against

the wall as people streamed past. A cyclist was precariously weaving through the slow lines of cars and buses. A man sat in a doorway sipping from a can of lager. His clothes were filthy but he was wearing brand-new blue-and-silver trainers.

Katherine looked down at her phone as though it didn't belong to her. She waited for the ringing to stop, walked up to Stephen and kissed him. They kissed slowly, exploring each other, their eyes shutting out the world.

They walked to Hyde Park and climbed over a fence. It was getting dark. In the distance, a police car was patrolling slowly along a path, its headlights illuminating the trees. They walked to some shrubs and parted the leaves. They spread their coats on the ground and lay down next to each other. A car passed near them, its slow engine pulsing, its headlights briefly lighting them as they turned their bodies in towards each other.

12

David sat at the Formica table with a cold cup of coffee. He gazed out at the latticed ironwork of the station, the hanging baskets, the village post office opposite, the quaint signposts. The quiet affluence of Fairhampton, the wealthy southern village which Gregory and David's sister Charlotte had made their home, baffled and oppressed him. He felt annoyed with May for going off and leaving him to his thoughts like this. In their urgency not to be late for Gregory, they had caught an early-morning train from Northumberland, arriving at Fairhampton a full two hours before they were due at Willow House. They knew that to arrive early would be just as irritating to Gregory as if they were to arrive late, so now they had been forced to wait. May had insisted on profiting from the spare time to walk to Fairhampton beach over a mile away, and David had been left in the station café. He had already read through the newspapers and was now reduced to watching the taxi drivers leaning idly against their cars. He felt a creeping dread of seeing Charlotte after so long.

He was filled with memories of his parents' farm. It was near to Lancaster Asylum, and some of the less severe patients would help his father at milking time. He thought of them, simple men who would smile without cause as they moved slowly amongst the cattle. He remembered how unafraid and patient Charlotte had been with them. He remembered how affectionate she had always been with him, and felt again the bitterness of the day Gregory had first come to take her out. It was washing day. Each day of the week had its tasks: washing day, ironing day, baking day, shopping day, sewing day. There were piles of laundry in great baskets under the sink, and David, aged eleven, stood unsteadily on top of one and leant across the sink to see out of the window. Charlotte stood next to him, in her yellow dress, gripping his hand.

'It's him. It's him,' she whispered, excitedly.

A brand-new Hillman was bumping down the farm track towards them. Charlotte ran outside, and David had watched her climb into the car. Gregory, tall and slim, put his arm round her like a wing, and they drove away. He took her to Blackpool. In the evening she'd come home with the sea in her hair, and given David a stick of rock, pinching his cheek like she was a grown-up. Gregory had bought her a strapless evening gown at Lillies, the modern dress shop, and Charlotte went into her bedroom to try it on. She came downstairs trailing her hand on the banister like a movie star, and his parents had applauded. He had never seen her look so beautiful. For David, Charlotte remained frozen in that time, on the stairs in her strapless gown, a force of vitality and goodness. He couldn't face the truth that she was lost to herself.

The taxi made a three-point turn on the drive in front of Willow House, its wheels crunching the gravel, and disappeared into a tunnel of rhododendrons. David and May walked up to the front door. They hadn't been to the house for nearly twenty years. The last time had been for a summer party. Charlotte had welcomed them with open arms. They had brought the children and Charlotte had fussed over Katherine and given her brothers a remote-controlled aeroplane to play with on the back lawn. David and May had been seduced by it all. There had been a marquee on the lawn, a live band and hundreds of guests with men in tailcoats and women in brightly coloured taffeta like sweet wrappers. Despite the ostentation, the house had seemed a happy place, but today, as David stood nervously in the porch, it seemed cold and eerie. Its bricks were so dark, he thought, he didn't remember them being so dark. He was stroking down his hair as the door opened.

'Gregory . . .'

'David, May . . .'

Gregory stood square in the doorway, his shirt tucked into his trousers which were pulled up high, making his long body seem oddly disproportionate.

'How good to see you.'

Their voices shimmered with nervous laughter.

'I hope we're not late,' said David.

'Come on in,' said Gregory, disappearing into the house.

May took off her coat and folded it over her arm. She tried to exchange a look with David but he was too pre-occupied.

'Come through!'

Gregory's voice bellowed from somewhere in the house. They walked into the vestibule. There was an overwhelming smell of polish. David had mentally rehearsed this moment many times since arranging the visit. He had planned to be deferential but wittily charming. Now that he was here he couldn't think of a thing to say.

'The great thing . . .' David started.

He'd turned left into a formal dining room with high-backed chairs around a gleaming glass table. There was no sign of Gregory.

'The great thing about Fairhampton,' he persevered, raising his voice a little, 'is that it never changes. It is preserved like one of Constable's great paintings . . .'

He stopped, unsure where to direct his voice.

The sound of clinking bottles came from behind a panelled door. David walked through to the kitchen.

'The church spire reminds me of his *Dedham Vale* . . .'

'Drink, anyone?' said Gregory appearing with a bottle of wine at the cellar door.

'Thank you,' said May.

'It's good to be here, Gregory,' said David, smiling and walking towards a painting on the wall, a bright orange gash scored across a black canvas like a bolt of lightning.

'Another Daniel Cole?' said David.

'A new one.'

Gregory had the bottle of wine by the neck and he screwed down the corkscrew in five firm twists. David looked at the painting. It was devoid of any merit.

'Bold,' he said, 'stark. The same unmistakable dynamism of the works in the flat.'

'I've got fifteen now. They've been a good investment.'

Gregory eased out the cork and poured out three large glasses.

'It's an impressive collection,' said David. 'As Redman said, a man who collects is a man of passion.'

'I don't know about that. If I like something I buy it. If it's part of a series I buy the lot. I do the same with shirts.'

David laughed politely. Gregory took a long swig of wine.

'There speaks the true collector!' said David turning, his eyes glittering, trying to cajole Gregory into conversation. Gregory laughed, disarmed for a moment, then heard himself laughing and stopped abruptly.

'Is Margery here?' said May.

'We are so much looking forward to meeting her,' said David.

'Marge! Margery!' shouted Gregory.

There was no reply. He went to the corridor and called again,

'Marge! Margery!'

They all waited, smiling tensely. Gregory paced back towards the wine bottle.

'I don't know where she's got to,' he said, unsettled,

pouring himself another glass. 'We'll have to set off soon; not that it's a long drive. We were lucky to find somewhere so close. It's one of the best like it in the country. Charlotte's lucky to be there. You will see for yourselves.'

'We've always known she must be in good hands,' said May.

'Twenty-four-hour care. Most of the nurses are from New Zealand. TV in every room. Not that she can watch it, of course . . .'

David smelt the polish again, strong and heady as petrol. He saw Charlotte in the room with a duster and canister of polish, spraying the surfaces, circling the duster, making everything gleam, just like his mother had done in the farm house.

'She's on a new regime,' said Gregory. 'The best doctors, not that they can do much of course, but at least we're doing everything we can.'

He looked at David for approval. May looked at him too.

'Of course,' said David, telling himself to sound more positive.

He could see the clear blue of the pool in the garden outside. Charlotte swimming up and down in it. He saw her drowning. There was a heavy silence in the room.

'The garden is looking lovely. Does Marge enjoy it?' said May.

As if on cue, Margery appeared from behind a shaped yew tree carrying a small yellow flower. She saw them and started laughing and talking, her head tilting back, mouth opening and closing, her hand gesturing with the flower. Gregory shoved open the sliding door.

'For God's sake, Margery!' he shouted, his voice harsh and clipped. 'We can't hear a bloody word you're saying!' He rapped his knuckles against the glass.

'Silly me! I was just saying that the man who blows the leaves blew over this little darling too.' She held up the flower, laughing. 'It's a wild primrose. Poor little thing. We'll put it in some water.'

She sailed into the house.

'Gregory has told me so much about you,' said Margery, offering her hand to David and May. 'So happy to meet you.'

She was not how David had imagined her; she was younger, more cheerful, bigger-boned. He couldn't help but feel the comparison with Charlotte, old, hospitalised, sick.

'There are wonderful flowers in Northumberland,' said May. 'You should come up. You'd enjoy the walks.'

'Margery hates walking!' said Gregory with a snort.

Margery seemed oblivious to his scorn.

'Gregory,' she said, 'May simply meant that it would be nice for me to come and visit her lovely home in the North.' She beamed at May like a warm sun. 'I would love to visit. May, could I?

Margery's warmth had a benign and stupefying effect on them all. They followed her to the kitchen and stood at the sink as she tended to the primrose. She filled a tiny vase with water and put it in.

'There. Now you'll feel happier,' she said.

David was acutely aware that all four of them were staring into the sink. He felt he had to say something. His mind was a blank.

'A daffodil drinks a glass of water a day,' he said.

'I'm not surprised,' said Margery, petting the flower's petals with her fingers. 'Yellow is such a happy colour.'

The time came for them to visit Charlotte. Margery came downstairs with freshly pinked lips. They all climbed into Gregory's car. David sat in the front with Gregory, May and Margery in the back. They drove down leafy lanes, glimpsing large houses behind high security gates, each with two or three parked cars on their forecourts. Margery chatted to May about the therapeutic effect of the colours of rhododendrons; their pink gives energy, she enthused. David winced as May said that she found the intensity of rhododendrons lurid and unnatural. He wished she would not be so opinionated, not now, when there was so much at stake. He wondered if this was the right moment, right now in the car, to mention Richard Seaton. He could drop it in effortlessly, casually. He rehearsed the words in his head: *Gregory, you'd be amazed, Northumberland is more and more civilised – a friend of mine has just opened a 24-hole golf course – all sorts of people have been tempted up to our backwater. Richard Seaton, who of course you know . . .*

The car slowed and turned into the Beaumont Nursing Home. David felt the sense of dread returning.

He hadn't expected it to be such a quick journey.

'So this is it,' he said, to say anything, and as the car cleared some boxed hedging, he saw the building for the first time.

A disorienting series of wings and annexes spread out over what seemed like a giant car park. There was a line of new birches in wire cages planted beside the drive. Gregory parked next to three blue clinical waste bins and they all got out. The air had the smell of the sea in it. They walked through the double doors, and Gregory led the way down quiet and empty corridors. A woman in a green hospital uniform walked silently behind them in white crepe-soled clogs.

The room was airless, the double-glazed windows sealed shut. There was a lingering smell of paint. A small TV stood next to a single bed. A door led to a small bathroom. David saw a handrail next to the toilet. Through the window two poplar trees stood as still as painted scenery. David stifled a gasp when he saw her. Charlotte sat in an armchair, wearing a pale green nightgown. Her back was hunched and he could see the bones in her bare arms. She looked straight ahead with unseeing eyes.

'It's the drugs, you see,' said Gregory, hovering near the door as if he couldn't bear to come any further.

'Lottie,' said David. 'Lottie.'

Charlotte didn't move. He walked over and laid his hands on her arm. She looked up at him blankly. There were purple patches under her eyes and her skin was as pale as chicken.

'She's gone, quite gone, you can see that,' said Gregory.

At the sound of Gregory's voice Charlotte's mouth clenched and she looked back at her hands. David stroked her arm.

'Lottie, Lottie,' he said. 'Lottie, Lottie.'

She looked up again at David, and suddenly she smiled, a great big beam. It was the Charlotte he knew. He saw her in her yellow dress at the farm coming out of her bedroom, her talking to the dairymen in the milking shed, walking into the kitchen carrying the milk, making a den for him by throwing a sheet over the clothes horse.

'Lottie, it's Davey, it's Dav . . . Dave . . .'

David started coughing. His words were stuck in his throat. Charlotte's smile passed. She stared ahead again, her gaze unblinking. David couldn't stop coughing. Tight bands seemed to close around his chest, and he had to loosen them. Charlotte started rocking backwards and forwards. The cough racked through him. He held his hand over his mouth and tried to stifle the convulsions. Charlotte started moaning.

'Stop bloody coughing, man!' snapped Gregory, and suddenly Charlotte screamed, a long sustained scream that passed right through her.

'Christ! For Christ's sake, David,' said Gregory. 'Get a hold of yourself, David!'

He rushed over to the bed and pulled the thin red cord. Charlotte screamed again. David was shaking his head trying to push the cough back down but it kept coming. He thought he would vomit. May was patting his back. Margery went to fetch water. Charlotte's scream was piercing and unbroken. A siren wailed in the corridor. Nurses appeared and David staggered from the room as the door was closed behind him.

No one spoke in the car to the station. There was silence, except for the occasional dry cough from David. Marge, next to Gregory in the front, turned her head and smiled at him sympathetically.

'Poor David,' she said turning back to him, 'poor you . . .'

They drove into Fairhampton, across the village green, past the perfectly painted shop fronts.

'There's a train in ten minutes,' said Gregory tersely.

A group of teenagers with school bags were congregated around a bench at the side of the road. Gregory had to swerve to avoid them. He stopped underneath the latticed ironwork canopy of Fairhampton station.

'Platform Two,' he said, holding the car door open for May. 'You have to cross under the line.'

'Thank you, Gregory, thank you, Margery,' said May.

'It's been lovely,' said Margery. 'I hope I'll be able to come and see you at your house soon.'

'Sorry about this,' said David stepping out of the car, still coughing. 'Thank you, Gregory. Charlotte is in good hands.'

Gregory didn't reply. David tried to smile, to relax. He had to do it now. It was now or never.

'Gregory, I wanted to mention . . .'

David started coughing, like an itch inside him.

'He should get that seen to,' said Gregory, addressing May as though he could no longer bear to talk directly with David. He moved towards the car and opened the driver's door.

'Honey and lemon is very good,' said Margery soothingly.

'Come on, we'll miss our train,' said May, leading David away. David turned back and stifling his cough, put his hand on Gregory's shoulder.

'Seaton . . .'

'What?'

'Richard Seaton.'

'What about him?'

Gregory looked at him sharply. David cleared his throat.

'I know that you used to work with him,' said David, smiling through his coughs.

'What's this about?'

'I wondered if you might help us reach him?'

Gregory paused for a moment. He looked at David with open scorn. 'Is that why you've come?' he asked.

'Of course not, Gregory. I just . . .' The cough stopped him going on.

'It is, isn't it?'

'Of course not,' said David, chest heaving. 'I wanted to see her . . . to see you . . . all.'

'Good God, David! Don't you ever stop? You didn't want to see any of us!'

He looked about him as if to gather support from a surrounding audience.

'This is how it always is with you, isn't it? Bloody hell!'

David's coordinates were vanishing. The cough racked him. This was not how it was supposed to happen. He didn't know what to say, how to defend himself. The cough kept exploding. Gregory's voice was rasping and bitter.

'You pretend you're interested in other people but you're not. You're only interested in yourself. You don't care about your sister. You only care about your precious memories of her. *Your* memories! I've put up with a lot from you, for her sake. Frankly you've got a bloody nerve coming here like this . . .'

He looked at May as though asking her to agree with him.

'You're quite wrong,' she said with quiet dignity. 'Quite wrong, Gregory.'

She took David by the arm. Gregory's temper was rising.

'It's all about you, isn't it? The fund-raising, the trips to London, the flat, they're all about you! Everything for your pleasure . . .'

May turned on him.

'Enough!' she said, vehemently. 'That is enough.'

A man and woman hurried past, a blur of red and brown coats talking loudly. Their voices faded as quickly as they had arisen. May's face was flushed. She took David's arm and led him into the station. The wind struck them as they walked into the stone entrance, and their steps faltered, but they adjusted to its force, leaning their bodies into it. David coughed harder as they disappeared into the tunnel.

13

They lay on a tide of sheets, two people washed up on a shore, exhausted, their heads close, faces blurring, seeing only each other. Katherine's thoughts were a slow chant inside her head.

'What is this?' she said, hardly aware that she was talking.

It could have been going on for ten minutes or forever. Stephen opened his mouth, and exhaled quietly. She kissed him and the touch aroused them both.

'I have to go.'

They kissed again, more insistently. She eased her body away from his, immediately feeling the lack of it. There was a small bathroom made from a plastic cubicle in the cheap hotel room. She needed to urinate and sat on the toilet; her pelvic muscles took a moment to find the right tension after so much sex.

Stephen lay on the bed and watched her, her breasts, her belly, her skin, her nakedness so unabashed.

'Stay,' he said.

Over the last three months they had met as often as they could. Stephen would come to London and they would spend afternoons in budget hotels in Bayswater. When he had a reading, Katherine would catch trains and buses to be with him wherever he was. She made excuses to Adam: teaching duties, seeing friends. She was amazed at how easy it was. She took time off work and phoned in sick. She would spend hours getting to strange destinations; she and Stephen would steal a little time together, then spend hours getting back home again.

One afternoon they met in Coventry; Stephen had given a reading in York the night before. It had been a frantic, last-minute arrangement, and they had arrived feeling desperate and wrung out. There wasn't time to find a hotel so they had sat in the station holding hands, kissing and talking for two hours. They told each other they had to try to understand the feelings between them. Why was it so intense? What was it? Mere infatuation? They told themselves they needed more evidence before they could agree what to do. They did not want to ruin their marriages. They told each other how good their lives were. They would look at each other helplessly as they questioned what they were doing. Every time they met, the connection between them felt like greed, and they wanted more. There was never enough time. They would spend hours kissing, making love, talking. They examined the frayed ends of all their thoughts. Their curiosity about each other was unbounded. Neither had ever known the same excitement about another person or felt the same urgency to explore their emotions. When they couldn't see each other they e-mailed. It became an extra dimension to their lovemaking, one that seemed to deepen and strengthen with it. They wrote of their pasts, their presents, their wildest thoughts and fears. Incidental details seemed immense to them. Stephen's writing began to flow again, his mind unlocked by their connection. Words for *The Crossing* poured from him, all his fear of the past transformed into excitement and energy. When they talked or touched, they were utterly unguarded. Each made the other brave, willing the other to go into their unknown, tangled places where, like floodwater receding, their communication exposed the mud flats, the green earth, the forests within themselves where they stood, naked, in the open, and fully knew each other.

'How can I stay?' said Katherine, her voice suddenly tearful as she started to pull on her clothes. They had never spent a whole night together. Stephen had dreamt of it, of waking up next to her. He reached out his hand. She lay down and curled into him and looked up at the curtains, the pattern's abstract swirls of orange and brown. There was a print of a windmill in a cheap gold frame over the bed and beside it a chipped brown cabinet, a plastic-coated Bible on its single shelf.

Katherine walked down the hotel corridor in a daze. She leant against a heavy fire door and stepped down the thickly carpeted stairs, past the reception and out on to the street. She felt as though she was plunging into a dark sea. She looked at her phone: ten past midnight. Her car was parked beneath some trees and she walked quickly towards it. She slipped into the driver's seat; the air was stale and cold. She turned on the heater and set off. As she drove home the tall London houses passed by like cliffs.

The following morning, she took Kieron to school along the busy Kingston Road. Her phone buzzed in her pocket with a text message; she knew it would be Stephen. Two workmen in luminous jackets were digging up the tarmac with pneumatic drills. She took Kieron's hand and they hurried past, breathing out as much as possible so as not to inhale the billowing dust. They passed the mums from the school tugging their children, grimacing in the dust. One of them smiled at Katherine as she passed. She looked similar to Katherine; in a rush, her coat undone, her hair unkempt. She wondered if she too was leading a double life.

After she'd dropped Kieron, she looked at Stephen's message. *Cambridge. Next Thursday. The whole night. Please.*

She got home, and checked her e-mails. There was nothing from Stephen. There was one from a dance company asking her if she would consider taking a class for them. She dragged it to the deleted items. It seemed to have come from another life. The breakfast things were still on the table. She put them in a pile beside the sink, went into the garden and sat on a stool by the back door. The garden wall had been rebuilt and she was enclosed once again within her private nook, a suntrap sheltered from the wind. The winter sun was warm on her skin. *The whole night. Please.* She felt the danger of it.

She took off her jumper, her T-shirt, her bra and leant against the bricks behind her, feeling the rough stone against her skin. She looked down at her belly rising and falling as she breathed; her nipples, warmed by the sun, wide and soft; her breasts tender and dumb as pink puddings. Is this why girls love pink, she thought lazily, the thought rising like a bubble. She touched her lips and remembered Stephen's kisses, their long bloom of lovemaking. She felt his presence. He was still with her, kneeling at her feet, kissing her body, his mouth covering a nipple with his lips, his hand gently pulling the other. The warmth spreading through her genitals deep inside her, the sunshine turning her liquid. Through half-closed eyes, she saw Kieron's bicycle lying on its side. One of its wheels was punctured; she had promised him weeks ago she would get it mended.

'What am I doing?' she said half aloud. 'What am I doing?' The sun went behind a cloud just for a moment, and she felt the chill of it.

On the morning she was due to go to Cambridge, Katherine kissed Adam as he went to work.

'I'll call to say goodnight to Kieron,' she said.

'Good luck,' he said.

She had told him that she was going away on a field trip with some of the boys from Ashwood. He never questioned her. In her more insecure moments, he would look at her and she would feel sure he knew. It seemed impossible, when she knew so much, that he could be so blind. She took a train to Cambridge, watching the land empty and flatten as she travelled east. She took a taxi from the station to the hotel. Stephen had already checked in and was waiting for her in the room. He was lying on the bed reading a book, a collection of short stories by Chekhov. After the torrent of e-mails they had exchanged since they last met, they were shy of each other, as though a whole night together was a new and unknown commitment. Katherine stood in the door. Stephen stood up and went to her. He kissed her neck and she touched his mouth with her fingers. Their readiness for sex was brazen and mutual.

'I have to give my reading,' he said.

He left, promising to be back in an hour. Katherine decided to explore the town. She left the hotel and wandered into the hushed stone quadrangles of one of the colleges. Academic worlds had always made her feel inadequate and defensive but today she felt curious. She crossed a stone bridge with arched windows, the last of the sun turning the sandstone to a buttery gold as groups of students ambled dreamily past. She walked across perfect lawns by a wide gleaming river. It excited her to be in such a rarefied world, and she smiled at people as they passed as though she knew them.

A perimeter path through a meadow led her away from the college towards low terraced streets. Katherine became disoriented. She wanted to get back to the college she had found so beautiful and seductive but didn't know which way to go. The streets became long and featureless and there was no one about. Her phone rang.

'Where's Kieron's swimming stuff?'
    'On the pegs.'
    'Right.' Adam sounded exasperated.
    'You okay?'
    'The shit has hit the fan at work. My client's going nuts. I'm fine. I'm busy.'
    'I'll be back tomorrow,' she said.
    She could hear his office phone ringing.
    'What time?'
    'In the morning.'
    'Where are you again?'
    'Wales. With the kids from school. They keep pointing at cows and asking if they are real.' The lies were ashes in her mouth.
    'Love you,' he said.
    'Love you too.'

She turned off the phone. Adam had sounded angry. Did he suspect her? His tone was often annoyed, especially at work. She frequently felt uncertain of him. He could be irascible one moment, and light-hearted the next. Katherine would be left wondering what had happened, whether she'd missed something. A part of Adam had always eluded her.

    At the beginning of their relationship, the mystery of

him had excited her. It had made her want to please him, win his attention. They had met at a friend's post-show party when Katherine was twenty-six, and Adam was thirty. Adam had gate-crashed with some friends. They had just finished law exams and were slightly drunk. Music throbbed through the room. Katherine was in the middle of the crowd with some other dancers. They were moving in and out of each other gracefully, with serious looks on their faces. Adam had walked right into the middle of the group, bold as brass, and started dancing with her. He moved outlandishly and made Katherine laugh. He jived with her, lifted her up and swung her round. He had no natural grace, but a winning charm. They danced together all night, and afterwards he walked her home.

They started to see each other. No one gave it long. Their worlds were poles apart. Katherine's dance friends seemed to Adam to be self-obsessed to the point of insanity. To Katherine, Adam's colleagues seemed rational to the point of desiccation, but something drew them together. What they couldn't express verbally, they did in sex. Adam found Katherine's body beautiful, not just physically but the way she knew it so well. Her body was how she expressed herself and she was confident and happy with it. In previous relationships, when he made love, Adam had never known for sure if the girl was enjoying herself, but with Katherine, he could feel her joy, so that he experienced her pleasure almost as much as his own. They would often dance together, and

Katherine cherished the fun they had, going wild together on a dance floor. After they were married, Adam announced that he didn't want to dance any more. It had been part of courtship, he said, that was all. He just didn't love it like she did.

Katherine couldn't tell which direction to take for the centre of Cambridge. She saw a spire in the distance and walked towards it through a modern housing development. A mini-bus had stopped on the road, its doors thrown open at the back. A disabled Chinese boy was being lowered to the ground on an electronic lift. He sat in his wheelchair, his head lolling to one side while a woman and child waited patiently on the pavement to receive him. Katherine guessed they were his mother and sister. Their hands were clasped in front of them like votaries. As the wheelchair reached the ground, the mother rushed forward to the boy, her face breaking with joy.

It took an hour for Katherine to find her way back to the hotel. Stephen was sitting on the bed writing in a notebook.

'I thought you'd gone,' he said.

The room had no view. The blinds were down. It was a sealed box. He looked deep into her eyes.

'I'm so happy,' he said.

She looked away, resisting him. She wasn't ready. He had so much power over her: she felt the damage of coming, and of lying to do so.

'What is the point of this?' she said with accusation in her voice.

She went to the bookcase, and paced restlessly back and forth.

'I've had to lie, and lie again. I don't know what I'm doing any more. I know this has happened to so many people,' she said helplessly, looking over at him, 'but I don't know if I can do this any more.'

Her anxiety and frustration steadied him. He understood it. He knew it too.

'Katherine. I've been invited to America.'

She stopped and searched into his eyes, trying to understand.

'I wanted to tell you. It's something I applied to do before I met you.'

He told her how the Rockerman plan had been in motion for over a year. It was something he had started when he couldn't write. He told her how he had longed to live in the desert again, to find a place where he could feel free, a place in which he might find the inspiration to finish *The Crossing*.

Since he'd begun writing again, he'd hoped the Rockerman might not offer him a place at all. He took Katherine's hand and played with her fingers, and for the first time, they spoke of the future. Their fears and hopes rose to the surface. They agreed they were sliding into an intensity they could not contain. They knew that together they could cause irreparable damage to their children and their spouses. Their relationship was nothing more than a valve for their marriages, they told each other, a safe space where they each could rediscover precious parts of themselves that had become lost. They told themselves they had brought goodness into their lives, sweetness and inspiration. Their love wasn't infatuation, it was transformation, an experience they would never regret, an exploration not just of themselves but of life itself, and how to live it. Katherine told Stephen that he should go to America, carry out his plan. It would be a test. If their feelings for each other were real they would endure.

He lay down next to her and she turned away. He curled into her.

'I love you,' he said.

He had never said it to her before.

They had both thought it many times. She turned to face him. He was smiling. She understood this smile. She was smiling too. His breath seemed to touch hers. She cried as they kissed and he tasted the salt of her tears. Katherine lengthened against him and his arms swept down her back, grasping her buttocks, her thighs. She gave in to her desire, opening herself to him completely. Her back arched like the curve of a guitar as he entered her.

When they woke it was the middle of the night. It seemed impossible that the bed and the hotel room were still in the same place. It felt like they had gone on a journey over a vast and changing ocean. They made love again, and talked in the quiet shelter of it.

'Our talking is like the sex and our sex is like talking,' whispered Stephen. 'There is so much I want to give to you, show you.'

Katherine could say nothing. She went to the end of the bed. She picked up his shirt and trailed it up her body, stretching her arms high above her head. Slowly, in silence, she began to dance, her arms making slow patterns in the air, her muscles strong and tensed, her fingers unfolding, her hips rising and falling. She danced for him, and for herself. They were the same thing. She no longer knew where he ended and she began. Her passion was uninhibited and a sense of pure love coursed through her body. Her openness was a gift to him, to them both, and he watched her without shame.

They woke early. Katherine and Stephen walked to the station. It was packed with commuters. Stephen was anxious in case they might be seen by someone he knew, so they sat on the ground, out of view, at the end of an unused line with the buffers in front of them. The old track stretched away from them into the level distance of the fens, petering into nothing. They held hands and waited. The courage of the previous night had evaporated. Katherine felt only panic.

'Don't go to America,' she said. 'Don't go.'

After she'd gone, Stephen bought a black coffee from the buffet and sat down with his notebook. Next to him was a row of slot machines, their lights flashing, their three wheels cascading up and down. Stephen was in turmoil. A few months ago he had longed for the desert, but now his mind was filled with confusion. He was standing between two lives, like his grandparents. He took out his notebook and started to write, hoping to catch the urgency of their dilemma in his. He wrote about Anna and Victor in Warsaw, the secrecy of their meetings, how danger stalked them, and how their elopement was born out of desperation to love each other openly. He wrote of their addiction to each other, and their thirst to find themselves through each other. He wrote of how they tried to give each other up, and how when they did, their love grew only stronger. He wrote all day in the station buffet without looking up. The sound of the slot machines churned his thoughts, and the poetry poured from him. When he finally caught the train home, it was night.

Alison was standing in the hallway. At first Stephen didn't see her but when he closed the door behind him, she was right next to him as though she had been waiting a long time.

'God! You gave me a shock,' said Stephen.

She looked pale and tired.

'Stephen, what is going on?'

His heart sank through him like a weight.

'The Rockerman Trust called.'

He looked at her in a daze.

'You haven't sent off the form for your work permit.

We can't go without it. I didn't know what to say to them. I couldn't get hold of you.'

'I'm sorry. I've been so busy with all these readings.'

'You said you'd done it weeks ago!'

'It's the writing. I've been writing. I'm sorry, Alison.'

'Christ, Stephen! Have you changed your mind?'

He didn't reply. He put down his bag.

'I'm just going to take a shower,' he said.

'Stephen! What the hell is going on?'

'Alison . . . it's just I've hit a good streak and I don't want to break it. When I think about America, I feel . . .'

She grabbed his arm, suddenly furious. It shocked him how upset she was.

'It's too late for this! Far too late! I've paid the bloody deposit on the house. I've found a school. I've rented out this place. You can't do this to us.'

He was heady with lack of sleep. He could still sense Katherine like a cloud around him, the smell of sex like fresh milk.

Alison broke away and sat at the kitchen table. She leant against a wooden slatted cupboard behind her. A friend had made it for them when they moved into the house. They had finished the kitchen's interior themselves. Stephen remembered how happy she had been just eighteen months before when they were doing it up. He'd never seen her so opinionated and spirited. They hadn't much money, but Alison had been inspired. She shopped everywhere for furniture, bought the dresser online from a shop in Normandy, rescued the marble worktop from an old butcher's. She'd stencilled the wainscoting with graceful lines and flowers. The table she had found in a skip, a solid piece of beech, as long as a coffin lid.

He moved towards her, but she uncrossed her legs and stood abruptly.

'It's up to you, Stephen. Whatever you decide will be fine. It'll be fine,' she said, all the emotion gone from her voice.

He watched her leave. It would be fine. She would make it fine. Once Alison decided to make something fine nothing would change her mind. Her emotions froze over in an instant. She had always been like this. Even when he had asked her to marry him, she had shown nothing more than cool detachment. 'I thought you would never ask,' she'd said, her tone deadpan like Katharine Hepburn, and had put her arm through his, like a china handle.

On their wedding day, Alison's sisters stood outside the church in big hats, smoking cigarettes and laughing. They had done everything, chosen the church, the hymns, the dress, the vows, but they treated the whole day as though it was an amusing piece of theatre. With Alison's family there was never any way of knowing what truly mattered to them. It was part of their allure. Alison and her sisters had insisted on Stephen including a Jewish ritual in the ceremony. Stephen had declined, making a joke of it, telling them he was hardly Jewish at all, and all he wanted to reflect the part of him that was, was to have rollmops at the reception. His mother and father came. It was the first time they had been at an event together since he was a child. His mother arrived alone in a taxi, wearing an oddly tight-fitting dress. His father stepped out of his old Ford with a new girlfriend on his arm and greeted Stephen in the graveyard. He had hugged him tightly to his breast, making him a little boy again. The hug went on for too long, and Stephen wondered whether his father was trying to tell him something important, but he wasn't sure what it was; perhaps that marriage was a futile construction, or to ask forgiveness for the long absent years.

In the year that followed their marriage, Stephen was more depressed than he had ever been in his life. Alison was supportive, stable, loyal, and beautiful, but she was always so cheerful and untroubled that in comparison Stephen felt completely inadequate. He couldn't admit to Alison that his true feelings were always charged and shifting. For a while he feared his family's curse of unhappiness had come to haunt him, but after the births of their children, the darkness lifted. Alison proved to be a wonderful mother. Alison and he were not the same kind of people, but perhaps that was why they were together. They appreciated each other. She anchored him, and he challenged her, just enough. As he thought of his solid life with her, Stephen felt the madness of Katherine. Katherine was the inspiration of his soul. Theirs was a shocking, immediate love, the kind most people never have, a communion so intimate and complex it seemed unfathomable. He put his hand to his face, and remembered their lovemaking that morning in Cambridge, the way she had slowed her rhythm to his. He felt an immediate desire for her, and hated himself for it. He went to the sink, and splashed water on his face. Katherine was too seductive. She had too much power over him. It could never last. She took him away from the person he was supposed to be.

He found Alison in the garden under the white glare of the outside light. She was at the rose bush holding a thorny stem and snapping off the dead heads. It was typical of her to be getting on with something useful at such an emotional time. She never moped, never wallowed in her feelings. She was uncomplaining and resilient, but he had also come to know that she was an innocent, and that under her cool demeanour she needed him. He wouldn't put her in jeopardy. Or the children. The idea that Molly and Frank might go through the same torment he had suffered as a boy was inconceivable.

'We're going,' he said. 'We're going to America. I'll get the visa tomorrow.'

14

David and May sat in the Alnwick surgery waiting room, glancing anxiously towards the receptionist. They had been waiting for twenty minutes, and David was restless. He was coughing and held a white cotton handkerchief tightly to his mouth to suppress the convulsions.

A mother and her baby were sitting opposite them. The mother wore a thick purple coat and had the baby wrapped in a woollen blanket. It was crying, and she kept repositioning it trying to quieten it. David could see it was too hot. He exchanged a look with May, the unspoken complicity between them earned through the long years of their children's infancies. David had always been good with babies; he instinctively knew how to comfort and distract them. He would hold them over his shoulder and make clicking sounds with his tongue against the roof of his mouth. He would walk up and down for hours in this way as May lay exhausted in bed. He seemed to have an endless patience for it, as though he were lulling himself as much as the baby with his ever-changing repertoire of rhythms. David had enjoyed the babyhood of all three of his children; it was when they developed personalities that they had begun to baffle him.

The baby wailed louder, arching its back as it tried to escape its mother's clutches.

'Let's go,' David whispered to May. 'I can talk to Dr Hegarty on the phone.'

'We can't. He needs to show you the results of your X-ray. He said he had things to discuss.'

David did not want to discuss anything with Dr Hegarty. He had hated having the X-ray taken, hated going to Carlisle Hospital, hated stripping to the waist behind a plastic curtain while the radiographer gossiped with a nurse. The radiographer had hardly spoken to him, just closed the cold panels of the machine around his chest and left the room. David had found the lack of control humiliating and frightening.

He shut his eyes tight and went through everything he had to do for George Gull's opening at the Jackson Gallery that night. Two of his trustees would be there, Paul Trent and Lionel Treader. Both had approved Geraldine Henderson's suggestions to cut back the artist-in-residence programme and suspend work on the library. It was vital that he talked them round.

'It's a nuisance you having to teach in Carlisle tonight.'

'I can't cancel a class,' she said briskly. 'You'll have plenty of supporters.'

David was silent. May never seemed to understand how much he needed her support. She could really make a difference, lighten his load, talk to guests and share his anxiety. He tried to imagine which of the guests might make a donation but gave up, defeated by the sheer hopelessness of it. He didn't have his old energy, now when he needed it more than ever, when doors were closing all around him. It was this damn cough. He was anxious about the X-ray, about what the cough might mean.

'Come, May,' he said, standing. 'Matthew is waiting outside.'

'It's what he's paid to do,' said May, staying in her chair.

The receptionist slid back her window. 'David Freeman? Dr Hegarty will see you now.'

'I'm sorry to waste your time, Christopher!' said David brightly as he entered the consulting room. 'May insisted on me coming.'

'It's quite all right,' said Dr Hegarty shaking his hand, his bright dentures flashing as he gave May one of his conspiratorial winks. 'Good to see you both.'

Since his aneurism, David had had regular check-ups with Dr Hegarty and got to know him well. He had told him about the Broughton Foundation and persuaded him to attend various openings and poetry readings, which the doctor had done with enthusiasm.

'Let's have a listen to that chest of yours.'

'I hope I'll see you this evening. You got the invitation, I trust?' said David, taking off his shirt.

Dr Hegarty placed a stethoscope against David's back.

'Breathe. And again. Breathe. Yes, I got it. Your artist-in-residence, isn't it? I met him at the last poetry evening. Sulky fellow.'

The stethoscope felt smooth and cold on his back, like a sea-washed pebble.

'That's right. George Gull. His work is conceptual, very abstract,' said David, knowing this would provoke the doctor.

'Art has to look like something for me, I'm afraid. Breathe in.'

'Artists like George Gull need you, Christopher.'

'What on earth for?' said the doctor, laughing. 'Cough for me. Cough again.'

He pressed his hand against David's lower back.

'They need to be rejected,' said David.

Dr Hegarty laughed. 'I see. The perversity of the artist. Longs for success but thrives on disdain. You can put your shirt on now.'

'The reception is at six. I'll expect you.'

'David, you are the most dogged man I've ever known,' said Dr Hegarty affectionately.

May sat on the chair at the side of the room watching them, her mouth turned down in disapproval. David's charm with other people masked his nervousness, and it annoyed her.

'How is he?' she broke in impatiently.

Dr Hegarty smiled his impossibly white smile. 'This is not an ill man!' he said. 'Not at all! I thought there might be a little pneumonia but the X-ray seems pretty clear. It's a little chest infection.'

David let himself absorb what the doctor was saying.

A chest infection. He looked to May, his face suddenly open and relieved. He realised now how much it had affected him. One morning, after a night of coughing,

David told May he'd dreamt his lungs were infested with maggots. He couldn't shake the feeling that something was festering inside him. It had alarmed them both, and now here he was, being told he had little more than a common cold.

'Antibiotics will clear it up,' said Dr Hegarty, scrawling on a pad.

'A chest infection! This northern weather is to blame,' said David, chuckling as he tucked his shirt into his trousers. 'I suppose there have to be some disadvantages to living at the centre of the universe. We'll see you later, Christopher. Six o'clock. Don't be late!'

David took May's arm, and they left the surgery. He was elated as they walked down the slate-coloured streets of Alnwick, shining with recent rain.

'Richard Seaton is not the right person for us,' he said, a new enthusiasm surging through him. 'I am going to call Paolo Giordano, the shoe designer. He is the one. He and his wife were genuinely enthusiastic. You can't put a price on that. We must work on him, arrange a visit. I'll invite Stephen to come and read for them . . .'

May listened to the familiar sound of David's plans. She too was relieved at the diagnosis but had wanted Dr Hegarty to tell David to take some time off. She had hoped the cough might mean they could spend more time with one another. After his aneurism, David had convalesced at home, and together they had enjoyed a period of calm and reflective companionship. May would read him P. G. Wodehouse, and they laughed out loud. David would sleep in the afternoons while she prepared him small and nutritious meals. It was a precious time for May, a rare moment in their lives when she didn't have to share him with other people. She had felt central to his life and cherished by his need for her. It had been all too soon that he had gone back to work.

Matthew was waiting for them, leaning against the bonnet of his car, reading a book. David raised his arm in salute.

'Clean bill of health!' he shouted.

'That's what they said about Bellingham and he was dead within a week,' said Matthew. He closed his book; it was a collection of Yeats.

'On which does the imagination dwell the most,' said David provocatively, 'the woman won or the woman lost?'

'The woman lost. You always want what you can't have. Although I don't see why people think Yeats is a poet of such great insight. He's basically just saying that the grass is always greener.'

David laughed as he got into the car. May sat in the back, piqued by David's delight in Matthew's shallow cleverness. These endless directionless young men with their constant need for his attention – she hated their intrusion into their lives. David had always surrounded himself with young men. He loved being their guide, mentor, father figure. Their older son William had once told her that he felt he was only one of the hundreds of sons David had. His children had had to learn to share their father with many others, but what galled May about his young assistants was the spark they inspired in him. It was a spark which neither she nor the children had ever been able to ignite in him.

She leant forward in her seat and tapped David on the shoulder.

'David,' she said impatiently, 'we have to get your prescription.'

'I suppose you want me to get it,' said Matthew, 'and mop your fevered brow.'

'We don't want you to do anything of the sort!' snapped May clumsily, her anger breaking out. 'I'm quite able to get it myself!'

Matthew glanced at David. Her tone had broken the skein of playful banter. David wished she wouldn't display her anger. He hated any show of emotion. He had struggled all his life to control his feelings. It was the root of his love for art. Art was the supreme response to difficulty and pain. It was the transformation of all unwanted feelings – love, anger, lust, disgust and fear – into something controlled, even beautiful.

'Of course, May,' said David, hoping to smooth over the awkwardness of the moment, 'it's only that you're going to Carlisle. Together with Shakespeare, May is setting Carlisle alight, Matthew. People flock to her classes.'

'Drop me here,' said May.

Matthew pulled to the side of the road near the car park where she had left her car. David searched for eye contact with her but she wouldn't look at him. She wasn't ready to be reconciled.

'I'll pick up the prescription at Boots and bring it with me when I drive back from Carlisle tonight,' she said, adopting her habitual defence of being extremely busy, with no time to confront what had upset her.

She walked down the cul-de-sac of pebbledash houses to where her car was parked. Beyond Alnwick, the Northumbrian hills were shrouded in clouds, and there was a sense of rain everywhere. The air was wet. Leaves hung heavily on the trees. An old couple were walking along the pavement towards her. The man had a collie on a lead. 'How do,' he said, nodding as she passed. She nodded back. They probably took their dog on the same walk every afternoon. May imagined their lives, conventional, their marriage so faithful and unchallenging. They were perfectly moulded to each other, like two bowls on a kitchen shelf. She could never have chosen a life like theirs, but as she got in her car to drive to Carlisle, she wished for a small measure of their contentment.

15

The Jackson Gallery was a converted farmworker's cottage. Its four small, whitewashed rooms were crammed with an eclectic crowd for the opening of George Gull's exhibition: locals enticed by the free wine, friends of the Broughton Foundation and a smattering of local artists and journalists. George Gull's huge canvases only just fitted on the walls of the small gallery, and the guests bumped into each other as they tried to stand back and admire them.

'I wouldn't want one in my living room,' said Barry Worthy, a publican from the village. 'All those funny bits sticking out. They're like teeth.'

'Nothing on the outside, vast meaninglessness in the centre,' said Charles Finch, a local businessman who sold hot tubs. David smiled. He had invited George Gull to the Broughton Foundation to capture the Northumbrian landscape, and respond to the hills and valleys that surrounded them. What George had painted over the past six months looked nothing like mountains or valleys. The paintings may have had titles such as *Bastlegyle*, *Lyne Top*, *Heron Hole*, *Bizzle Tarn*, but each consisted of the same identical protuberances, meticulously painted thumb-like shapes that crowded the canvases like villi, each excrescence identical to the last.

'Little penises,' said Lady Highsmith, laughing.

'If they're penises, I would prescribe medication for every one of them!' said Dr Hegarty. He wore a bright pink shirt and was slightly drunk.

'David,' he said, jovially combative, as he pointed at one painting, 'tell me how on earth is that Bastlegyle?'

'Anyone can do likenesses,' said David. 'I didn't ask for likenesses. I asked for George Gull's response to Northumberland.'

'It's a very odd response.'

'Perhaps his genius is to confirm your own perception of Bastlegyle to you,' said David, relishing the challenge.

He smiled at George who was sitting in the corner by the door looking like a tortured gallery attendant. For David, his paintings had compact intelligence, and he was pleased that everyone was so unsettled by them.

The door opened and David saw Stephen Jericho come in wearing a thick coat with a rucksack on his back. He looked as though he had been running. George saw him and smiled for the first time that evening. He and Stephen were natural opposites: Stephen charming and sociable, George introverted and difficult, but during their time together at the Broughton Foundation, they had found an affinity, and enjoyed the differences between them.

'I'm going to buy one of these paintings!' said Dr Hegarty, pulling at David's sleeve. 'This one!'

'You can't be serious!' cried Lady Highsmith.

'I am. It's perfect for the surgery. It reminds me of a diagram of the stomach.'

'What about you, Barry?' said David turning to the publican who was staring at a painting of what looked like a row of little green eggs. 'Are you going to buy?'

'This one's called *Kield Hope*,' said Barry Worthy in disbelief.

'Do you see?' said David, undaunted. 'Each shape looks the same, but look at the brush strokes.'

The publican peered closer.

'They're all different,' he said.

'Exactly!' said David. 'Is Kield Hope ever the same? The weather changes it by the hour. We all change by the hour. Perhaps our opinion of what makes a painting should change as often,' he added, smiling mischievously.

The publican looked at the little price sticker next to the painting.

'Three hundred pounds?' he said, indignantly. 'I wouldn't pay that for a bloody Picasso.'

By ten o'clock most of the guests had left. David had worked hard all evening, enthusing to them about the paintings, using their disquiet as the grit of discussion, but in the end, not one picture had been sold. Dr Hegarty's wife had dragged him off into the night before he could get out his chequebook. David had talked with officials from the North East Development Agency about increasing their grant to the Broughton Foundation, he'd spoken at length to the two trustees about future plans, he'd charmed Lord and Lady Barrington, and in general

193

provided bibulous and lively company for everyone. They spilled out into the quiet valley, tipsy and satisfied, with the inimitable feeling they always got from David's company, that they were part of something genuinely important.

'A triumph, David,' said Lady Highsmith exuberantly, as he led her towards her car. 'The paintings were ghastly but it was an absolute triumph.'

A group of younger people were gathered around George Gull, trying to console him. David felt an arm on his shoulder. It was Stephen.

'David . . .'

'Stephen, I'm so glad you could make it back for George. How are you? How are you getting on with *The Crossing*?'

'It's going incredibly well. Better than it's ever gone.'

He looked well. There was an enthusiasm in him David hadn't seen for a long time.

'I look forward to reading some. Don't forget us!'

'Of course not,' said Stephen.

'When do you leave for America?'

'Soon,' said Stephen. David felt an acute exhaustion. He longed to confide in someone how hard it was to keep the Broughton Foundation going, to acknowledge how close they were to collapse, and Stephen was the perfect person, but he also knew that Stephen, like everyone else, wanted his counsel and encouragement, wanted him to be the enabler they all needed, full of optimism and vision.

'The land of possibility. Embrace it, Stephen.'

'To the Back Rooms! To the Back Rooms!' George Gull stood drunkenly in the doorway of the Jackson Gallery, waving his arms as though conducting a symphony.

'Come with us,' said Stephen.

'You go,' said David. 'I'll just finish up here.'

David locked up the gallery and walked back to Sellacrag. On the kitchen table were an assortment of medicines; he had asked Ken to go to the village to buy him over-the-counter cold remedies. He boiled the kettle and emptied a sachet of Lemsip into a cup, watching the yellow powder fizz in the water, listening to its wet gasping sound. He believed in Lemsip: it was succour at the click of a finger, something he could trust.

He sat in the armchair by the fire, and felt the old familiar ache rise within him. Stephen was leaving. Another departure. People were always leaving. America. America. The word seemed to sing to him, to call to him from his youth. The vastness of it, the freedom. May and he had been happy there. David had a sudden flash of their rented rooms in San Francisco in the painted house on Broderick Street, which plunged down to the ocean: him sitting in the bath tub with an old Remington typewriter balanced on a plank, working on his PhD, while May read books in the bedroom. He thought too of the days after William was born, when May had pined for England and eventually had gone back on her own with the baby, leaving him alone in America to finish his research. When it was complete he'd hitched across seven states to New York to catch the boat home. He saw the empty roads stretching to the curve of the horizon through the cornfields. He saw himself, his briefcase leaning against his leg, his thumb out, waiting to see an approaching car. He remembered the small towns with their wooden houses, black men laughing at the side of the road, the university towns where young women in bright sweaters and long-haired men read newspapers and argued the politics of change. He remembered the rides he got and the joy he had felt at hearing people's stories: a trucker who hoped one day to own a builder's yard, the Jewish labourer working to study physics at college, the salesman who was a part-time actor, the preacher who hated the Bible, the Italian barber who cut David's hair as he sat on an old bottle crate at the side of the road.

David took a sip of his Lemsip and let the acrid sweetness soothe his throat. He stared into the coals of the fire as he remembered his final ride into New York. He was picked up just outside Allentown, Pennsylvania, by a blue Cadillac. The driver was a journalist on his way back from writing a story in California about the new surf craze. The man talked of the exhilaration of catching the wave as it swells and riding the breaker all the way to the sand. David loved the way he talked, loved his curiosity. He had asked David a thousand questions about his life, his family, his education, his wife, his politics, and by the time they arrived in New

York, David knew they didn't want to say goodbye.

Gazing into the fire, he saw the man's face against the chequered tiles of the Oyster Bar in Manhattan. He saw the cliffs of the tower blocks rise up as they walked in Central Park and felt the steady hold of the man's arm on his back. They had gone back to the car and kissed in the back seat. It was like no other kiss David had experienced before.

He picked up the poker and stirred the coals. A wave of scorching heat billowed up from the fire. He put on his overcoat and set off into the village. He could hear the occasional movement and breathing of cattle in the dark fields. The rain had filled the air with the smell of grass and earth, and he could hear the swell of the river Rathe, nearby. After twenty minutes he reached the edge of the village – the teashop, the Co-op and the telephone box, and crossed the lane towards a low pub with a hand-painted sign of a swan. David only rarely visited the Back Rooms. It was a local haunt frequented by farmworkers and many of his younger staff, and it was infamous for its lock-ins.

He pushed open the heavy door. Hot smoky air spewed out into the night to the sound of raucous, drunken shouting. Bedlam bloomed. The low-ceilinged room was packed with people screaming as they crowd-ed round an unseen game.

'David! Over here!' shouted Stephen. He waved through the crowd, his face glowing and animated.

David pushed his way towards him. A man with a

huge belly was standing in front of a blackboard.

'Lay your bets!' he bellowed. 'Lay your bets!'

A pool table had been covered in a plastic sheet marked out as a race track. Five lanes had been divided into squares in which stood five big plastic animals – a baboon, a lion, a Tyrannosaurus rex, a giraffe and an elephant. Each had a different-coloured ribbon round its neck. A woman in a low-cut silver top with a deep cleavage stood on a chair at one end of the table. Above her head, she held two huge home-made dice. People were shouting and laughing, waving their money in the air.

'Two pound on T-rex!'

'Fiver on Monkey!'

'Lucky Lion! Ten pounds!'

'Is it rigged?'

'Of course it's rigged!'

The man by the blackboard gave a piercing whistle and the woman threw the dice to the floor. The room erupted in a wild cacophony. Some began chanting, 'Elephant! Elephant!' Stephen was among them. The big man picked up the plastic elephant and started to move it forwards along the track, animating its movements, bouncing it up and down. He turned the head of the Tyrannosaurus rex making it look back at the elephant's progress, while like a demented sports commentator, he spewed out an endless manic patter: 'Eddy the elephant's getting away! T-rex won't take this! He's mad! Eddy's ahead and T-rex can't stand it! He's coming out of his lane – would you believe it! He's trying to trip up Eddy! . . .'

David pushed through to the bar and ordered tumblers of whisky. He drank his quickly and handed round the others. George Gull was leaning over the pool table shouting drunkenly at the Tyrannosaurus rex. David had never seen George so happy. There was a roar as the elephant crossed the line.

'I won!' shouted Stephen, gleefully pushing his way through the crowd to collect his winnings.

'More whisky! Stephen! Whiskies all round!' shouted George. The man at the blackboard started calling out, 'New race! Lay your bets! Five to two on the baboon to win!' The woman picked up the plastic animals and set them back at the starting line.

Something in David loosened, intoxicated by the atmosphere. The unabashed hedonism reminded him of clubs and bars he had visited in London. He had always stayed on the outside, never able to fully lose himself like the others, but he had loved their sense of freedom, their wild abandon, seeing men become whoever they chose to be. He sat at a table.

'George! Tell him,' said Stephen, grinning at David, and dragging George away from the betting game. 'Tell him your idea!'

'Daniel Boulens!' cried George knocking back his whisky, his eyes gleaming. 'Daniel Boulens!'

'What about him?' said David, laughing.

'You know him?'

'Of course,' said David. 'He paints a line, doesn't he? A single line.'

'Wherever he goes,' cried George, beside himself with excitement. 'Always the same, the same colour, the same width. It's brilliant! He's never changed what he does, just the place, and the context. David, he's just bought three of my paintings.'

David clasped George's shoulder and beamed. He knew exactly what a great affirmation this was. Daniel Boulens was one of the most famous abstract artists in the world, a pioneer of minimalism in the seventies.

'I told him about the Broughton Foundation. David, I asked him to come. I asked him to paint his line in Braymer.'

'What did he say?'

'Over my dead body!' George roared with laughter then came close to David, whisky on his breath. 'The truth?'

David nodded.

'He said he'd come if I'd curate it,' whispered George. 'What do you think?'

'Yes! Yes!' David shouted. The crowd around the pool table erupted again as a plastic giraffe was hurled into the air. 'Yes,' he shouted. 'It's a fantastic idea!'

The valley was black, the air smelt of soil and moss. Ahead of Stephen, George and David reeled home, their drunken, exultant voices breaking the silence. The moonlit sky was shattered by the branches of the trees. Stephen could see the gleaming line of Lake Braymer and the glowering shapes of the hills beyond it. He felt drunk and happy. He hadn't seen David since St Mark's. When he had first walked into the Jackson Gallery, he'd felt troubled and guilty about Katherine. David had nurtured and inspired him as a poet, and he had repaid him by having an affair with his daughter. As soon as they started to talk, the fear fell away. David had been as warm and enthusiastic as always. There was no awkwardness, and Stephen found it easy to separate his feelings for David from those he had for Katherine; neither had anything to do with the other.

George turned off towards his cottage, bidding the whole valley good night with a sweep of his hand.

'A line!' he shouted. 'A constant line! Right across the valley!'

David waited for Stephen to catch up. 'A nightcap?' he asked.

Stephen accepted gladly. In Sellacrag he watched as David lit a fire in the grate and produced a half bottle of whisky. They sat, as they had many times before, in the two battered armchairs that flanked the chimney-breast as the fire kindled, sipping their whisky from china cups.

'I've never seen George so happy,' said Stephen.

'He's in love.'

Stephen lowered his cup in surprise.

'With his work,' said David, 'the only thing worth being in love with. Are you in love?'

'I'm writing like I've never written before,' said Stephen. 'I'll finish *The Crossing* in six months, maybe less.'

He reached for the whisky. The fire was blazing, the flames stretching up as they were sucked into the chimney. On the mantelpiece, amongst the clutter, Stephen saw a flyer for one of Katherine's dance shows. It must have been nearly eight years old.

'I worry that America has come at the wrong time,' he said. 'I'm writing so well here in England.'

'Your best writing is yet to come, Stephen. You must go.'

They discussed *The Crossing*. Stephen explained to David that he'd found a new dynamism in the love story. He'd excavated his grandparents' sense of displacement and found a way to write forcefully of his parents' divorce. David's questions were penetrating, probing into Stephen's imagination. They spoke of the wide landscapes of America and how they might influence Stephen's work. Stephen felt the same passion he had felt before when he spoke with David; the burning imperative that his work was more important than anything else in the world, more important than love, than family. David invested his work with value. He challenged Stephen to hone his words, to cherish them, sucking them dry of every possible meaning, as though it were his sacred task.

It was two in the morning when they finished the whisky. The wind was blowing outside. They stood unsteadily. As they reached the door they said goodbye to each other, the whisky slurring their words. Stephen leant forward for a hug and felt David's arms lock round him. David sighed, and Stephen felt David's chest heave against his, his weight lean into him. He felt David's lips against his face.

'Stephen...'

Stephen pulled back. David looked at him, full of fear. Stephen understood everything in an instant.

'It's okay,' said Stephen. He put his hand on David's arm to reassure him that it didn't matter, but David could not look at him. Stephen turned and slipped out into the night without looking back.

May pulled up outside Sellacrag, the headlights catching the glittering shards of rain. David was sitting in the armchair, half asleep. She saw the two china cups on the fender.

'Who was here?' she said

'Stephen is going to America.'

He was drunk.

'My antibiotics,' he slurred.

She saw a piece of paper on his lap. It was the scrawl of an unfinished poem. David's poems were private, never to be read, never to be seen or known by anyone except May. He wrote of his raw desire and masked it in a dense web of allusion. In his words she saw his longing for all of them – Stephen, Matthew, Paul, the countless others; the men he met on trains in London, America, in places she never knew. He used poetry to write himself into another life, and the sight of it filled her with the old jealousy.

'You're drunk,' she said. 'Take them in the morning.'

She went upstairs and lay down on the bed. The wind blew and rattled the window. He'd left the poem lying on his lap like that, for her to see. Over the years there had been so many tortured poems. He would always ask her to read them and she did, absorbing a passion never meant for her. She could sense him downstairs, brooding, nursing his unhappiness. It didn't help to reject him, it never had. She tried not to judge him; she knew he needed to confide in her, to again confess his craving. She should stifle her jealousy and go down to him, but as she lay in the darkness, the anger and shock of it all came rushing back to her. It was before Katherine was born when he first told her about his feelings for men. May had been utterly bewildered. She thought David was describing a book he had been reading. He had taken her hands and begged her forgiveness, but her heart had pounded so loudly in her chest it was all she could hear.

He implored her to understand that it didn't affect his love for her. They told themselves it was a momentary aberration, a strange fluke, a puzzle, a madness. She was frightened. She felt the shame of homosexuality. David felt it too. They feared the law, his being caught, the horror of it all.

She heard him climbing the stairs. The sound of his footsteps comforted her. There was no one with whom she could talk like him; no one she loved like him. He was the father of her children and she felt a devotion to him that could never be erased. She had colluded in keeping everything secret. No one knew, no one should ever know, especially not the children.

He slipped under the covers and lay next to her. His sadness and vulnerability were part of her. She turned and cradled him in her arms.

16

A fire door opens and she walks along corridors with yellow walls past a boiler room into a toilet, where she looks at herself in the mirror and dabs a powder puff on each cheek, leaving a patch of white dust. In a low-lit bar, Stephen waits for her on a velvet stool. She puts her arms round him, and he falls into her. A boy runs up, terrified, and begs her to throw him into the river. She picks up the boy and throws him in, and he floats face down in the shallows, shaking and screaming, his head vibrating like a wind-up toy.

Katherine woke, breathless, her head in the pillow. Since Stephen had gone to America all her dreams were nightmares.

She turned on to her side and lay there waiting for the fear to pass. She could hear Adam and Kieron laughing in the front garden. It was morning but she couldn't face getting up. She turned over in bed and listened to the shush-shush of the yard broom beneath her window. She got up, pulled on a T-shirt and looked out. Adam was cutting the hedge and Kieron was sweeping the leaves with his own small broom. She undid the catch and pushed open the window to call down to them, when something stopped her. The air in the street was so still and so hushed that it seemed she could hear her own voice before she even called out. It was a restless and dissonant voice that did not belong to that quiet domestic world. She felt a sharp longing for Stephen. It caught her breath, and she closed the window quickly.

She went to her chest of drawers and took out the pill box. She had put Stephen's ring in it and buried it under her tights and pants. She remembered the sweetness and desperation of buying it. It had been on their last time together.

They had gone to the New Horizon Hotel in Bayswater, a place they had been to several times before. They made love silently as though they were trying to disappear into each other, realising it would be the last time. Three hours later they left the room key at the reception and walked to the station.

It was the Friday before Christmas, and the streets were busy with shoppers and drunken office workers. Gusts of freezing wind blew thin snowflakes through the air. They put their arms round each other, pulling each other in tight. Neither of them spoke. They stopped at a shop window and stared in at trays of jewellery.

'Let's buy something,' said Stephen.

The shop was tranquil after the bustle of the street. There was a smell of incense. The shopkeeper was arranging jewellery in a case, and they waited quietly, watching her. She had a mane of red hair and her eyes were narrowed with concentration as she reached to the back of a glass shelf and took out a necklace. It was made of pink stones, like amethysts but rougher and more crystalline. She smiled warmly at Katherine and Stephen, and gestured for them to come closer.

'I only use uncut stones,' she said. 'These stones are exactly as they were found.'

She held up the necklace. Each stone was a different shape. Each looked as though it had been hacked out of the rock or picked from a stream; they were jagged and had a naked, ungainly beauty. She showed them a tray of diamonds, rubies and emeralds.

'If you cut a stone you kill its soul,' said the woman.

Katherine and Stephen picked out two rings; a ruby and a diamond. The ruby was no more than a sliver, a crimson shard set into yellow gold. The diamond was like no other they had ever seen. It was smooth and cloudy.

'It is alluvial,' said the woman. 'It has been washed in the Indian Ocean for thousands of years.'

They put the rings on their fingers, Stephen the ruby, Katherine the diamond. Somehow they felt it was all meant; the jewels, uncut, whole, precious, like what was between them.

They paid for the rings and left the shop. Two days later, Stephen left for America.

In her bedroom Katherine put the ring over the tip of her finger. She thought of the Indian Ocean, the massive weight of water smoothing the stone over thousands and thousands of years. She looked at it closer and saw that beneath the glassy clouds of the stone's surface were hard prismatic lines, like deep cracks in the ice. The diamond's true nature could never be smoothed away, no matter how much the ocean pounded and washed it. She pushed it down over her finger and went downstairs.

Adam and Kieron were still sweeping in the front garden.

'It's nearly lunchtime,' said Adam, not looking up.

'Mummy, why do you sleep so long?'

'I'm tired, Kieron.'

'You are always tired. We went to Sainsbury's.'

'Great,' she said, trying to sound breezy. 'I'll make lunch.' She held open one side of the bin bag while Adam pushed the leaves down. He saw the ring on her finger.

'Where did you get that?' he said.

'Camden Market. Do you like it?'

'You never wear jewellery,' he said.

'I just liked it.'

'Sometimes I don't know you,' he said. He lifted up the bin bag, tied it firmly in a knot and hoisted it over the hedge on to the pavement.

'I bet you're both hungry,' she said.

She walked back inside the house. She opened the fridge.

'Adam! What's going on?'

She could see a chicken, a whole salmon, a leg of lamb, several huge pots of yoghurt, stacks of butter and cheese, enough vegetables to feed a family of ten.

'It's too much! You've bought far too much . . .'

'What?'

He came inside, defensive and perplexed.

'It's too much,' she said.

'Katherine, it's just a shop.'

We're on the edge of a cliff, she wanted to shout. A high cliff and we're going to fall.

She could feel Adam waiting for her to speak.

'What's wrong?' he said.

She couldn't speak. He stepped towards her and she turned to him, resting her cheek against his shoulder. He put his arms around her, loosely, without commitment.

'Dad! A beetle!'

Adam went to Kieron, relieved to be called away. She watched the slump in his shoulders and the weariness of his step. Maybe he had bought the food in the fridge to compensate for something not provided in their relationship – warmth, connection, for love. The thought of it was unbearable.

She walked out into the back garden. The new yellow bricks that had seemed out of place in the ramshackle of their neglected garden now seemed normal. Cement had dried on the patio flags; roses and herbs grew side by side in pots in a strangled mass of twigs and ragged leaves. A tomato plant-in-a-bag that Katherine had bought for Kieron a year ago. She stared at it all as if it had nothing to do with her. Every thought was about Stephen. She thought of him in a whitewashed house in the desert mountains walking into a simple kitchen, swinging a child. She saw Alison, smiling, saw Stephen walking alone amongst huge American pines, heard him whispering her name. She went back upstairs and lay on the bed and conjured him into the room. She could feel him touching her. She sat up abruptly, ashamed of her obsessive thoughts. How had this happened? How had she become so removed from her own life? She knelt down by her bed and waves of pain moved through her. Adam and Kieron were chatting outside, and she forced herself to think of them, her husband and her son, right there, on the other side of the wall, tending to their home, but in her mind they were gone, their home was gone, and all that was left of it was a blackened gap in the street, the charred roof beams of the house exposed to the sky. Some force had blown her made-up life apart.

She reached into her pocket for her mobile. She would call Stephen in America. She couldn't bear it any longer. Why had he gone? He had left her to a life she could no longer understand. Anger rose inside her. She went into her text inbox and found the number of his cellphone in America. They had agreed not to be in touch, but he had sent the number 'just in case'. She tapped in the number, pressed the dial button and heard the slow pulse of the foreign ringtone. A woman answered.

'Hello?'

It hadn't occurred to Katherine that Alison might answer.

'Hello?'

Her voice sounded sleepy. Katherine breathed lightly, high in her lungs.

'Is anyone there?'

Katherine felt a rush of power. Her anger consumed her. She had only to speak a few words and everything would change forever. She would destroy Alison, her children, Adam, Kieron, smash their worlds forever, rid herself of her torment, and drag them all down. She stared at the phone, trembling with an immaculate rage. The line went dead.

She sat on the edge of the bed, frightened by what she had done. She could no longer trust herself. She had to get away, to find time to think.

Adam was resolutely silent as he watched Katherine bundle Kieron into the car.

'It'll be good for Kieron to see his grandma,' she said brightly. 'I'll call you tomorrow morning.'

She'd told Adam her father had a special exhibition in Braymer and had asked her to drive up for it. She'd phoned Ashwood and lied about a family emergency. Kieron sat quietly in the back listening to a talking book as she drove the four hundred miles north. The motorway was clear and the speed made sense to her. The world around her was still and suspended, but she was barrelling through it. On the final thirty miles of the journey, as she zigzagged along the roads into Northumberland, the hills folded themselves in behind her, as if to stop her turning back.

It was late and raining heavily when she arrived at Sellacrag. She carried Kieron from the car under her coat and laid him on a bed in the spare room. She fetched blankets and tucked them round him.

She sat in the kitchen amongst the banalities of her father's daily life. An old porridge bowl on the table alongside a powdered milk drink, its flap open, a caked spoon next to it, a plethora of cough syrups and Lemsips, on the sideboard a cluster of jams, vitamins and medicines, all ancient and dusty. There was a stack of mint cake and an array of little vases. An upturned aerosol lid was filled with broken pens, chewed pencils, and several old toothbrushes. Rain drummed on to the roof and the gutters gushed with rainwater as the wind blew the trees wildly round Sellacrag. Katherine listened to its thunderous hissing, the sound entering her feverish thoughts about how to forget Stephen, how to live as though she'd never met him, how to re-enter her life.

When she got up the next morning, David had already gone to his office above the museum. May had arrived from Carlisle early. She had cleared the kitchen and was cutting open an orange at the table.

'It's nice that you have come up,' called May in a voice that said that she wasn't sure it was. 'I have to be back in Carlisle this evening.'

'We don't need looking after,' said Katherine, coming through to the kitchen.

'Where is Adam?'

'Working. He sends his love.'

'Shouldn't Kieron be at school?'

'It's fine. We just wanted to get out of London.'

'It was a long way to come.'

Katherine noticed the delicate broken capillaries on her mother's cheeks and the creases around her mouth. May was seventy now. She looked outside where the storm was still raging. The hills beyond the lake were indistinct behind grey screens of rain. Katherine had been hoping to leave Kieron and go for a long walk, but the rain was too heavy. They were stuck inside. Kieron was sitting on the rag carpet in front of the fire playing with the wooden Meccano Katherine had played with as a child. She sat next to him, in a daze, looking at the black and white print of a sultan riding on an elephant and, beside it, the lamp with a cone-shaped shade with a brown scorch mark. The objects in the room seemed chaotic and random, reaching back through the years. Along the low mantelpiece were invitations dating back to the 1980s, a school photo of her brother William, and a flyer for one of her old dance shows.

'Mum, I want to go in the garden,' said Kieron.

'All right. Put your wellies on.'

She watched him trudge outside into the rain. He bent down and picked up a stick. Katherine heard the front door open, and went through to the kitchen.

'You've brought the weather,' said David, shaking off an umbrella. He looked lost in worry. He picked up some papers from the table and turned back to the door.

'George Gull's exhibition is a triumph. You must take a look, Katherine.'

'I will,' she said.

'Time waits for no man,' he said, sighing as he turned back to the door.

'I'll leave some fresh bread and sardines in the larder,' said May.

David grunted a response. Katherine felt suddenly helpless. Some profound need rose up in her and she burst out,

'I'm in love. I've fallen in love.'

May stopped at the table. David turned and looked at Katherine. He stepped back into Sellacrag, and as he did a surge of hope coursed through her that he would listen, would help, that they would talk it through, as he had talked things through with so many others.

'All love is madness,' he said.

'I know. No, I don't know,' she stumbled. 'He's gone away and I feel lost. With him, I could do anything, I was transformed. I don't know how to give him up.'

'These are just feelings, Katherine,' said David. 'They will pass.'

'I don't want them to pass.'

'Does Adam know?' said May.

'No.'

'Love is a distraction,' said David.

'From what?'

'Work lasts forever, but love . . .'

'With him I could work. I could even dance again, be myself, be my real self . . .'

She stopped, aware her words were hackneyed and

inadequate. Her parents were looking at her with something like pity.

'Who is it?' said May quietly.

'Stephen Jericho. You introduced us up here, don't you remember, Dad? We met again that night at St Mark's.'

She couldn't stop. Now she'd started speaking she couldn't hold back.

'I feel I've known him all my life. He feels the same. He's been able to write because of me. Our meeting has brought so much love . . .'

There was a loud crash. She didn't know what had happened. Something had fallen to the ground. Her father had dropped his cup. A white cup. Katherine saw it lying in jagged pieces on the floor in a small pool of water.

'You fool, Katherine.'

Her father was shouting at her.

'You blind, stupid fool!'

Katherine instinctively looked to her mother; she was staring at David, openmouthed.

'You think you can do what you want?' he railed. 'You chose a life with Adam. You chose marriage. You can't do what you want! No one can. Do you hear me? No one!'

'David,' said May, stepping forward.

He rounded on her, his eyes blazing with anger. 'I will say what I want! You think this is special, Katherine? This is not love! It is not even fantasy! It's pathetic!'

Katherine pushed open the door. She walked quickly from the house, up the track, past the reed pond, through the kissing gate, through the tunnels of rhododendrons and out on to the open fell. Her mind was racing. She was in shock. She had never expected her father to react that way. She didn't recognise him. That was not her father. Her father was urbane, controlled, charismatic. She'd never seen him so angry, not with anyone, not with them as children, not with May. She marched on through the rain and mist to Fallowbeck, forcing back the tears. The stream was in torrents after the downpour and roaring like an engine. She reached the zigzagging path and climbed upwards, stopping to catch her breath by the waterfalls. It was where she and her brothers William and Michael had played as children, spending whole days absorbed in making dams with sods and stones. She had been expert at ripping the great clods of grassy earth from the bank, never caring about her aching hands or the freezing water as she wedged the clods into place and dragged the heavy stones on top of them. She stood watching the water crashing down. Her life seemed small and stupid. She saw herself, the fierce little girl desperately trying to dam the stream to be accepted by her brothers. She had never succeeded. She had always been invisible.

She cut up Bracken Fell on the faint sheep paths. It was steep and her legs burned. She was glad when at last she reached the plateau of grass at the top. She stopped by the sheepfold.

She remembered being on this fell with her father when she was a teenager. It was a beautiful summer day, and May had persuaded David to leave his office and come for a walk with the whole family. They'd come across the hill, and William and Michael had gone ahead with May. David rarely took any exercise, and stopped to rest by the Blind Pool. He took off his shoes and socks, rolled up his trousers and put his feet in the water. His skin was white as bone, his toenails uncut. He lay back on the green earth and closed his eyes in the sunshine. Katherine sat next to him on the bank. It was a precious moment, a rare occurrence, just her and her father. She started talking like she never had before, full of adolescent passion about her dancing, about technique, about the next performance with her dance teacher, Gelda, about the costumes she'd made from Lycra off-cuts, about how inspiring Gelda was, how Gelda danced not for fame and fortune but just for the sake of the madness of dance . . . Her father lay there next to her with his eyes closed. He chuckled as she talked on and on. Katherine had enjoyed herself. She felt he was laughing because she entertained him, but now she wondered if he had been laughing at something else, if he had heard her at all.

A dead sheep lay in the grass below her, its wet wool still clinging to the bones. The mist had cleared, and the hills flattened towards the white salt haze of the sea at Barrow. Her father was wrong; her love for Stephen wasn't just fantasy, it was a connection between two souls. Defiance rose in her. She would not let it go. She climbed again towards the summit, scoring her own path through the dead bracken and across the punishing scree.

17

He could hear that she was scared.

'It's like London to Cairo,' Katherine said.

'Not so far . . .'

Stephen knew it wasn't the length of the flight that frightened her, but what the trip would mean. She was in New York waiting for her connecting flight to Phoenix. She had rung him a few weeks ago after the outburst with her father to tell him she wanted to come. He had been overjoyed, and they had arranged it for a week when Alison and the children were going to the mountains to visit friends in Colorado. Now she was having second thoughts.

'I should go home. Adam will find out.'

'What did you tell him?'

'That I'm visiting an old dance colleague in New York.'

Stephen didn't like her fear. It was small and collapsed their experience to something troublesome and mundane. He wanted to maintain the surprise of their relationship, the joy of it, to feel how astonishing it was to be married, halfway through life, with kids and plans for the future and mountains of work, and to meet someone new and to feel so much love for them, a pure, joyful love. He wanted her to feel the same.

'Please, Katherine,' he said. 'You've come this far. You're more than half way. The flight from New York to Phoenix can't be more than five hours.'

He was talking on his cellphone by the mailbox at the end of the drive.

'Frank! Molly! It's ready!'

It was Alison calling for the kids. Stephen could hear them tearing up and down the muddy slope among the pines. The slope had enthralled them ever since they'd arrived in America. It had been covered with snow when they first arrived, and they'd bombed down it on tin trays in their thick coats. Now spring was here, it had become a red dirt run. It was a world away from the small, orderly lawn that had served as their wilderness in England. They let loose dust bombs, skidded down the bank, ran wild through the woods, and came home filthy, their eyes bright, like lizards, quick and lithe.

'Come on!' Alison shouted again. 'There'll be nothing to eat on the way.'

She already had a slight American accent. Frank and Molly's shouts and shrieks came closer as they ran back to the house. He could feel their happiness, the certainty of their world, and he was painfully aware of his absence from them, standing at the edge of their rented property, hidden from view, talking to another woman.

'I've got to go, Katherine,' he said. 'Please come.'

He put the cellphone in his pocket and looked out at the wide breadth of earth and sky, stretching flat to the mountains streaked with snow. There was pink blossom on an apricot tree. The scent aroused him. The thought of being with Katherine made him breathless.

'Stephen!' Alison was calling him, her voice exasperated.

'I'm coming.'

He walked back to the house.

'Molly won't eat,' said Alison.

His daughter sat at the table with a bowl of pasta.

'Don't be such a baby, Molly,' said Alison. 'Finish your food and let's get going.'

He hated the way Alison skated over the children's feelings. Difficult emotions were always left unexamined, feelings unexplored. He felt each unresolved moment like a knot and saw a rope of them wreathed around his family. He carried their bags to the car.

'You're going to have a great time in the mountains,' he said, hugging Frank and Molly. 'I wish I could come. I'll miss you. I love you.'

Alison was already in the car. She was still nervous about driving on American roads.

'I'll call when we get there. Work hard!' she said brightly.

The car doors slammed shut. His whole family seemed suddenly vulnerable, sealed inside. For a moment, he didn't want them to go: they meant everything to him. He wanted to call them back and confess everything to them, to tell them about Katherine and beg their forgiveness and never lose sight of them again. The car drove off and Frank and Molly waved from the back window. He felt afraid as he watched them disappear, but it changed nothing. He knew he had to see Katherine.

He walked into the town through the red-walled streets. Blossom was drifting like lazy snow from the trees. The Blue Cliff Café was a haphazard place with armchairs and sofas and three or four computers on wooden tables. They made brownies and muffins every morning. The owner, Ed, a tree of a man, was at the till and smiled when he saw Stephen. 'Been expecting you,' he said, tossing him a set of keys.

'Thanks, Ed,' said Stephen.

Ed was lending him his car.

'Did you use my recipe?' Ed clucked like a chicken and laughed.

'No way!' said Stephen.

It was a joke between them. Alison and the kids had got gastric flu, and Stephen had bought a chicken to make them soup. He'd stopped off at the Blue Cliff and put it on the counter while he drank a beer. He and Ed had started swapping stories. Ed had tried to give Stephen his recipe for chicken soup. Stephen told him he didn't need it, that chicken soup was his heritage, in his DNA. His grandmother had bribed her way out of Poland with chicken soup; his mother had won his father's attention with it. Chicken soup wasn't just in his blood, it *was* his blood. Stephen found himself referring to his Jewishness in America in a way he never had in England. Everyone seemed so much more relaxed about where they were from. When he'd left the Blue Cliff an hour later, he'd left the chicken on the counter. Ed had come running up the road after him with it, flapping his arms and clucking like a rooster.

He drove to the airport in a dream. Ed's car was a big old Buick with wide seats. Ed didn't have children to mess it up and the seats felt cool and smelt of leather. As he parked at the terminal Stephen realised he had forgotten his cash card. He didn't want to pay for anything on credit in case Alison found the statements. He walked through the terminal building, past expensive shops, and leant against a gift-boutique window, looking up at the monitor above an escalator. People drifted listlessly past. Stephen had spent a lot of time moving around, writing travel pieces, but it was still exciting to be in an airport, a suspended world of polished glass and luxury.

At the arrivals gate, Katherine was already there, talking to a Texan in his sixties. There was a small gathering of other people waiting for passengers to arrive. He hung back behind a couple of drivers in creased suits, half-heartedly holding up pieces of card with names scrawled on.

'Enjoy your stay, Katherine!' said the Texan.

'Enjoy London,' she laughed, 'if you ever get there!'

The Texan disappeared in a throng of people. Stephen watched as Katherine looked about her. Her face was prettier than he had remembered. She was wearing a summer dress and her eyes were bright with excitement. The full weight of what he had done in encouraging her to come struck him. Here she was, halfway round the world, come to see him. He recalled what she had said about travelling when they first met, how vehement she had been that it was a pointless thing to do. He walked forward and she smiled. They embraced, pressing into each other.

'What am I doing here?' she whispered into him. 'What am I doing?'

He smiled into her hair.

They held hands and walked out into the parking lot. They put her bag in the boot of the car and drove towards Phoenix.

'Where are we going?' She was excited. She seemed far younger than he remembered.

'A place a friend told me about, in the desert a couple of hours away. Subayato. There's a hotel there called the Lotus. It's quiet, out of the way.'

In the car, he put his hand on her thigh. She let him, tilting her leg outwards. He experienced the same intensity for her every time they met.

'I have to stop off at the house for my cash card.'

He pulled into the chalky drive, ran into the house and rummaged through his desk for his card. It wasn't there. He went into the bedroom and found it in a pair of trousers. When he came out, Katherine was standing in the yard looking into the house. There was a sketch of flowers by Alison on the wall and some paintings Molly and Frank had done on the fridge. Neither Stephen nor Katherine had seen each other's homes before, and as they got back into the car, Katherine was silent. They drove through the town and on to the freeway, the desert opening up in front of them like an unknown land. Katherine took off her shoes and curled up on the passenger seat, and it was a while before they talked. She told him of her shock at seeing his home, the pictures by the children.

'I hated it,' she said, 'it was too real.'

Stephen felt his shoulders and neck relax. He'd felt this before. It was the feeling he got when he was with Katherine that everything could be discussed no matter how serious, and because of that nothing could go wrong. They drove for two hours along the freeway into the desert. On the horizon, under a dark sky, huge rocks stood like massive chess pieces.

'It's further than I thought,' said Stephen.

The land became blank and unwelcoming, the grey sand stretching away. They fell into silence. Stephen kept checking the map to be sure of the turning. They passed a roadside casino with flashing lights, a big structure in the middle of nowhere, empty and pointless. After another thirty minutes, they turned off the freeway on to a small road towards low desert hills.

'Nearly there,' he said. Katherine smiled to reassure him.

They drove on. There were no houses to be seen. It started to rain, the raindrops battering the roof of the car like hail. The rain punched into the dust on the road, kicking it up like bullets. He drove on slowly. At last they saw a sign ahead: WELCOME TO SUBAYATO.

It was a desolate place, a few houses and a field with six or seven trailers. Above one of them flew an American flag. On the stoop of one house, a thin man stood staring out at the downpour. Stephen wound down the window.

'Hi there. I'm looking for the Lotus Hotel.'

He had to shout to be heard through the rain.

The man laughed and shook his head. Stephen drove on. There was a crack of thunder. The air was black with rain. It was impossible to see the road ahead. He stopped the car in the road. They decided to wait for the worst of the storm to pass.

'Perhaps you got the name wrong,' said Katherine quietly.

'We'll find it, don't worry. I'm sorry.'

Through the wash of rain, they saw a door of a wooden bungalow bang open against the timber frame. A man stepped into the doorway. He was holding a young child by the wrist and shouting as he pushed her out. She stumbled forwards and fell to the ground right near the car. She was maybe eight years old. The man went back inside and slammed the door. The girl picked herself up and sat on the front step, wet through, her clothes sticking to her.

'Shouldn't we do something?' said Katherine.

'Like what?' asked Stephen.

They sat in the car. The girl sat on the step. She never once looked at them.

When the rain eased, they drove back to the freeway

and checked into a motel. At the reception desk, Katherine put her hand on the back of Stephen's neck to reassure him. They walked along the porch to a small, airless room, happy to be inside four walls again, in a space that felt like their own. It didn't matter where they were. They drank beer and made love and slept for a couple of hours, wrapped in each others arms. When they woke up, the rain had stopped, and the afternoon had fallen away into darkness.

'I'm in the desert with you. It's like a dream.'

She kissed his mouth, drinking him in.

'I'm so happy. I've never done anything like this before,' she said. 'Have you?'

He heard the slight catch in her breath.

'It was never like this,' he said, regretting it immediately.

'Tell me.'

'It was before I met you. Three or four times. It was sex, never anything more.' He knew it would hurt her, but he couldn't lie to her.

Katherine listened as Stephen told her about the other women with whom he had been unfaithful. It happened after readings, he told her. He was usually drunk. He told her it hadn't happened for a long time. Katherine suddenly felt an overwhelming desire to curl up and sleep. She snuggled into Stephen's body to silence him. He took her embrace as an acceptance.

'I love you,' he said, kissing her as he moved down her body.

She tasted salty and metallic. He took her passivity as abandonment, and when she reached orgasm, he held her tightly as she shuddered against him.

Katherine woke in the night. Stephen was asleep next to her. It was the kind of moment they always longed for; to wake next to each other in a shared bed in the small hours. She got up and went outside into the night. Cars sped past on the freeway, their headlights spotting the darkness. Images of women drifted through her mind. She saw them undressing, curling themselves round Stephen like swans. She hated herself for her jealousy. What did it matter? How could she feel the wound of something that happened before they had met?

She sat on the ground at the back of the motel and stared into the desert towards the distant mountains, and for the first time with Stephen, she felt alone. She thought of his house and his children's drawings, the photos on the fridge, the torment of being in love with someone who was always out of reach. Stephen could only be with her by absenting himself from the rest of his life. Her father had been the same, absent, away, distracted, searching for his life away from the home.

The moon made metal of the mountains. Her father's outburst at Sellacrag came back to her. It had shocked her to glimpse his anger. It had been like a deep essence of him, some dark tincture. She had made the decision to fly out to see Stephen, diamond-hard in the face of his fury, as she had climbed the screes above the tarn. She had never really known her father. She had once found one of his poems scribbled on the back of a chequebook at home in Carlisle. Her mother had explained to her that he wrote poetry, but that it was private, and never meant to be read. Katherine had taken the chequebook into her bedroom like a thief. She had pored over his almost illegible scrawl. It was about a man in deep conflict, inconsolably longing for another life. The thought came crashing into her. She was just the same. A mystery to her own family, absent, halfway round the world with another man.

The following day Stephen and Katherine had coffee on the veranda of the motel. Stephen was relaxed, exuberant. For the first time he could remember, he felt a certainty, a sense of commitment that astonished and delighted him. He took Katherine to a pueblo and they wandered through an exhibition of Native American sculpture made from old cars and pieces of junk. They went to the hot springs and bathed in the clear pools and sat on the cracked earth to dry themselves. They drove to a diner on the edge of a small town. The sign above it said WELCOME TO GRACIE'S. As Katherine walked across the parking lot towards the door, Stephen watched her, her body strong and slim, her skirt loose against her legs. She turned, realising he wasn't beside her, and looked back at him. He saw her sadness and felt ablaze with love for her.

He went towards her. Her mobile rang in her pocket. She put it to her ear and walked to the far side of the diner. Stephen looked out over the desert. Two trucks roared past, their exhaust pipes belching black fumes. When they had gone, a new stillness had settled on the road. He would leave Alison. He knew it for sure now. He would start his life again with Katherine.

He looked round for her. She had ended her call and was standing at the side of the diner, her hands by her sides, suspended in empty space. He smiled as he walked towards her, but he could already see the news was bad.

'What is it?'

'My dad. He's got cancer.'

18

Katherine pressed the button for the fourteenth floor. Gregory's apartment block was shabbier than she remembered it, but the lift was exactly the same, the same plum carpet on the walls and small white buttons that illuminated in sequence as it climbed. Despite their differences, it seemed Gregory had agreed to let David stay there while he was out of town, so David could visit a doctor on Harley Street. Katherine felt the same tenseness in the pit of her stomach that she had felt as a child over twenty-five years before, during the family holiday in London. It was the only holiday the family had ever taken, and her memories of it remained vivid. May had announced they were going to spend a week in the capital. She had bundled Katherine and her brothers on to a train, each with a small rucksack. Katherine remembered her calling her father from Carlisle station. They had argued: for God's sake, why shouldn't the children see London? He saw it often enough . . .

It had been the greatest adventure of their lives. May had booked a cheap bed and breakfast in Finsbury Park. They hadn't been allowed to stay at Uncle Gregory and Aunt Charlotte's flat, for fear they might break something or dirty the furniture, but one afternoon they had gone there to meet her father and have tea with him. He was staying at the flat alone, an arrangement that had seemed perfectly normal to Katherine at the time. Looking back on it, she realised how strange the whole trip was. Not only had her father not stayed with them, but he hadn't gone on any trips with them, to the Houses of Parliament or Madame Tussaud's.

The lift climbed to the twelfth floor. She remembered the delight it had given to herself and her brothers. None of them had ever been in a lift before, and they had been beside themselves with excitement, infuriating May by running in and out as the doors were sliding shut.

At the fourteenth floor, Katherine got out and walked down the carpeted corridor. She glanced at her watch. Her father would be waiting for her to take him to Harley Street. Since she had heard about his illness, her memories of his outburst at Sellacrag had evaporated, and she felt only tenderness towards him. She longed to be useful to him, and had been delighted when May asked her to drive him to his doctor's appointment. Her brother William had already accompanied him to see the consultant in Carlisle, and Michael couldn't get back from Canada, so Katherine was to be the only one of the children to be with him. May had insisted that she be punctual; David was seeing an eminent oncologist, Dr Sorov, a friend of Lady Highsmith. Dr Sorov had agreed to examine David free of charge as a personal favour to her. May was teaching in Carlisle, but was coming down by train and would join them at the clinic.

The front door of the flat was open, and she saw her father standing at the window, his back to her. He was slightly stooped and clutched his hand to his head. Katherine's initial thought was that he was in pain, but as he turned to face her she saw that he was on the phone.

' . . . not the bed and breakfast. The Shenner Bay Hotel!' he shouted brusquely, looking straight at Katherine. 'The Shenner Bay! . . .'

She raised her hand in greeting, but he turned back to the window. His tone was frenetic, almost bullying.

'We'll pay. Of course we'll pay! Just book it. Giordano. Spell it right. We need to meet William Turner about the tunnel. William. Turner. Can't you hear what I'm saying? I need to know what we're doing with Boulens. Is George on top of it? What about advertising?'

He reminded Katherine of a politician on television, the same exasperated tone, the same forcefulness. She looked round the room. It seemed totally unchanged; the same seventies decor, the marble solitaire table, the deep pile cream carpet, the brown suede sofa, the garish paintings. She remembered the paralysis she'd felt as a child, standing with her brothers in the living room, terrified of touching anything. Despite herself, she felt it again now.

'Katherine!' David said, pocketing his mobile phone. 'Good of you to come.'

He spoke to her as though there were other people in the room.

'Hi, Dad.'

He coughed and she moved towards him, wanting to soothe him.

'Don't be upset,' he said brightly. 'It's how the cancer works. It makes me cough, and sometimes I feel a little stiff. That's all. Usually I feel fine.'

'Right.'

'The cancer has to get on with its life just like anybody else.'

His phone rang and he snatched it up.

'Terry? Thanks for calling back. I want to set up a meeting with you and Meadowbank, the structural engineers in Manchester. A big project. Next week? No, no, this week. I'm getting the funding structure in place.'

Katherine watched him in amazement. David was not as she had expected to find him. He seemed well, better than when she had last seen him, cheerful even, and brimming with energy.

She walked into the hall to wait. In an alcove near the door, there were some gold ornaments on a glass shelf. Below them was a pale wooden box inlaid with pearl and curlicues of silver. She recognised it at once; Aunt Charlotte's vanity set. She crouched down and lifted the lid. Inside was the silver brush and mirror. She held the brush in her hand, remembering the feel of it exactly, the slim handle, the balanced weight. Memories came to her, not exact but visceral, of fur collars, sweet perfume, leather gloves, the snap of a clasp on a bag. She pressed the straw-like bristles into her palm; there was something intimate and disturbing about the feel of them.

They must be from a real animal, a horse perhaps, she thought. It struck her how much she missed her aunt.

Charlotte, with no children of her own, had always doted on Katherine. Katherine was used to living in the wake of her brothers and her busy parents and wasn't used to the kind of attention her aunt gave her, but during the all-too-rare times when they met she blossomed. Charlotte's friendliness continued as Katherine had grown up and moved to London. She would take her shopping at Selfridges or Harvey Nichols, and they would have lunch in the shop restaurant. Katherine was never the feminine companion her aunt longed for, one who relished clothes and fashion and gossip, but despite this they had remained close. On the last occasion they met before her illness, Charlotte had bought Katherine an expensive leather handbag with gold buckles. Katherine thanked her aunt effusively, even though she knew she would never use it. Charlotte had drunk a bottle of wine over lunch, and when the time had come to say goodbye she pulled Katherine close to her. 'You're a special girl. I love you very much, I love you,' she said. Katherine had looked into her eyes, unable to respond. Her mother and father never spoke to her like this, and it frightened her to feel she had the same reserve. She sensed a terrible numbness inside her and forced herself to embrace her aunt. 'I love you too,' she said, the words as strange as shells in her mouth.

She could hear her father concluding his phone call. She slipped the brush into her pocket, the feel of its weight gave her a vague sense of comfort. She would give it to Aunt Charlotte when she next visited her.

She drove her father to Harley Street. Katherine feared he might mention Stephen, or want to talk about his outburst in Sellacrag, but he seemed to have forgotten all about it. He sat in the back, making one phone call after another. She parked the car on a meter, and David stepped on to the pavement and looked up at the Georgian buildings.

'Elegant, don't you think?' he said. 'Come on! We mustn't be late. Your mother will have something to say! What number is it? Where is your mother?'

'She's meeting us there. It's number 39.'

'Good. Good of you to come, Katherine,' he repeated. 'How's Adam?'

'Fine. He sends his love.'

His phone rang twice, then stopped.

'Dad?'

'What? Yes?'

She hesitated. 'I thought you'd stopped work.'

'Why on earth would I do that?' he said. 'The cancer does its work, I must do mine. This is an exciting time, Katherine. I have plans! So many plans! We are going to build a tunnel under the lake at Braymer.'

'What?'

'Oh, and Daniel Boulens is coming. Katherine, you must not miss him.'

'Who is he?'

'The world's greatest abstract minimalist. He's coming

to Braymer. He is going to paint a line, a constant line across the lake.'

Katherine looked at her father, amused.

'A line across the lake? How?'

'That is a secret! You mustn't miss it, Katherine! Here's May . . .'

She was standing in the doorway. David bounded up the steps to meet her.

'May, Katherine has never heard of Boulens! How did we manage to breed such ignorant children?'

Dr Sorov pushed a disk into his computer, swivelled the screen towards them, and moved his mouse across a pad of Hampton Court. Black and white shapes swirled through grey clouds across the screen.

'This is the right lung,' he said pointing to a mass of white.

A dark egg-shaped patch appeared in the top right-hand corner of the screen.

'The grey area is the tumour. Behind it is David's spine. You can see the nodes are quite bulky.'

He pointed to more grey areas. Katherine tried to absorb the fact that she was looking inside her father's body. Her instinctive reaction was one of shock and dis-comfort. It was too intimate, it seemed to infringe on his dignity and privacy. Her father and mother seemed unflustered, and sat like obedient pupils taking it all in.

'What does it mean? That the nodes are bulky?' asked May.

'The cancer has spread beyond the lung,' said Dr Sorov. 'It's not beyond treating with chemotherapy and radiotherapy. The good news is that there is no secondary cancer. I had been worried it might have spread to the liver, but as you can see it is spotless.'

'Good,' said David.

A dark shape spread across the screen in a tangle of tendrils.

'What's that?' asked Katherine quietly.

'Your father's heart,' said the doctor. 'There is nothing wrong with that.'

There was a pause as they all gazed at the strange shape on the screen.

'How did you feel during the scan?' asked Dr Sorov.

'A little uncomfortable,' conceded David.

'It's to be expected. The tumour presses down on the nerves when you lie completely flat,' said the doctor, 'and constricts the air to the lungs. It can be fatal to lie flat, but not at your stage. Are you sleeping with extra pillows to prop you up?'

'Yes,' said David.

It was the first time that day that Katherine had seen him vulnerable. She looked again at his heart on the screen and in the vegetable-like shape with its roots and tendrils she saw a fragile beauty, complex and unfathomable. Dr Sorov pushed his seat back from the desk to indicate the appointment was over.

'I want to keep the day job,' said David in a slightly self-mocking tone as he stood up.

238

'There's no reason not to,' said Dr Sorov. 'Chemo-therapy can make you feel a little tired and nauseous. You may lose some hair. You will be vulnerable to infections, but it's nothing you can't live with.'

'I've got something big coming up. I can't take time off right now,' said David.

'You must start your treatment when you are ready.'

'He doesn't need to start straightaway?' said May, surprised.

'It's important that David should be ready,' repeated Dr Sorov, careful not to inflect any opinion in his voice.

'This is great news, doctor,' said David. 'Great news! Have you ever been to Northumberland?'

'I'm a sailor, not a walker.'

'Sailing? We have some of the best sailing in the country at Kielder. I will expect to see you,' said David, handing him a card.

'I would love to come,' said Dr Sorov. 'Louise has told me about your wonderful work there.'

'To be told is nothing. To experience is everything,' said David.

Dr Sorov smiled, succumbing to David's charm.

'Until you start your treatment, David, keep taking the steroids. You can get another prescription from the front desk.'

As they came out on to Harley Street, David was already on his phone. Katherine turned to her mother.

'Steroids?' she whispered. 'Is that what's making him

so high? He's no idea what he's doing, Mum. He's talking about a tunnel under the lake. And what's all that about a line? Someone painting a line across it?'

'The steroids make him feel better,' said May.

'Mum, he's ill. He's got to slow down.'

May looked at Katherine and said nothing. It was clear the conversation was over.

May insisted that she and David catch a bus back to Gregory's flat. It would do them good to walk to the bus stop, she said. Katherine watched her parents walk away; her mother's upright form, her father stockier, one hand gesticulating wildly as he spoke on the phone. Their insouciance about his illness disturbed her. There should be some change, some acknowledgement, some letting go. As they turned the corner on to Upper Regent Street and disappeared, Katherine suddenly felt fear. It was like a hand round her heart, as though someone might tear it clean out of her body.

19

'My usual table, please!' said Gregory as he strode into the busy restaurant. A waiter came over, smiling professionally.

'Sir, we have this table here.' He indicated one in the middle of the room.

'I always sit by the window,' said Gregory. 'You must be new.'

'I've been working here for. . .'

Gregory didn't wait for the waiter to finish. He knew what was going to be said and the exact timbre in which it would be spoken; the inevitable tedium of the exchange meant there was no point in pursuing it.

'Yes, yep, yep, yep,' he said, punching out the words, waving his hand impatiently. He marched over to the table in the window. 'Well, that's good, very good.'

The silver cutlery on white linen gleamed in the last of the evening sunlight. Gregory sat down, beckoning the waiter to him.

'You're doing well,' he said, glancing round at the other customers. The waiter seemed unsure whether Gregory was giving him a compliment or making an accusation.

'Are you going to give me the menu or not, young man?' He raised an eyebrow and cocked his head on one side to show he was making a joke; being charming was necessary to expel sadness and pressure, which was important to do, especially now when things had gone so wrong.

The waiter was unresponsive to Gregory's humour so he provided the laughter himself, in five short bursts. The waiter must be foreign, he decided, Lithuanian perhaps, or Polish.

He was handed a leather-bound menu.

'Will anyone be joining you, sir?' said the waiter.

'No! No! God, no!' cried Gregory. 'Right, young man! Two bottles of Burgundy. The Grand Cru, yes, the Valmur.'

Wine was also important at the moment; it was helping him sleep. For the last four nights he had lain in bed wide awake in a state of nightmarish obsession. How could Marge have done it? How could it have happened? That phrase she used about him: 'old man'. *Old man*. She was right, he was an old man, a retired old gentleman trying to make her happy. How could she? In his mind he saw her note again. That note. How could she have been so cruel? It had been on the glass coffee table. He hadn't bothered to read it straightaway; it wouldn't be anything important, just another note about popping into the village for dry cleaning or, more likely, to visit their local health food shop. Margery had become fixated with the health food shop, the House of Heather, and was forever trying out new remedies for her various digestive disorders.

The waiter brought the two bottles of wine and

opened one of them. Gregory waved the man away and poured himself a large glass. He wondered if Marge's remedies had had anything to do with what happened. Her latest curatives had been linseed, flax oil and black-currant tablets. Perhaps they had altered her state of mind. He drank his wine thirstily. Six months ago, they had wandered into the House of Heather on one of their village shopping trips. They had been browsing the bewildering rows of vitamins and herbal remedies when a voice behind them asked if they needed help. An Indian man in his fifties stood behind the counter in a white coat. Margery shyly asked him if he had anything for indigestion. Gregory left to wait in the car; he found the articulation of all medical complaints acutely embarrass-ing. He sat listening to the cricket on the car radio. When Margery came out, she was carrying a bag full of pills and potions. She excitedly told Gregory that the doctor made a great deal of sense. 'He's not a bloody doctor,' Gregory said. 'Not a real one!' 'He is to me,' Margery replied sim-ply. She told him how the doctor had explained to her the connection between body and mind, and how most peo-ple were off-balance and needed to undertake a journey towards harmony. He had told Margery that this journey began in the intestine. It was a great sadness, he said, that people in the West were so scared of their intestines. Margery had bravely confessed that she had suffered from digestive complaints all her life, and as she listened to his calm voice reassuring her, she felt a great weight lift from her.

Gregory had laughed at Margery's account of the doctor but he hadn't forbidden her from continuing her visits to him. It had all seemed so harmless; as long as Margery was there at his side when he needed her, he didn't mind what she did. Now he wondered if the doctor had been an evil influence.

Margery did not come home. Afternoon turned into evening, and eventually Gregory opened the note and read it.

Gregory,

I am leaving you. I am going to spend some time with my daughter in Canada. I'm sorry this hasn't worked out. Please don't contact me. I feel sad about Charlotte. I am an old woman and you are an old man and we must find peace of mind before we die. I am sorry.

Love and best wishes,

Margery

Gregory had laughed at her childishly simple words. The echo of his laugh bounced off the sliding glass doors to the garden and over the swimming pool. He laughed again and it echoed through the trees. Margery could go to hell! He was fine. That night he had taken a bottle of Pontet-Canet '97 from the cellar and gone to bed. The next day he had read the note again. He realised he was going to die alone, and the pale monsters inside him began to stir.

In the restaurant Gregory called the waiter over. He

asked him to open the second bottle and ordered a rare steak. He looked at the bottles of wine on the table in front of him. Their shape pleased him, like two little maidens he thought, with good curvaceous figures, waiting to do his bidding.

He ate half of the steak, paid the bill and stumbled out into the street into the early evening. He walked down the high street with its hanging baskets over the doorways. He stopped outside the village post office and vomited in the gutter. The sick came out easily, purple with burgundy.

He got in the car and set off towards London, the windows open, driving fast through the country lanes. His car never let him down. He turned on to the motorway. A police car on a bridge was hovering like a hornet and he slowed down. He was too clever to get caught by those bastards.

He drove into South London. The street lamps were shining yellow and white down the long high streets. Gregory knew exactly where he was going. He passed a queue of young people stretching round a corner. They wore dark clothes and seemed strangely mirthless and silent. He swung over to the left by the lights and turned off the engine. He opened the door and stepped unsteadily on to the kerb. There were smells of takeaway food and petrol. It felt good to be here at eye-level with the real, dirty people. He felt thrilled, like a child at a funfair sensing danger in the swirling lights. His weight shifted from one foot to another slowly at an uneven rhythm. He reeled towards Sunset Parlour.

Two men on the door looked at each other as Gregory approached unsteadily.

'Coming in?' said one of them.

One of the men was black, the other white with a diamond stud in his nose.

'Certainly,' he slurred.

They opened a space for him to squeeze through. Gregory stepped inside, his eyes adjusting to the gloom. He made his way down a black-walled corridor. A neon arrow pointed the way downstairs. He held the rail as he descended. Heavy drum and bass throbbed louder at each step. Gregory's heart seemed to bounce inside his rib cage.

At the bottom, he turned a corner into a dark room. There were women chatting and moving to the music. He felt frightened, but the alcohol in his blood kept him strong and he walked forward. He didn't dare look at the women directly but sensed their breasts, their shoulders and bare arms. His eyes focused in the darkness; there were six or seven of them. A large white woman brushed her fingers against his cheek.

'Hey, lover,' she whispered. Her words sang to him. He looked up at her. Her features were large, her eyelids sparkled as she blinked. The way she touched his cheek was lovely. His face softened. He felt a tightness behind his eyes which might produce tears. He let his head loll and push into her shoulder, then her breast.

'All right, love,' she said.

'Mmmmm . . .'

'Come on then . . .'

She led him up a few stairs into a small room. She closed the door behind them and they stood under an ultraviolet light. She sat on a bed covered in a crimson sheet and began to undress him. Her hands were big and sure as he swayed. She peeled off his vest, undid his trousers and pulled them down, sliding his underpants down his legs.

'Now then, what do we do with you?' she said softly.

He was naked except for his shoes.

'I need . . .'

'What, love?'

His penis sat in the fuzz between his legs, hiding in its skins. He felt scared but when she reached down and held him he flushed into life. I am a stallion, he thought.

The woman laughed. He didn't want her to laugh. She should be sweet. He was a man in his prime. He shouldn't be laughed at. He saw her big face laugh, the dark fillings in her mouth. He couldn't bear it and pushed her away. She fell heavily.

'You fucking little shit! Dren! Dren!'

The next thing he knew, he was being dragged out. His feet were scraping along the floor. One of his shoes came off. Two men threw him through a door and he fell heavily against tarmac. They kicked him hard in the stomach, and he curled instinctively as they raised their fists. His cry was tiny in himself, God help me.

*

247

At Gregory's flat, May made sardines on toast in the spotless kitchen. It was two in the morning but David couldn't sleep. From outside the flat came the sound of the night pleasure boats on the Thames, their low horns sounding as they passed under the bridges. David sat at the table, his eyes closed in sudden anguish. May opened a bottle of wine and poured two glasses. She took his hand. She took a drink of wine and looked down at his hand in hers. Two such old hands, she thought.

'It's very good of Louise to do this for us. If the treatment goes well you can have an operation and recover fully.'

She rambled on, trying to sound practical, going over the points of the case, her hand gripping his.

'Isn't it odd, David? You never smoked. Never. We know it's small-cell carcinoma. That's what they told us at Carlisle and that's what Dr Sorov said, isn't it?'

'I did smoke. I smoked in London . . . '

May put a morsel of sardine in her mouth. It was dry so she took a sip of wine.

'Do I look ill?' asked David. 'Do I?'

May looked at his face.

'You look tired.'

'Once the chemotherapy starts, we'll know where we stand,' he said. 'Then we can plan.'

'Yes.'

'After Giordano, we'll start.'

'Yes.'

'I will lose my hair.'

248

'Yes.'

'We'll have to tell people.'

'Yes.'

A horn sounded on a boat on the river. May reached for David's hand again. He let her take it.

The phone rang, a bright chirping tone. David growled in the back of his throat, cleared the phlegm and picked up the phone.

'Hello?'

There was no reply. He was about to put the phone back on its cradle when he heard a weak voice.

'David?'

'Gregory?'

May looked over at David sensing his urgency.

'Camberwell . . . Hendon Street . . . phone box . . . please . . . come quickly.'

Half an hour later, a taxi pulled up outside Sunset Parlour, its blue and red lights flashing *MASSAGE*, and *SAUNA* on the blackened windows. There was no one on the street. The low thump of music was coming from the doorway. The cabbie turned to David and May.

'You sure this is where you want?' he said.

'Twenty pounds,' said David, passing through a note to the cabbie. 'Wait for us.'

They walked into Hendon Street. There was a phone box next to the railings of a patch of scrub land. Gregory was huddled on the floor.

May put her hand to her mouth. They opened the

door. There were cuts on his face. He had no shirt under his coat and he had only one shoe. There was a pool of vomit on the ground. David tried to help him stand, putting his arms round him.

'Nothing to say,' muttered Gregory, 'nothing to say.'

'Of course not,' said David.

Supporting him either side, they staggered back to the main road. The cabbie rushed out to help and they laid Gregory on the back seat. David and May sat on the fold-down seats.

'The nearest hospital,' said May through the window.

David took off his jacket and spread it over him.

'I'm sorry', said Gregory. He was almost delirious. 'So sorry. So sorry to . . .'

'What happened?' asked May.

Gregory groaned and buried his head.

'What on earth happened?' she repeated.

'Not now, May,' said David. He reached over and stroked Gregory's head. 'You're safe now.'

May was moved by David's gentleness. He acted as though the scene was entirely normal and expected. He didn't judge or question or betray the slightest censure.

Despite everything, David could still amaze her. Gregory, in his most difficult hour had reached out to him, and rather than gloating, David had responded with immeasurable humanity.

'Adventure,' said David, smiling at Gregory.

She watched as Gregory looked up at David with something like gratitude.

20

Kieron raced ahead on his scooter, rattling over the paving stones. Katherine was walking him to school through the sprawling housing estate behind their house. It was already hot and the windows of the tower blocks gleamed gold in the morning sun. A group of women in bright saris sat on fold-out chairs outside their flats. They watched Katherine without curiosity as she walked slowly past, consumed with her own thoughts.

She was thinking of Stephen, and of her father. Since she had returned from America, Stephen's e-mails had become increasingly exuberant and urgent. Her visit seemed to have transformed him. The lying had to stop, he said. They had a chance for happiness, and should seize it. He would tell Alison he had fallen in love with someone else. He would separate from her, and he would find a place where he and Katherine could live together. Katherine barely knew how to reply. She couldn't think clearly. Her father's illness infected everything. The shock of it was still with her. She experienced sudden rushes of desperation, shapeless fears, as she imagined his pain, and his rage. She wanted to spend time with him, but even now, he was always too busy. He didn't seem ill at all. When she discussed him with her brothers, they told her not to worry. He would do things his own way, they said, he always had.

Katherine wanted to confide in Stephen, like she had before, but she couldn't. She wrote back to him, wishing she could echo his enthusiasm but found herself composing her replies. For the first time she began to lie to him about her feelings.

Kieron had reached the playground. He was circling a see-saw on his scooter, enjoying the smooth run of his wheels on the tarmac. She walked towards him through the narrow passageway leading from the estate. It was overgrown with holly bushes, which blocked out the sun and made the air cooler. Her phone rang.

'Hi. Is it okay? Are you alone?'

She stopped in the shade, the chill of it entering her.

'It's not a good time, Stephen . . .'

'I'm coming to England, to Braymer. In a few weeks. Your dad is flying me over to read for the Giordanos. Please come, Katherine. I need to see you, I have to . . .'

They hadn't spoken since America. The sweetness of his voice pulled at her, and she longed to dissolve into him. Kieron was by the swings, looking back at her.

'The Rockerman has offered me an extension to stay in America for two more years. I'm going to turn it down. I'm coming home, to be with you.'

She walked out of the gloomy nook. There were iron railings billowing with spiders' webs, their silver threads shining in the sun. As she listened to Stephen, she looked at them, amazed at their delicacy. Each thread was connected to another, the concentric lines held apart by radial filaments like spokes on a bicycle wheel. They were blowing in the breeze, but for all their fragility they did not break.

'I read you a story once,' he said. '"The Lady with the Lap Dog"? The two married people who fall in love?'

She remembered it, her lying on the bed in Cambridge.

'At the end of the story, they don't do anything,' he said. 'They don't change their lives. They remain tormented. They lead double lives for the rest of their days. I don't want that to happen to us, Katherine. I'm going to tell Alison about us. I'm going to tell her tonight.'

She could see Kieron at the far side of the park. He had stopped at the road.

'I'm not ready,' she said.

'When will you be? A week? A year? Five years?' His voice was hurt and accusing. 'Are you going to pretend to be happy for the rest of your life?'

'I can't talk now,' she said. 'I need more time.'

Cars were tearing past. Kieron stepped off the kerb to cross the road.

'Kieron!'

She ran towards him, her heart racing.

'No!'

A lorry roared. She couldn't see him. She sprinted. A car horn blared. He was standing in the middle of the road. She ran to him and a voice she barely recognised ripped out of her.

'You bloody fool! Don't you ever do that! D'you hear me!'

Kieron shouted back at her, defiant, tears in his eyes.

'You take too long! You always take too long!'

'Okay, okay. Sorry. There. No more phone. Sorry.'

She switched it off and put it into her pocket. She held his hand tightly and they crossed to the other side. Kieron scootered off towards school where a throng of children and parents were gathering. He went up to another boy who also had a scooter and they rode off together.

'Love you,' she called after him, but he didn't seem to hear.

She sat on the top deck of the 14 bus on her way to Ashwood. Low branches whipped against the windows. She looked down at the King's Cross development site. The crane stood motionless against the sky. The gates in the high fence were flung wide and a cement truck lumbered out on to the road. She saw a bulldozer ramming at the soil, backing up and ramming again. The earth opened up in deep pits, exposing the guts of the past, cracked sewers and the black sinew of electric cable. Huge segments of white pipe lay in a broken line waiting to be lowered into the ground.

At Agincourt Road she got off the bus and walked towards the gap in the red-brick wall. At Ashwood, she tapped in the code at the security gate. She nodded curtly to Michelle as she passed. Her mobile buzzed in her pocket; two messages. The Beaumont Care Home had rung to say she could visit her Aunt Charlotte the following week, and Adam had managed to arrange a baby-sitter. He was taking her out after work and would pick her up at Ashwood. Katherine had tried to put him off but he insisted he wanted to see where she worked. Katherine felt uneasy about the night ahead. She couldn't be sure that Adam didn't suspect her, and for the hundredth time, in her mind she saw him asking her if there was something going on, something he should know about, his face full of anger and disbelief.

She climbed the concrete stairs on to the half-landing and past the smell of disinfectant and sweet liquid soap from the toilets, the mingling institutional odours unchanged for generations. She pushed away memories of her own school days; girls in slit navy skirts, their legs mottled purple by the cold, boys chewing paper into small wet bullets. She'd tried hard to fit in, customised her school uniform like every other girl: the tight pencil skirt, the court shoes, blouse undone to the third button, tie slung low and knotted tight. She'd spoken with a strong Northern accent despite her parents' more stud-ied voices at home, and lied about her father's job. He was a bus driver, she'd said, never admitting that he ran a museum for poetry.

A boy slouched out of the toilets and brushed past her as he walked downstairs. Katherine marshalled herself to stay in the present. Memories seemed to come at her without warning. They came in flashes, as though someone was riffling through the cards of her past, and holding them to her face.

The afternoon dragged by. She saw Conrad Obadino, Liam Baldwin, Mason Fletcher, and finally, to her surprise, Jared Hinton. He walked in without a word and stood silently by the door. He looked almost haggard. There were deep grooves of tiredness below his eyes. His lips were mouthing numbers; he was counting as usual, everything he could see.

'Jared, have you ever played a piano?' she said, holding eye contact with him.

He looked down and counted the keys, one white, one white, one black, one white, one black, one white. Katherine played a chord. The sound resonated around the room. To Katherine's amazement, he came over to the piano. In all the lessons they had had, it was the first time he had actually entered the room. Katherine felt pleased. He put his fingers on the keys and pressed them down; the notes crunched together discordantly.

'Let me show you.'

She played a C-major triad.

'You try. Put one finger here, one here and one here. Now press down . . .'

He managed to get his fingers on the notes and pressed again.

'A C-major triad. You hear how it's a nice sound? A positive sound?'

She played another two octaves lower. 'You can play them higher or lower,' she said. 'Try again.'

Jared pressed his fingers to the keys again but this time the sound was discordant.

'Almost,' said Katherine. 'Move the bottom finger up one.'

He tried again but the chord came out badly again.

His face clouded.

'We'll do something else. That was just to start,' said Katherine.

He ignored her and tried again, his fingers clumsy on the keys.

'Very good, Jared,' she said.

He started bashing the keys.

'All right,' she said, 'stop. Don't get frustrated. Let's try it together.'

Their hands were about the same size. He had a line of warts along the side of his index finger. She put her own fingers on top of his to give him the shape.

The moment she touched him, he lashed out.

'Fuck! fuck! fuck!' he shouted.

She screamed involuntarily. He had hit her. Had he hit her? There was a deafening noise. He was hitting the piano. He was smashing the piano with flailing hands.

She had been told that Jared could become violent but this was the first time she'd seen it and she didn't know what to do. She'd been sent on a short course prior to starting the job and remembered being told to stay calm.

'It's okay, Jared,' she said.

'Jared Jared,' he echoed, 'Jared Jared Jared,' smashing his head down on the keys. 'Fuck fuck fuck fuck!'

His skull struck the keyboard, then the hardwood corner of the piano.

'No!' Katherine shouted.

She tried to get her hand between his head and the wood to stop him hurting himself but he pushed her away.

She stood back. She couldn't move forward or back. She wanted to help him but she couldn't. He sat there, his forehead was bleeding, one hand hanging limply at his side, the other clenched in a fist. He stood up abruptly and walked out, slamming the door behind him.

Katherine walked over to the window barely breathing. The school was eerily quiet. She leant against the glass, still unsure if he had hit her. She put her fingers to her face. He pushed me, she thought. Violently. He hurt me. She brushed her fingers against her lips. No, I pushed him. I pushed him to play the chord. She reached for her coat and put it on, her fingers slowly working the buttons through the holes. She stepped into the corridor, half-expecting to see the other teachers marching towards her in alarm, but the corridor was empty. It was as if nothing had happened. There was nothing but the ticking of the radiators.

She looked down into the playground. She didn't know where Jared would have gone. She imagined him hiding his face against a wall. Violent incidents were supposed to be reported to Henry West, but she didn't want to get Jared into more trouble. She went to the school nurse and told her what had happened. The nurse barely raised an eyebrow. She said it wasn't the first time Jared had lost his temper and thanked Katherine for letting her know.

Katherine walked out of the building, holding herself upright, as though she was being scrutinised for signs of weakness. She was a music teacher at the end of her shift on her way to meet her husband. What could be more normal? As she left, she willed her heels to click on the hard floor but her shoes were crepe-soled, and her steps were silent.

Adam was waiting on Agincourt Road by the gap in the red-brick wall. He was on his mobile but switched it off as he saw her coming.

'So this is the madhouse?' he said. 'Do I get a tour?'

She kept walking, the shock of what had happened with Jared inside her.

'What is it?'

'I've had a bad day. My dad . . .' she said, turning to face him, grasping at something to say. It was a shock to make eye contact. She realised how distant they had become. They related now entirely through Kieron.

'Katherine, it's more than that.'

'I don't know what I'm doing,' she said. 'I don't know what I'm doing.'

She couldn't stop herself. Her eyes welled with tears.

'I hate it,' she said, 'my work. I hate everything about this place. I'm kidding myself. Today one of the . . .'

She stopped and wiped her eyes briskly.

'It doesn't matter,' she said. 'It's just been a bad day.

Let's go, wherever we are going.'

'Some of the Armenians from the Shushen case are getting together, and we're invited.'

Adam had started working for Legal Aid and was helping an Armenian family fight for UK citizenship.

'It'll be different. We haven't been out for so long. There's a dance,' he said.

She was surprised. The idea of her and Adam dancing together again seemed strange, but she recognised the gesture he was making towards her, expressing a desire to be close. They walked silently by the long stretch of buildings and gateways of Felling Hospital. An ambulance's siren pierced the air, drowning all other sounds. They watched from the pavement as it drove in to Accident and Emergency, and its lights stopped spinning.

Adam put his hand on her shoulder. 'Tell me what happened today. Please, Katherine. It's important to me.'

His tone softened her. She had almost ceased to think that she mattered to Adam as anything more than one half of their child-management team. They went to a pub and found a quiet table in the corner. She told him about Jared, about his counting, his head against the piano, the blood on his face, how she had been powerless to stop him.

Adam sat back in his chair, and was quiet for a while.

'Jesus,' he whispered. 'You didn't sign up for that.'

Katherine suddenly felt very awake. Jared's movements replayed in her mind. He had wanted not just to hurt himself, but for her to see him do so. The sound of his head smashing into the wood of the piano had been a pure, astonishing sound, and as she heard it again, she was thrown into a deeper sense of herself.

'That turmoil, Adam, that madness . . . it's part of me.'

She felt choked. She couldn't speak. A memory came to her, vivid and sharp.

A dark airless space below a pub. It smelt of dust, cigarettes and stale beer. On a small stage under three low spotlights, she was dancing. She was nineteen years old, and it was the first piece she ever choreographed. Her father was in the audience. He had come alone, unannounced. Katherine had seen him through the curtains of the dressing room, but as she'd stepped on to the stage, she didn't think about him. As she danced she was lost to herself. There was no vanity, just a raw energy. She felt free, exhilarated. She started to improvise, spiralling and falling, spiralling and falling until her body was pounded and bruised.

Afterwards she remembered her father, and was horrified to see that he was crying. After the ten or so people in the audience had left, she had pulled a jumper round her shoulders and gone to him. She sat awkwardly on the chair next to him, hugging her knees into her, waiting for him to speak.

'Well, Katherine . . .' he started, struggling to find words.

She'd never seen him like this, unable to speak. She realised she had moved him. For a reason she did not understand, and he could not convey, her dancing had touched him deeply. She hated it. She could not bear to see him so powerless, so emotional.

'What's the matter?' she said, her voice hard with reprimand.

Her father was silent, looking down, struggling.

'I've got to go,' she said, and stood up.

Slowly, he regained his self-control. He looked up at her and raised an eyebrow.

'You certainly got a lot out of your system,' he said, reverting to the guarded mockery she knew so well.

His face lost all its openness, and Katherine was relieved. She left quickly and disappeared up the stairs.

Neither of them had ever spoken of that evening but as she sat in the café with Adam, as she thought of how cold she had been towards him, a darkness broke inside Katherine and she wept. She'd wanted all her life to be seen, to be heard by him, to matter to him. The one time she had managed to reach him, she had rejected him. It distressed her to think he had never again shown such openness to her. Her father, so loved by all yet so hidden to his family, had tried to connect with her, had given her an opportunity to see him as he really was, and she had missed it. She had been as incapable of seeing him, as he was of seeing her.

Adam had brought her a glass of water. On the other side of the pub, a group of young men and women were at a table, drinking, flirting with each other. Behind the bar, a woman was pulling a pint of beer. A man leant against the counter. Everything around her – the tables, the chairs, the customers, the upturned spirit bottles – was a layer of the world, but it was not the truth of it.

Everything collapsed to a terrifying clarity. Everything she had ever done in her life – her dancing, her marriage to Adam, her love-affair with Stephen – seemed nothing more than attempts to find her father, and it was always an impossible quest. Her father would always be out of reach. She herself had conspired to make it so, addicted to the turmoil, to the madness of it all.

She took a sip of water to calm herself.

'You've got so much to offer, Katherine,' said Adam. 'There are so many other things you could do. You just don't know what it is yet. You should leave that school. We've been so distant. It's my fault. I've made you unhappy. We'll get away.'

The simplicity of his plan touched her. She didn't speak. She felt how little she knew herself, how little she knew anything.

He put his arm gently round her, and she let him pull her close.

That night, after Adam was asleep, Katherine went downstairs and sat in the blue glare of the computer. The house was quiet as she typed.

Dear Stephen,
The woman who finds the shell on the path. I know now she cannot have it. It is not hers. It was never

hers. She has to leave it where it lies.

He wrote back many times, three times a day, but Katherine didn't open any of them. Eventually the e-mails stopped, and the silence that followed was like death.

21

'Beautiful! Beautiful!' said Ilana Giordano, stepping from their Mercedes and surveying the lake and the sun on the hills. '*Bellissimo!*'

'You've brought the weather with you,' said David, kissing her on either cheek. 'You must come to Braymer more often!'

Ilana laughed. She wore a red silk dress, Paolo a dark blue linen suit. Both were glowing with health. He looked more handsome and she more beautiful than David remembered from St Mark's.

He had planned their visit down to the smallest detail. His aim as always was to make the past vital, breathing and present. He took them round the museum, stopping at every painting, introducing them to Poole and Shawn, painters who had become captivated by the Northumbrian landscape in the eighteenth century, explaining their use of tints and washes, encouraging them to notice the subtle greens and blues and the pencil lines beneath. The pictures came alive with his commentary. He told Paolo and Ilana anecdotes about the poets and artists in the Broughton Collection.

He encouraged Paolo and Ilana to ask questions, to feel involved. He took them to the cramped manuscript room and gave them Coleridge's notebooks to hold, letting them feel the thrill of history as they turned the brittle, fragile pages.

Afterwards, he sat with them in Sellacrag garden. He gave them mint cake, joking that it was a Class A drug to which they would become instantly addicted. He spoke passionately about how essential it was to complete the new library and inspired them with his mission to make poetry accessible to all. He pointed out the hills that surrounded them, Kield Hope, Stone Baron, Iron Fell, and told enthralling stories about them. He suggested they take a stroll around Lake Braymer so they could enjoy the beauty of the hills and watched them go off, hand in hand, like young lovers.

'Be back by six!' he called after them. 'I have a surprise for you.'

They waved as they rounded the point. David felt supremely happy. He had stopped worrying about his health. He enjoyed his visits to Dr Sorov in Harley Street. Unlike the weary doctor at the oncology department at Carlisle General Hospital, Dr Sorov respected David; more importantly, he prescribed him steroids. David was deeply grateful for them. They gave him lucidity and limitless energy. They made him the man he wanted to be.

David galvanised everyone at the Broughton Foundation. There was a new optimism, a whirlwind of possibility. Daniel Boulens's visit to Braymer was confirmed. George surpassed himself, working day and night to organise every detail. Boulens had expressed his desire to paint his line across the lake. David was delighted and amazed by this intriguing proposal and he was not alone: the prospect of Boulens' line in Northumberland captured people's imagination and began to attract nationwide publicity.

For strategic reasons David confided in a few of the Board of Trustees about his cancer. Not out of any sense of defeat; on the contrary, he considered it a tactic. The mere mention of cancer made it impossible for them to veto his plans. At the June board meeting, David won the vote to appoint new writers and artists-in-residence and commit the Broughton Foundation to a daring programme of exhibitions. He threw his energy into what he felt would be his greatest project, the tunnel under Braymer. It would divert all traffic and return the valley to its bucolic past. May told him he was mad, but David brushed aside her scepticism. A tunnel would make Braymer a perfect Eden, attracting visitors from around the world. It would secure the Broughton Foundation's future for generations.

He knew his drive relied upon Dr Sorov's steroids. When their power faded, the cough returned, and he felt vulnerable and frightened. Once, when he had visited an engineering firm in Birmingham to discuss the viability of the tunnel, his train home had been delayed. His steroids were back at Sellacrag. After half an hour, the guard's voice had crackled over the tannoy and apologised for any inconvenience. The reason for the delay was a passenger incident on the track near Crewe. David knew what it meant; someone had thrown themselves in front of the train. His thoughts plummeted. He closed his eyes and tried to calm himself, trying to silence the deafening noise inside him, to stop himself seeing it all: the person falling, the train roaring towards him, the rush of air, arms reaching, body smashing into blinding pain, churning in the wheels along the track. Without the steroids, he was stripped of his objectivity and left like a scared child.

At six o'clock that evening, the Giordanos returned dressed for dinner. Ilana wore a green cocktail dress with pearl earrings, Paolo a black silk suit. David met them outside the museum in the grey evening light. The air was warm and fragrant. Everything was ready. Like a theatre director, David had prepared his stage.

'Follow me,' he said.

He led them towards the unfinished library across the mud-smeared boards. Ilana stepped carefully in her high heels, perplexed and amused. David opened a studwork door and they walked into the site. A magical space greeted them, ethereal and primitive. The roof of plastic sheeting had been removed and the library was open to the sky. Clusters of candles had been placed on the unfinished walls, on the rough alcoves and the concrete floor. The shape of the space was like a boat, tapering at one end, and rounded at the other. The candles threw their guttering light on to every surface, transforming the breeze-blocks to rippling surfaces of shadow and illumination.

Paolo and Ilana were silent as they looked about them. Above them, the dark blue canopy of the evening sky was speckled with stars. Other guests could be heard talking as they approached, and as they stepped inside, they too fell quiet. Stephen was amongst them. Ilana saw him and her expression confirmed to David that he had been right to ask him to fly over from America. When he had first asked him, David had detected a hesitancy in Stephen's response. He didn't know whether it was because of their drunken night in Sellacrag, or because of Katherine, but when Stephen had arrived in Braymer that afternoon, there had been no hint of any reluctance or embarrassment. Stephen had greeted him warmly, and together they planned the night ahead, which they hoped would change the future of the Broughton Foundation forever.

Stephen stepped into the middle of the space and addressed the small circle of people.

'Building work began on this new library while I was living here in Braymer. It stands for everything I believe in. I want to read you part of my new poem. It is called *The Crossing*. It is about a family, a people crossing from one country into another, from one century into another, one life into another. My hope is that this building too will cross into a new life, and become a beacon for the future.'

He began to read, his voice deeper than David remembered. He felt a rush of excitement that Stephen had found something truly authentic. The passage was of two lovers, his grandparents, before the war in Poland, and the brutal collision of their love for each other. Stephen described their connection as a collision. *The Crossing* was far from romantic, it insisted on the pain of sex, of lies, of not belonging. The poem held a new intelligence. The language was arresting, almost disturbing, as though he had pounded and bullied the words, pushing them to the limits of making sense. It was a raw excavation of the human need for love and the struggle to sustain it.

He listened to Stephen, surrounded by the group, their faces still in the flickering light, and as he did David witnessed the purity of the transaction between the poet and his audience. It seemed that every word was shaped and given life not just by their creator but by the collective imagination of his listeners. Together they gave birth to the words and created worlds with them, magnified, new.

After Stephen finished reading the group stood in silence under the stars.

They made their way to the Broughton restaurant and ate a simple dinner. The enchantment of the library and Stephen's reading permeated every word, every look amongst the guests. David sat back in his chair as the conversation rose around him and smiled; it was the triumphant evening he had wished for.

As the Giordanos were leaving, Paolo tapped David on the shoulder.

'Come to our hotel. Bring Stephen. Ilana and I would like to share a drink with you.'

There was warmth in his voice and David knew this was the moment. He and Stephen would go to the Shenner Bay Hotel. They would sit with Paolo and he would make his donation to the Broughton Foundation.

Stephen sat at the table and looked over at David standing in the door saying goodbye to the guests. He hoped he had not detected any of his awkwardness when he had arrived, but at first it had been almost unbearable to be in a place so suffused with Katherine. While they were preparing the library for the reading, he had stepped outside to gather himself. He had wild thoughts that she would suddenly appear. He had looked up at Kield Hope towards the Dungeons and Stickles and seen her on the skyline in her long unbuttoned cardigan, her heavy boots, walking in long strides. She had walked down the flanks of the fell and round the crystal edge of the lake towards him. He'd seen her coming into focus, the details of her face, her cheeks red, her cold nose burrowing into him, the smell of lanolin in the damp wool, the straw of her sweat. She looked at him with that mixture of defiance and love he had come to cherish.

Stephen had felt such an acute sense of loss that he could barely stop himself from trying to contact her, but as the evening unfolded, a subtle transformation occurred. His yearning for Katherine subsided and was replaced by a sense of the power of his work. It was the same feeling he had felt before under David's guidance, that his words mattered, that his poetry was at the heart of everything, that in Braymer there was a shared purpose which reached beyond himself.

David's hand on his shoulder.

'Stephen,' he said, 'Giordano has invited us to his hotel. This is it.'

David was glittering with victory. Together, they set out across the car park and walked through the valley in silence. As they stepped through a line of trees, the knowledge of what they had achieved and the gratitude they felt for each other could not be spoken. They walked past the river Rathe, the sound of rushing water filling their ears. An owl cried out like a lost child, and in that instant it seemed to Stephen that with David anything was possible, that he had a hand in making the clouds break and the moon shine on to the water, as though he were orchestrating the whole wide beauty of it all.

May was reading by the fire when David returned to Sellacrag two hours later. He sat down and put his head in his hands. May went to him and anxiously put her hand on his shoulder.

'It's time,' he said.

David laid a cheque gently on the table. For a moment she allowed herself to dream.

'Time?' she said quietly, picking it up.

'Twenty thousand pounds,' he said without looking at her. 'What can I do with twenty thousand? I need three million. It's time to start the chemotherapy.'

'I'll ring Dr Sorov in the morning.'

He was completely exhausted, the fight gone out of him. He laid his head on the table and the cough started to rack through him. He took her hand and held it to his face so hard it twisted her wrist. It hurt, but she said nothing.

22

Katherine, Adam, and Kieron were walking along the beach. The waves crashed on to the shingle, pounding and dragging it in endless rounds of motion. Kieron ran on the wet sand and screamed as the sea chased him away. Adam caught him and threw him up like a rag doll. Katherine looked out over the ocean and let the wind roar in her ears.

She had thrown all her energies into being with Adam and Kieron. She had organised trips to the circus, to Kew Gardens, to wild-water rides and a pick-your-own farm in Kent. She had invited friends over for homemade pizzas and bought marshmallows for the children to roast on the barbecue. Adam and Kieron seemed surprised by her vigour and her desire to be with them.

Today she had brought them to Fairhampton so they could spend the morning by the sea before she went to visit Charlotte at the Beaumont Care Home. It was time for her to go. They walked back up the beach, their steps sinking into the pebbles.

A small crowd was gathering further along the seashore. A dark-haired boy was laying a metal chain on a concrete walkway, marking out an area. Kieron and Adam ran ahead to see what was happening.

Four acrobats in shorts and vests flick-flacked across the space the chain defined. They were a family, a father and his three sons, all with olive skin and black hair. They began a sequence of balances, building shapes with their bodies. They stood on one another's shoulders and leaned in like rafters of a human house before collapsing it and cartwheeling away. The sons rolled out a metal pummel strapped with grubby tape. The father lifted himself into an inverted position. He stood on one arm above the crowd without wavering, beautiful in his stillness. His sons watched him, unfaltering in their gaze, supporting their father unquestioningly, their purpose clear, their skill transparent, as he held himself above them, frozen in space, his hand gripping the pummel.

Katherine stood behind Adam and Kieron but saw nothing. It seemed nothing could stop her thoughts flying to Stephen. She longed for him to be watching the acrobats with her. She reached forward and put her hand into Adam's pocket to warm it. The feeling would pass.

As Katherine left, the acrobats were starting up a slow handclap in the crowd as they built up to their final trick. The father took his position, legs wide, body braced. The next son stood on his shoulders and then the next until they made a ladder of three bodies. The youngest boy, ten or eleven years old, stayed on the ground and pulled a face of mock fear to the crowd. The eldest of his brothers, joining in the showman's game, shouted at him fiercely in a foreign language, making out he couldn't hold the position for much longer. Still, the boy shook his head.

The father gave a piercing whistle and suddenly the boy scampered quickly up the tower of his family and stood at the summit, beaming, his arms raised to the sky, and as he did Katherine knew that somehow she would dance again.

Katherine entered the Beaumont Care Home, a bland building in a wind-blasted garden. She pushed open the double doors and was hit by the smell of warm food and soap. She walked along white corridors, through a dark-ened sitting room full of plastic-covered armchairs. They were empty except for one by the window where an old woman sat hunched over, her back so curved that she stared at the floor, the chair offering her no support.

'Katherine, nice to see you.'

A nurse came into the room.

'We haven't seen you for a while,' she said.

'I've had a lot on,' said Katherine.

'Charlotte's had a bath. She's been a good girl today.'

Katherine left the room. She hated hearing her aunt spoken of as though she were a wayward child. She walked down the corridor and opened Charlotte's door.

She was sitting in her chair wearing an absurd pink nightie; her motionless face framed by fancy frills and ribbon borders. Charlotte had always had impeccable taste. The secret, she once had told Katherine in one of her girlish confidences, was to avoid anything that over-powered. Always stay in control, she said, never let the clothes wear *you*. Katherine hoped her aunt was unaware of how she looked now, like a pet dressed up by a child.

She sat next to her. Her aunt's eyes were dark shadows and she was staring at her hands, her knuckles moving slowly round and round each other.

'Aunt Lottie.'

Charlotte didn't look up. She closed her eyes almost disdainfully and rested her head back against the chair as though Katherine was just another exhausting hallucination. Katherine felt at a loss. She hadn't expected such a dramatic deterioration. The last time she had visited, Charlotte had recognised her immediately.

'I've brought something for you,' said Katherine, and held out the silver brush.

Charlotte's body tensed and reared backwards. Katherine could only wonder at what her aunt was seeing. Once when Katherine had visited, Charlotte had seen people hiding in the bathroom and had spoken to them like naughty children, shouting at them to get out and leave her alone. Katherine had consoled her, whispering softly, and she had slowly come back to herself.

'It's me, Aunt Lottie, it's Katherine.'

She put the silver brush on Charlotte's knee and took her hand, unclenching her fingers and resting them on the handle. Charlotte opened her eyes and looked at it but did not respond. Her body was tense, as though she was holding her breath. Her hand let go and the brush clattered to the floor. Katherine picked it up and walked behind her. Gently, she began to brush her aunt's hair. The brush moved easily through the thin strands. She repeated it, stroke after stroke, and Charlotte's breathing steadied and deepened. Katherine continued to brush and as she did she thought of Charlotte's childhood on the farm with her father. She thought of her marriage to Uncle Gregory. She thought of her drinking. It seemed her aunt had paid a terrible price for having to pretend that everything was right when it had all been so wrong. Her whole generation seemed to live with so many lies. She thought of her father and mother, how they struggled to appear correct and acceptable, of how punishing they were to themselves, how deeply they buried their true feelings, as though their real selves were somehow unbearable to them.

Charlotte began to snore. Katherine sat on a low stool at her feet. She rested her head on her aunt's lap.

A knock roused her from sleep. A figure stood in the doorway holding a bunch of flowers.

'Katherine?'

It was Gregory. In all her visits, their paths had never crossed. She'd heard from the nurses that he only visited occasionally when there were papers to sign, and never stayed long.

'The nurses said you were here.'

A man with a trolley of toilet rolls trundled past in the corridor behind him. Gregory stepped into the room.

'I didn't realise it was so late,' said Katherine, standing and reaching for her coat.

'I brought her these,' said Gregory awkwardly. 'Not that she'll notice.'

He laughed without opening his mouth and laid the blue irises on the table. One of his eyes was cloudy as though he had a cataract.

'Don't go,' he said. 'I'll buy you tea.'

They sat in a teashop in Fairhampton at a table in the window. There were few customers and a lingering smell of bleach. They were served by a woman in a plastic apron. Gregory ordered tea and toasted tea-cakes from a laminated menu.

There was nothing to say. Katherine watched the butter melt on her tea cake and wished she could leave. She knew her uncle was trying to be kind but felt no connection with him. He seemed eager to please her. He asked after Adam and Kieron, her house, her job. He asked how she got about in London and complained about the inadequacies of the London transport system and how poorly it compared with those of other capital cities. After an hour, Katherine made her excuses and stood up to leave. He reached forward to touch her, brushing his hand against the front of her coat.

'Good,' he said. 'Well, I'm glad to see you.'

'It's good to see you too.'

'Your father . . .'

It was the first time Gregory had mentioned him.

'I hear his treatment is going well,' he said.

'Yes,' she said.

'That's good,' he said and moved abruptly to the door.

From nowhere, Katherine suddenly wanted to cry. The

stiffness of their exchange had exhausted her, the false-ness of it. She stopped in the doorway.

'Uncle Gregory,' she said. 'My father's treatment is not going at all well. He has not responded well to the chemotherapy and they've stopped it. He hasn't long to live.'

Gregory stared at her, helplessly.

'I must go. Adam and Kieron are waiting,' she said. She quickly opened the door and went out on to the street. A man was unloading boxes of tins from a van into the local Spar.

'Katherine, wait . . .'

Gregory was coming after her. She had no choice but to turn and wait for him.

'Your father,' he said, his voice strained. 'We didn't always hit it off as you may know, but I want to do some-thing for him.'

She looked at him blankly.

'Tell him, would you? Tell him I'll talk to Richard Seaton.'

She saw him smile. It was as though a huge weight had been lifted from him, and Katherine saw him as though for the very first time.

23

The wind blew across Lake Braymer, strong and warm. A gaggle of small sailing boats creaked and bumped softly against the wooden jetty. On the shore, people were putting up trestle tables. Katherine watched a man struggling with a white tablecloth as it flapped against him in the wind. She could see George Gull and Daniel Boulens by the boats. Boulens had white hair and wore a thick duffle coat and next to him, George Gull, who seemed to exist only in his head, wore nothing more than an open shirt. Normally so diffident, he was speaking animatedly to Boulens, his long limbs pointing to the boats and the hills beyond. Katherine thought of her father and wished he could have seen them together. George looked over to her and waved.

'Katherine!'

She walked along the shore towards them.

'Have you met Daniel Boulens?'

She shook him by the hand, and he smiled, his eyes sharp and intelligent.

'David's daughter,' said George.

'I did not know him of course,' said Boulens. He spoke with a heavy French accent. 'Only on the telephone, but everyone talks of him so much I feel like I do.'

'The kids will be here soon,' said George excitedly. 'Fifteen of them. One kid for each boat.'

'How did you find them?' asked Katherine.

'The Outward Bound club. They've lent us the boats too. They arrived yesterday on lorries. We've been attaching the sails all morning.'

Katherine looked at the boats. Boulens had painted his line, in blue paint, on each sail, each one at a different angle and level.

'Did you make the sails here?' she asked.

'I make them in Switzerland,' said Boulens. 'They come by aeroplane. George and your father arrange everything, every detail, where the boats will start, where the people will watch.'

He smiled, as though the thought amused him.

'Here they come,' said George.

A crocodile of children wearing life jackets was making its way towards them through the trestle tables. George and Boulens left Katherine and went to meet them.

She looked out over the lake. On the shoreline Kieron and Adam were skimming stones with her brother Michael, who had flown in from Canada. Kieron managed to make one bounce twice and gave a jubilant cry. Michael smiled, and she saw something of her father in him, like a shadow passing over his face. She wondered how long he would stay in England this time.

The guests were beginning to arrive. Since her father's death, the Boulens installation had turned into the biggest event the Broughton Foundation had ever known; over a thousand people were expected. Katherine had been amazed by the mass of letters that had arrived. They all expressed shock at David's sudden illness, awe at his public achievements and gratitude for how he had inspired, challenged and uplifted them. She wondered if he ever knew how much he was loved.

The last time she saw him he was sitting up on a makeshift daybed in the sitting room in Sellacrag, propped up on cushions. His eyes were wide and staring. He wore a striped shirt that was too big for him, his body shrunken away inside it.

'Hi,' he said brightly.

His voice was clipped and staccato.

She sat at his side and held his hand. She gripped it like there was nothing else in the world. There was just his hand; only that mattered.

'I want to say some things,' he smiled, 'because I'm dying.'

Her eyes filled with tears before she could stop them.

'Stop,' he said firmly. 'Stop that.' She saw the effort of it.

'Katherine. Katherine,' he said more gently, resuming his Lancashire lilt.

He repeated her name as though to be sure of it.

'Katherine . . .'

He was in a fine and exact state, like a high note sustained on a violin. It was the final stages. He was breathing an air different from hers. She sat there holding his hand, taking him in, willing him to speak.

'Look after Kieron,' he said.

The cry caught in her throat. His remembering her child took her by surprise. 'And Adam. He is changing. Things change.'

Katherine leant forward to him.

'Dad, I met Uncle Gregory when I was visiting Aunt Charlotte. He's going to talk to Sir Richard Seaton. He wanted me to tell you.'

David smiled.

'That's good,' he said.

'Dad, about Stephen . . .'

He waved his hand impatiently. She could see the pain surge through him. His breathing was laboured. The structures of his life were dropping away.

'Nothing matters,' he said.

He looked down at their hands, the fingers intertwined. She felt a clear connection run between them, like a light passing through her.

'Nothing matters,' he said, 'except you. You must be happy, Katherine.'

He smiled into her eyes with the deepest certainty. She knew what it meant; he was seeing her, only her, his daughter Katherine, seeing her as a father and loving her as his child.

Her hand in his. His daughter's hand. This is his daughter's hand, yes, her hand, so strong, full of life. Wonderful. He lets it go. It's not so hard to let it go. She stands. His daughter by his bed. Her shadow.

Katherine. She's gone, and May is here, her lovely face. Her hair.

'Come,' she says. 'Once you're up you'll be fine.'

He hears himself speak. It is as though someone else is speaking. He cannot make out what he is saying. She heaves him to the edge of the bed and puts his feet into trousers.

'It's all right,' she says softly.

She pulls his body to standing, this body that is collapsing. He sees the trousers round his ankles, the big shirt hanging down. He reaches down to pull the trousers up. His hands can't reach them. The bottom of the trousers are not fully over his feet. He must get the left trouser leg over his left foot before he can pull it up. He has shoes on. He must have had them on in bed. How strange. It will be difficult to get the trouser leg over the shoe. The shoe will have to come off. He looks down at his own feet and sees his black shoes. The laces are untied. He sees the squat little foot inside, and inside the foot, the air inside him. It doesn't matter about the shoes, the trousers, or going down to the lake. Nothing matters. His feet are air, and he knows this air will fill him now.

'Come,' she says.

He looks up at her. He wants to tell her about the air, about what he has seen in his shoes. I can see it, I can see the air, he wants to say but stays quiet, and she helps him into the trousers.

*

Ken is with him. Ken the gardener, who had worked for him since the beginning. Ken is taking him down to the lake. He's been wrapped in a big coat and hat and Ken is walking him down to the lake. Ken's big arms support him. They arrive at the lake. Ken unfolds a chair on the shore and sits him in it. He looks out over the water. He feels the valley surround him. He looks up to where Kield Hope and Lyne Top meet and sees a young man cycling into the valley. It is himself.

He cycles into Braymer, freewheeling over the brow, the hills before him painted rust and yellow, the sunlight piercing through the clouds on to the flanks of Bastlegyle. He's never seen anywhere so beautiful, so fierce. May is in the terraced house back in Carlisle with two small children squabbling at her feet, and another big in her womb, but he is here, liberated from babies and domestic squalor, and it's all just for him: the black lake, the raging wind, the grey screes as though the hill's flesh has been ripped away to reveal the bone beneath. Nothing is out of place. He is within its perfection, and part of it.

He climbs the path. The little museum is nothing more than a barn. Dust swirls in pale streams of light. The floorboards creak. He opens the glass-topped cabinets and lifts out the yellowing papers. Treasures beyond value. A vision comes to him, a place built on manuscripts here in these hills, a foundation, alive, bridging past and present.

*

That night, David asked for the cushions in his bed to be removed. He wanted to lie flat. He lay down and let the tumour restrict his breathing. He was holding May's hand tightly when he died. She lay down next to him and took him in her arms.

Cars were parked all along the road into the village. A crowd stood on the shore of the lake waiting to see a line, a line through space. It was a line created by the great artist Daniel Boulens, but they had come because of David. It was the last of his events, and they came to honour him. The waiters from the hotel served drinks as people stood discussing the event. A line? Across the lake? How? People were intrigued and amused. Some American academics from David's days in San Francisco stood chatting to Lancashire farming people from David's family. Harold Flacker watched unsteadily on the shingle, Lady Highsmith next to him in a wide-brimmed hat. There was a sense of occasion, a day out. Ladies with cut-glass accents, local farmers, taxi drivers, poets, journalists, politicians, shopkeepers and sports-men had gathered on the shore, and they were all thread-ed in and out with running children, oblivious to everything but each other. Kieron was amongst them, playing happily with his cousins. They ran down to the water and took turns balancing on a stone in the shal-lows, the water lapping around their feet. Along the shore, the boats were being prepared. The children from the sailing school stood round their teacher, receiving last-minute instructions. They climbed into the boats, helped by mums and dads. Boulens walked along the jetty adjusting sails. On each was his line, a single bold stripe.

Katherine took Kieron's hand and he jumped to the shore. Behind them, May stood at a small microphone. Adam was talking with her, and as Katherine approached she noticed the warmth of their exchange, an ease between them that had always been there. She let them talk, and turned towards an elderly man standing behind her. It was Bob Clayton, an old friend of her father's from America. He told her stories of her father when he was a young man living in San Francisco.

'He went everywhere on this old bicycle with no brakes,' he said, chuckling as the memory came to him. 'I'll never forget seeing him on that bicycle, careering down a hill, singing at the top of his lungs, barefooted!'

It seemed such an unlikely vision of her father that Katherine laughed too. In the pause that followed, the American asked about her family, her work.

'I'm having a break right now,' she said, 'but next year I'm going to choreograph something. It's for a youth group in Carlisle.'

Katherine looked along the shore. Stephen and Alison were by the boathouse. They were talking to George Gull. Their children stood next to them, the boy kicking stones, the girl shivering in a short-sleeved T-shirt. Stephen was listening attentively to George, his hand raised to his face to shield his eyes from the sun, a slight smile on his lips. Alison took a scarf from her neck and tied it round her daughter.

Katherine felt her heart stop. She hadn't known they would be there, and for a moment she didn't know what to do. She knew she had to speak to him. She turned back to Adam.

'I want you to meet some people,' she said. 'Stephen Jericho and his wife. Do you remember, we met up here a couple of years ago? Kieron played with their kids.'

They walked over to them. Stephen was still listening to George Gull, and they shook hands with Alison.

'David was a wonderful man,' said Alison. 'I'm so sorry.'

Katherine thanked her. Stephen laughed at something and turned towards them. Their eyes met and for a moment she experienced the same rush of openness and recognition she'd always felt with him, the astonishing sensation of being wholly known, but something was different too. The feelings she had for him no longer overwhelmed her. She felt a new certainty. All the unravelled threads of herself that had spooled on to him, she took back. She felt a lightness in herself, a happiness, and she smiled at him. She knew the luck of their connection, the rarity of it. It had been like finding quartz in a stream.

'How are you?' he said.

'I'm well,' she said.

She looked away and slipped her arm through Adam's. A woman's voice rose into the air. It was May addressing the crowd.

'Thank you all for coming. David would have been so happy to see you all. Because he can't be here, I'd like to read a poem by Auden,' she said, 'one that he loved.' Her voice was impossibly soft, it could barely be heard. Katherine turned into the wind to catch the words.

Doom is dark and deeper than any sea-dingle.
Upon what man it fall
In spring, day-wishing flowers appearing
Avalanche sliding, white snow from rock-face
That he should leave his house,
No cloud-soft hand can hold him, restraint by women;
But ever that man goes
Through place-keepers, through forest trees
A stranger to strangers over undried sea,
Houses for fishes, suffocating water,
Or lonely on fell as chat,
By pot-holed becks
A bird stone-haunting, an unquiet bird.

For the first time Katherine heard the poetry. She let the words in. They became untethered from their meaning. They seemed to come to her surrounded by space and air. She heard the music of them, their beauty, and they delighted and consoled her.

George Gull pushed past and ran down to the water.

'It's starting,' he shouted, as excited as a schoolboy.

Everyone turned towards the lake. The boats were setting sail across the water, each manned by a child in a luminous jacket. They kept one hand on the tillers and

moved their sails to catch the wind. Some boats raced
ahead, others veered off and had to make small circles,
leaning back almost horizontally, to get back into position. One child lost hold of a rope, and his boat pitched
on to its side. The triangle of his sail slapped the water
and he tipped into the lake. An adult paddled over in a
canoe and righted the boat. The child laughed as he
scrambled back in and waved to the shore.

'What on earth is going on?' said Louise Highsmith,
her voice carrying in the wind.

The boats pulled away into the open water, becoming
smaller to the eye. They kept no shape but sailed higgledy-
piggledy, the line on their sails broken and making no
coherent pattern. Katherine stood on the shore taking it
all in. Suddenly she felt a connection with her father, as
though his hand were in hers again, and she absorbed
every detail around her because he couldn't. He couldn't
see the expectant faces stretching along the shore, or
Daniel Boulens standing apart, delighted by the chaos, or
Gregory walking towards the lake with Sir Richard
Seaton, or Kieron laughing on Adam's shoulders, or
Ken's unbreakable smile, or George Gull jumping up and
down, or May's pale face at the water's edge. He couldn't
see the sails on the lake suddenly connect, but Katherine
could, just for a moment, and they formed a single
unbroken line.

Acknowledgements

I would like to thank all my family, especially my mother, Pamela Woof. I am grateful to everyone at Faber, especially my editor, Hannah Griffiths. Thanks to Rebecca Carter for her inspired suggestions and friendship, to Jamie James for his comments and assiduous reading. Also thanks to Wes Williams, Deana Rankin, Nikita Lalwani and to Francesca Simon for her great generosity. Thanks to Claire Paterson and Tina Bennet at Janklow and Nesbit for making it all happen. My deepest gratitude is to my husband, Hamish McColl, whose encouragement and insight have helped me more than I can say.